# MURDER MOST IRRITATING

## A CAROLYN NEVILLE MYSTERY BOOK 2

## JOHN DUCKWORTH

**Murder Most Irritating**
John Duckworth

Print Edition
© Copyright 2020 John Duckworth

CKN Christian Publishing
An Imprint of Wolfpack Publishing
5130 S. Fort Apache Rd. 215-380
Las Vegas, NV 89148

eBook ISBN 978-1-64734-698-0
Paperback ISBN 978-1-63977-093-9

# MURDER MOST IRRITATING

MURDER MOST IRRITATING

*To all the editors I've ever met,*
*especially the grouchy ones.*

# PROLOGUE

"Okay," Stephen said, frowning. "Just found something on CNN.com. Posted fifty-seven minutes ago." He poked again. There was a pause as he read the article.

He gasped. "Oh, God. You won't believe this."

"What?" I asked.

"He's dead."

He looked up from his phone.

"The guy is dead."

"How?"

"Nobody seems to know. But everybody knows who did it."

I had to admit, though not out loud, that my feelings were mixed.

On the one hand, I was sorry his life was over.

On the other, I had the feeling mine was about to get a lot more complicated.

# CHAPTER 1

THE ONLY TOLERABLE PART OF MY ANNUAL PHYSICAL COMES when it reaches the end.

Unfortunately, it hadn't.

That part would be the one where Dr. Thomas Garabedian, M.D., shakes my hand and says everything looks good and he'll see me next year.

This time, though, there was a surprise ending.

He was sitting on his stool, staring at the laptop that balanced on his thighs, tapping away, his bald head glistening under the bleak fluorescent lights. Finally he hit ENTER and looked up.

"I always leave the most difficult part for last," he said.

"The debate about single-payer health coverage?"

"No, the discussion of your lifestyle."

"Oh, that." I could feel my hackles rising, though technically I didn't know where my hackles were.

He flipped the sheets of paper on his clipboard back to the nurse's preliminary notes. "I see you've gained a few pounds this year. Been exercising?"

I shrugged. "Editors tend to lead sedentary lives. Does vigorous erasure of proofreading marks count?"

"Afraid not. I have at least two other patients who are editors. They claim to hit the gym six days a week."

"Liars."

"Do you perform any physical activity at all?"

"Of course. I take walks."

"How often? How far?"

"It varies. But I have one of those step-counting things."

"And how many steps a day do you take?"

"I don't know. It's broken."

He sighed. "Would you say you're careful about what you eat?"

"I would say that, yes."

"Would you be telling the truth?"

"Not exactly."

Sighing, he flipped to another page, the one with test results. "Your blood pressure is up about ten points. I can put you on a pill, or you probably can handle it with exercise and diet."

"What kind of diet?"

"Same kind most people need. Low fat, whole grains, limit meat, lots of vegetables and fruit, high fiber. For a lot of people, cutting sodium helps."

"No salt?"

"Most Americans get way too much, at least three thousand milligrams a day. Better to get about half that."

I frowned. Salt was good, one of God's Top 10 inventions. People in the Bible ate it. Some of them, like Lot's wife, even turned into it.

"Your LDL cholesterol is up, too. That's the bad kind. Let's put you on a statin to see if we can bring it down."

I shook my head. "Statins are too dangerous. It takes a three-page spread in *Parade* magazine to list the side effects."

"It's a tradeoff, Carolyn. Statins can reduce the risk of heart attack and stroke by up to thirty-five percent. Your grandfather had a heart attack, didn't he?"

I folded my arms across my chest. "Yes, but he practically lived on butter, bacon, and bourbon. My vices are limited to doughnuts and being judgmental."

He stroked his chin. "I can't force you to take my advice, but that *is* what you pay me for."

I unfolded my arms, trying to look friendlier. "I don't mean to be a problem patient. It's the drug companies I'm worried about. Look at the UniMerritt case. Everyone else is."

"The one with the whistleblower."

"Exactly. The company said Millenitor . . ."

"Milletinor."

"Yes. They said it was revolutionary. Worked miracles for diabetes. Too bad it also caused pancreatic cancer."

"So I've heard."

"How many people died? Sixteen?"

"Something like that."

"The company knew and covered it up. No wonder so many people are suspicious of Big Pharma."

He leaned forward, still balancing the laptop on his thighs. "All very disturbing, if true. But to put it bluntly, you're eating and editing yourself into an early grave."

"You say that like it's a bad thing."

He looked down at his computer and started tapping the keyboard again. "I'm going to write you a statin prescription. Prevenutab. Don't worry, UniMerritt doesn't make it. We'll start you on a low dose. Even if you'd rather not take it, maybe your survival instinct will kick in and convince you otherwise before it's too late."

"Survival is overrated. I expect the next life to be an improvement."

He just kept tapping. Then he hit RETURN, and the order sped to a pharmacy about a mile from my home, unstoppable.

His smile was triumphant. "If you have any concerns, just call the office. Otherwise, let's check your levels in about three months, shall we? I'd recommend getting a blood pressure monitor. Any kind you want, but not one that goes on the wrist. Isn't accurate. And try reducing that sodium."

He stuck out his hand.

I shook, but planned to wash it as soon as possible.

* * *

On the way out I sought to make a follow-up appointment with the help of a young woman who seemed not to understand how the days of the week worked. While she squinted at her computer monitor, I checked my watch.

It was 10:04.

No, that couldn't be.

The Acquisitions meeting was at 10:30.

I was going to be late.

But I was never late. I knew cleanliness wasn't next to godliness, but punctuality was pretty close to cleanliness.

The girl behind the counter, having at last deciphered the intricacies of the calendar, handed me a card with my appointment time scribbled on it. Stuffing it in my purse, I started working on my daily steps by power walking through the waiting room where I'd so recently wasted at least half an hour watching HGTV.

My lateness was the doctor's fault. How could he expect me to take his advice, much less his prescription?

In the parking lot my red RAV4 cowered between an Escalade and an Explorer. I checked the dashboard clock, hoping my watch had been wrong. No such luck.

After driving past the UPPER MANHATTAN PRIMARY CARE PARTNERS sign, I injected myself into the clogged artery of downtown traffic. I went as fast as I could, about three miles per hour. As usual it was stop-and-go, mostly stop. And as usual it gave me a chance to brood.

I wondered why I still commuted from Connecticut in a car instead of a train. No sane person did that. More to the point, why did I keep showing up at Pendleton House Publishers at all?

Wasn't I tired of hearing my bedside clock radio spring violently to life at 5:15 a.m. with an ominous traffic report about I-95 South? Wasn't I weary of gulping instant coffee in my half-lit condo kitchen and wolfing down a waxy brown supermarket doughnut?

Did I still love slipping into my tweedy brown editor's blazer? Why did I keep putting up with 137 minutes of arduous brake-mashing from the picturesque seaside village of Hensford to the grimy Oz of Manhattan?

I looked at the clock again. What I saw made me grip the wheel more tightly, a move that did surprisingly little to increase the speed of traffic.

I fished my phone from my pocket and placed a call to Stephen Ames, the young senior editor who reported to me, or pretended to.

"Carolyn," he said. "Where are you?"

"On the way. I'm running late for Acquisitions."

"But you're never late for anything. I thought it was like your Prime Directive."

"I need you to stall until I get there."

"How? Go around the room and have people name their favorite color? Pull the fire alarm?"

I squeezed the wheel harder, but the driver in front of me seemed not to notice.

"Are you in the meeting room yet?" I asked.

"Uh-huh. People are starting to show up."

"Who?"

His voice dropped to a whisper. "Two from Marketing at the other end of the table . . ."

"Which ones?"

"I think these are new. They're always new. They never seem to stick around for long."

"Because they all have ADHD," I said.

"There's a middle-aged lady with gigantic hoop earrings. And a young guy who looks like he's having a really bad hair day, only it's probably an actual style he paid seventy-five bucks for."

"What about Our Friends in Finance and Our Friends in Legal?"

"One of each. Ed Kraft and Bob Whatshisname."

"Is Hunter there yet?"

"No, but I'm sure he will be."

I knew what he meant. Hunter Thicke never missed a chance to run a meeting; it gave him something to do. As vice-president of content development, he was not a member of the working class.

"Any editors?" I asked.

"Just me."

I considered reprising my classic speech about how editors had sunk to the bottom of the publishing food chain. How we were trapped on the wrong side of history, like pagers and Betamax. But we'd addressed this subject many times, since editors liked nothing better than complaining about their pending extinction. There seemed to be little new ground left to plow.

"I hope you brought something to present," I said.

"Two proposals. One about the geology professor who returns to the small town he grew up in, where he has an affair with the woman who runs the bed and breakfast. Not very original, but I like what he does with dialogue. I told you about it last week."

"Of course," I said, not wanting to admit I hadn't been listening at the time.

"And a young adult dystopian series, except that it's not. It's actually utopian, only in an angsty way. Does that make sense?"

There was a long pause, during which I tried to think of a response other than "No."

"Guess you had to be there," he said finally.

"Unfortunately, I'm not. But I will be as soon as I can." I hit the END button and dropped the phone back in my pocket.

I checked the dashboard clock again. If I were lucky, I might be less than half an hour late.

Even so, Hunter wouldn't be happy when I got there. Two proposals weren't enough to justify his attendance at Acquisitions. The one I'd planned to present had been held up by an agent's eleventh-hour monkey wrench—a demand to retain electronic rights.

I had to come up with something else, and soon. Before my fingers touched the doorknob of Conference Room 3C.

By the time I finally parked in my appallingly overpriced space two blocks from the office, I'd failed to brainstorm even a minor cloudburst. Grabbing my briefcase, I looked up at Pendleton Tower. The gritty, gray granite monolith had been absorbing soot from the tailpipes of MTA buses for as long as I could remember. So had I, probably.

After pushing my way through the brass-and-glass revolving door, I crossed the mostly deserted lobby and pressed the UP button on one of the four elevators. I could imagine what was going on without me in 3C. Hunter's mouth was open, and from it flowed a steady stream of the latest buzzwords he'd seen in *Businessweek*. Or maybe he was quoting an inspirational anecdote about Walt Disney being fired from his childhood paper route, or the story of a courageous dog with one leg, or something else cribbed from a newsletter packed with ideas for executives who were determined to try the patience of their employees.

The elevator door rolled open, then closed behind me. Any moment now I'd be walking into that meeting, unarmed.

I looked up at the recessed light in the ceiling. Why did I subject myself to this? Did I *have* to be an editorial director, a position commanding the respect of exactly no one who understood twenty-first century publishing?

Sometimes I fantasized about being a *real* editor, the kind I'd been long ago and far away, unburdened by having to interact with anything more unpredictable than a pencil sharpener. But Pendleton House didn't need me to do that.

And I needed the money. But thanks to the assault and battery committed on my investments by certain politicians and stockbrokers, I could only imagine financial security.

The elevator shuddered to a halt. The door slid open. I stepped out, having indulged in enough self-absorption to choke the average teenager.

Before me the empty hallway unfurled, full of possibilities.

None of them was good.

* * *

"And that, my friends, is the story of how the kindness of a little girl with a really bad speech impediment helped Winston Churchill become the leader of the free world."

When Hunter finished, he looked down at his hands, which were folded with great solemnity on the table in front of him. His head was lowered, the slicked-back black hair gleaming. A long silence followed, though not because the other attendees seemed to be pondering his words deeply. They were all looking at me, probably because I was standing there with my hand still on the doorknob.

Hunter raised his head. "Well. So glad you could join us, Carolyn."

"Pardon my . . . tardiness," I said, barely able to force out the T-word. I sat down next to Stephen, who looked away. His wrinkle-free millennial face did not have a smile on it.

"We were all amazed at your lateness," Hunter said.

I looked around. No one seemed very perturbed. "Yes, I can see that."

"But we managed to make good use of the time." He picked up the one-page agenda. "We've heard from Mr. Ames about a fiction proposal. Frankly, it didn't get much traction."

"Oh," I said. That explained Stephen's pout.

"But it reminded me of a story about Winston Churchill," Hunter added, "which I think has given us all something to think about." No one nodded in agreement.

He flashed the disarming smile that, as far as I could tell, was his sole qualification for upper management. "And now I believe Mr. Ames has another proposal for us to consider."

Stephen stood. His cinnamon-colored hair was frizzier than usual. I wondered whether he'd been in a rush to leave his apartment or whether it was an outgrowth of a distracted mental state. Either way, he wore his Presentation Smile as if it were radioactive and he could barely wait to tear it off like a piece of Velcro.

He handed me a sheaf of papers. "Please take one and pass the rest on." I did, then started to read. It was about that non-dystopian YA series, something called *Echoes of Tomorrow*. From the subheads I could see the agent had touched all the usual bases—concept, primary and secondary and tertiary markets, author's platform, affinity groups, potential endorsers. I wondered whether the sample chapter was any good. If my experience was any indication, the answer was no.

"*The Hunger Games,*" Stephen began dramatically. "*Divergent. Maze Runner.* Young adult dystopian series are old news. Time for something completely different."

I nodded, trying to look supportive.

"You might even call it utopian," he continued. "*Echoes of Tomorrow* takes the cliché and turns it on its head. Yet it still—"

"Just a second," Hunter interrupted. "You're saying this is exactly the *opposite* of all those successful books?"

"In a way, yes. But it still has enough—"

"Seems to me we shouldn't mess with success. We should be talking about imitating what's worked already."

Stephen took a deep breath. His Presentation Smile looked ready to go askew. "I think we'd all agree the market is saturated with series like those. We need a new direction. People want something fresh."

Frowning, Hunter shuffled through the proposal's pages, perhaps looking for something he could understand, like pictures. "What kind of research do you have to back that up?"

Stephen cleared his throat. "It doesn't take research to see that the more imitators you get in a category, the lower sales go. Everybody knows that."

"Ah," Hunter said. "Well, *everybody* used to know the earth was round. But we don't know that anymore, do we?"

There was silence as the rest of us pondered his statement.

"Whatever," Hunter murmured, still scouring the proposal for a cartoon or at least a pie chart. "Carolyn, what do you think?"

I scratched my chin, hoping to appear thoughtful. "The . . . principle is sound. The pendulum swings. The audience tires of one thing, then wants the opposite." I paused. "Whether *this* is what it wants, of course, is another matter."

"Exactly what I'm saying!" Hunter declared. "We need research. Numbers. There's too much at stake to go with your gut."

Stephen didn't bother to set his smile aright. "The problem is that people don't know what they want until they see it. Our job is to create it and show it to them."

Hunter set the proposal down. "No, your job is to show this *committee*. Do the research. Get . . . you know . . . measurable." He tapped his temple with his index finger, perhaps hoping to convince us there was something inside. "Let's table this 'til next time."

Stephen sat down and said nothing. Neither did anyone else. His expression was unreadable, but only if one were legally blind.

"Okay!" Hunter said, breaking out the grin again. "What else do you guys have for us? Carolyn?"

I swallowed, twice. The first time was involuntary. The second was stalling.

"Research," I said finally. "Yes, research is indispensable." I had no idea where I was going with this. "I've been thinking a lot about research lately."

Then I remembered. The researcher. The whistleblower. At the drug company. The one I'd brought up at the doctor's office. It hadn't done me much good there, but maybe it could here.

That was when the idea began to come together in my head, like crazed Black Friday shoppers converging on a marked-down designer dress. It was a terrible concept, but the only one I could call my own.

"How many have heard about UniMerritt? The drug company cover-up?" I asked. Most raised their hands. Stephen, still looking unhappy, did not raise his very high.

Hunter went beyond the call, raising both of his. "Big Pharma," he said, sounding disgusted.

"A multinational corporation invents a drug that kills people, then hides the evidence," I continued. "One of its researchers blows the whistle. One brave man against a giant."

"Like David and . . . that big guy," Hunter said.

"Goliath," I said.

"That's the one."

I leaned forward, trying to look impassioned. "What if we could get the whistleblower's story?"

"Oooh," said the Marketing woman with the hoop earrings. There were goose bumps in her voice.

"Everybody's heard of him, but nobody seems to have gotten an interview—let alone a book."

Stephen, who was doodling in the margins of his tabled proposal, did not look up. But Hunter's face was alight.

"I love it!" he said. I hadn't seen him this excited since the last time he'd been quoted in *Publishers Weekly* on one of the many subjects he knows nothing about. "It has to be an instant book. Ripped from the headlines."

*Uh-oh.* I closed my eyes. I should have known this would happen. Hunter thought short-term when he thought at all, always poised to exploit every half-baked but supposedly timely idea that came his way. This one certainly fell into that category.

"Maybe we can get your old buddy to do it," he said. "The true-crime writer, the black guy."

"Marvin Ainsley Pitts? Oh, I doubt that. He's retired. And he doesn't like instant books. He says quality takes time."

"Whatever. The important thing is to get it done." He leaned back in his chair and nodded at me. "We need somebody heavy-duty, somebody we can trust. I want you to write this book personally. You and Mr. Ames."

Stephen, still doodling, made a choking sound.

I would have swallowed once more, but I was out of saliva.

"But we can't drop everything and—"

"Sure you can," he said. "Hire a couple of freelancers and an intern to cover for you. If you want something done right, do it yourself. Or, if you're me, get somebody to do it for you." He turned to the rest of the group. "Time to take a vote. Who wants Carolyn and Mr. Ames to co-write this book ASAP?"

All hands went up.

Except mine. And Stephen's.

"Motion carried," Hunter said. "Now, I want you two to go talk with this whistleblower in . . . ." He paused. "Anybody know where he lives?"

The young Marketing guy with the messy hair spoke up. "Seattle, I think."

"Okay, Seattle. Go get the rights from him. *Now*, before somebody else beats us to it."

Stephen put down his pen but said nothing.

"This is gonna be big, people," Hunter said. "My gut tells me."

Stephen rolled his eyes.

"I want to see this book in stores four months from now," Hunter added.

I shook my head. "But that's—"

"Don't tell me it's impossible. People said it was impossible to turn lead into gold. But did those Middle Ages guys give up trying? No."

The members of the committee were very quiet, no doubt having been overcome by his powers of inspiration.

I, meanwhile, was thinking about the assignment Stephen and I had just been handed.

We'd been commanded to strike a deal with the whistleblower, thereby saddling ourselves with an impossible deadline.

It was much like being forced to dig our own graves.

I could only hope that if we failed at the former, we wouldn't have to do the latter, too.

# CHAPTER 2

I DECIDED TO FORTIFY MYSELF FOR THE JOURNEY BY EATING comfort food and proving that Dr. Garabedian didn't know squat. I was fit to travel without his witch-doctor prescription. The only way to do both, of course, was to eat and run with my BFF, not necessarily in that order.

Mikki Flaherty and I knew each other from church. Our plan was to meet at the park halfway between my condo and her townhouse, where the jogging path was. I'd never used it before, but she spoke highly of it. We'd run to Roundelay's, the doughnut place nearby.

I spotted her powder blue Mini Cooper Clubman in the lot at the park. It was the ultimate car for her slender self, a body that could have inspired Elton John's "Tiny Dancer." Unlike me, she needed no shoehorn to squeeze therein. It was also the perfect way to determine whether she was around, considering her preference for changing looks every couple of weeks. Today it was a bleached-white ponytail that would have done Edgar Winter proud, sticking out the back of a metallic gold cap.

She was doing stretches when I got there, the kind of

thing she probably did backstage before her "creative move-ment" numbers in the Saturday night worship service. Few people could get more inspiration out of a fistful of silk scarves.

"Long time no see," she said, bending down and touching cheek to thigh in a totally unnatural way she made look perfectly natural. "I'm sure the running path would say the same thing."

I picked lint off my blue sweatsuit, the one I'd bought last year that still had the tags until this morning. "Like I said on the phone, I've got something to prove. Surely you've had that feeling."

She straightened up. "Yeah, I once had to prove I could do cartwheels down the aisle at church during the offering. Put Mr. Halperin, that perfectly nice deacon, in an elbow brace for a month."

"Well, you're the expert. How do you jog?"

"Haven't you *ever* done this?"

I thought for a moment. "Maybe I did and just don't remember."

She shook her head. "Well, let's not overdo it. Speedwise, you should be able to carry on a conversation, but not sing."

"Okay."

She started running in slow motion. I followed. So far, so good.

"So let's carry on a conversation," she said. "You're going to Seattle?"

"Yeah. Hunter wants me to."

She shook her head. "One of his dopey ideas?"

"Actually, mine."

"What's the thing you have to prove?"

I lifted my chin. "That my doctor's wrong. He wants me to go on a statin for cholesterol. Doesn't like my blood pres-sure, either."

"Some reason you can't do what he says?"

"I'm fine. I don't like side effects. And I don't trust drug companies."

"I'm the same way. But I exercise. Just sayin'."

"Well, now so do I."

I was starting to breathe heavily.

We both fell silent. "Keep talking," she said.

"I . . . can do better than that," I panted. "I can sing."

"Show me."

"Goodbye, yellow brick road," I croaked. "Where the dogs . . . of society—"

I gulped, then ran out of air.

I stopped. An elderly couple walked past on the left, looking at me with concern.

Mikki waited. "You okay?"

"Sure," I said, hands on my knees. "I'll stick to talking."

"Let's just walk for a while."

I shrugged as if it wasn't necessary, but secretly breathed a sigh of relief.

We walked without speaking, taking in the smell of just-mowed weeds that edged the path.

"What would you do if you *did* have a health problem?" she asked suddenly. "I mean, when people like us are on our own, there's nobody to take us to the doctor or anything. We can get on the prayer list at church, but it's hardly the same thing."

I looked up at the sky. "Count on my friends, I guess. I'd take *you* to the doctor or wherever."

"Thanks. I'd take you, if you paid me."

I rolled my eyes. "Forget it."

"So how often are you planning to do this?" she asked, waving to indicate the path we were on.

I cleared my throat. "Not sure."

"Did the doctor say anything about your diet?"

"Maybe."

"You planning to change it?"

I frowned. "I guess I could give up doughnuts for a while."

Her eyes widened. "You're kidding. I thought we were going to Roundelay's after this."

"I'll start tomorrow. Maybe I'll do it for a week. Seven days. Seven's the biblical number of perfection."

She laughed. "Hey, the Flood lasted forty days and forty nights. How about that?"

"Baby steps," I said.

\* \* \*

The next day Stephen and I touched down at Sea-Tac Airport, which sounded as if it had been named for a marine adhesive. That seemed fitting since, as a little-known City of Seattle ordinance must have required, it was raining.

Stephen wasn't his usual buoyant self, having glowered out the drizzled window for much of the flight. The dismissal of his book proposals had clearly taken their toll, as had Hunter's enthusiasm for my abominable suggestion. He'd spoken maybe three dozen words to me in the 48 hours since the Acquisitions meeting, at least four of them accurate but unprintable assessments of Hunter's competence and character.

As his supervisor, I couldn't indulge my desire to do the same aloud. But I'd done my best to express solidarity with his cause by secretly and repeatedly envisioning Hunter being executed for crimes against literature and society at large. My favorite scenario involved the electric chair.

The relative silence between us lingered as we rode the airport's moving walkway past framed ads for the pantheon of Seattle icons—the first Starbucks, Pike Place Market, the

Seattle Center Monorail, the Washington State Ferries, Pioneer Square, the Mariners baseball team . . .

And, of course, the Space Needle.

I'd pondered that landmark just yesterday, after the whistleblower and his wife had warily agreed to meet with us. When I'd e-mailed that news to the committee, Hunter's blunt thumbs and Autocorrect had texted that we should take our "future parters" out for a "world-clash" dinner. The place to go, he wrote, was "that thing that spins around on top of the Space Needle."

Bound by duty and disregarding his spelling, I'd considered the possibility. Judging from Internet reviews hastily and resentfully compiled by Stephen, the lofty dining establishment was the subject of acrimonious debate. Some said the food was nothing special, and the rotation of the restaurant triggered motion sickness.

Too risky, I decided. Still, we faced a battery of unknowns. We were strangers to Seattle, and to our quarry. What did whistleblowers eat? How about this one in particular?

Stephen's online explorations hadn't helped much. All we knew was that the guy's name was Kelvin Rhee, age 51. He and his wife, Olivia, age 42, were second-generation Korean-Americans. Holder of a Ph.D. in biochemistry from Johns Hopkins University, Rhee had spent the last nine years managing one of three research labs at UniMerritt. There seemed to be only one photograph of him, which had appeared with most of the articles posted about the case. It depicted a very serious-looking man with tired eyes, black and bushy eyebrows, and short, salt-and-pepper hair.

As for his dining preferences, the Web was mum. In light of that, I'd suggested a Korean restaurant.

Stephen shook his head. "Stereotyping. They might be offended. Or bored."

Both prospects appealed to me, of course. After all, I didn't want them to greenlight the book. It was a sentiment I left unspoken, though, out of respect for the sensitivities of my bank account.

In the end we'd gone with what seemed like the safest option. After soliciting recommendations from Ms. Hoop Earrings and Mr. Messy Hair, both of whom claimed to have been to Seattle, we flipped a coin.

And that was why, at this moment, the four of us were being escorted to a booth at something called GreenGenes. It had been Mr. Messy Hair's choice, and I was already wishing he and the coin had possessed a little more foresight.

GreenGenes had sounded vaguely scientific, a trait we hoped would appeal to our guests. But one look at the staff and patrons made me cringe.

The young man guiding us to our seats sported a man bun, a look that said, "Samurai warrior with Quaker sympathies." So did a few other male employees, the rest having opted for Messy Hair of one kind or another. Most of the women, meanwhile, looked like the oppressed waif from the poster for *Les Misérables*, but wearing fashionably ugly, black-framed glasses. I saw no women buns, so to speak.

Too late to change the plan. We'd have to make the best of it.

As we approached our booth, Dr. Rhee surveyed the room as if he'd suddenly found himself in a mismanaged psychiatric hospital. If he knew his charcoal suit and cufflinks were out of place, he didn't seem to care. His wife, dressed in a gauzy, tie-dyed outfit that made her float instead of walk, looked mostly at the floor.

When the four of us were seated, I smiled at our guests. "Have you been here before?"

Dr. Rhee didn't answer, but frowned with great conviction.

His wife picked up the conversational slack. She returned my smile, though with less incandescence and more shyness. "I don't think we've been here," she said, her soft voice barely rising above the din. "I probably would remember that."

Dr. Rhee looked down at his menu, which was undoubtedly printed on recycled paper. He appeared reluctant to touch it. "GreenGenes," he said. "A familiar name."

We waited for him to explain, but he seemed to think it unnecessary.

Finally I spoke up. "The suspense is killing me. Why is it familiar?"

He sighed heavily, as if he were the smartest person in the room but didn't want to be. "GreenGenes is an RNA database. Part of the Second Genome Project. University of Denver, University of Queensland. I've used it only occasionally, but one must be conversant with such resources. The introduction of nucleic acid polymers through genetic therapy is the future of medicine."

"No question," I said, having no idea what he was talking about, and not really wanting one.

Suddenly our server appeared, his man bun bobbing like an untreatable growth on the back of his head. Grinning with a zeal that didn't seem quite normal, he introduced himself as Chandler.

"Here's our specials," he said with an appalling lack of subject-verb agreement, not to mention the speed of someone fearing the effects of climate change might cut him off at any moment. "Northwest Cedar Plank-Roasted Salmon with a Vermont Maple Glaze. Savory Kale Salad with Goat Cheese and Cider Vinegar Dressing. Gluten-Free Pasta—"

Frowning, Rhee looked up from his menu. "The cider vinegar," he said. "Is that raw, unfiltered, organic?"

"Well, I—"

"Does it contain the mother?"

The young man's brow furrowed. "Excuse me?"

"The 'mother' occurs naturally as linked chains of protein enzyme molecules. It's been praised for its health benefits since the days of Hippocrates. Surely you're aware of that."

The server's man bun began to tremble, as did several other parts of his body.

"Do the research," Rhee added ominously.

"I . . . I'll be right back," the young man said.

There was a long pause. I tried to come up with my next line. Mrs. Rhee lowered her gaze.

The scientist turned toward his wife. "I suppose I've embarrassed you again."

When his wife didn't reply, he turned toward Stephen and me. "Olivia and I have somewhat differing approaches to the younger generation. My parents challenged me, teaching me traditional values like self-control and precision. Call me out of touch, but I'm afraid too many of the current generation haven't received those values from their own families."

I nodded. "I'm a big fan of self-control and precision."

Stephen looked at the Rhees. "Oh, if you only knew," he said with a sigh.

Just then the server returned and took a deep breath. "Okay. Are you folks ready to order?"

"Did you do the research?" Rhee persisted.

The young man tried to smile. "I did. I looked at the vinegar jug. It's raw, unfiltered, and organic, but doesn't say anything about . . . the mother."

"Fine," Rhee said, looking down at the menu. "I actually wanted the Northwest Cedar Plank-Roasted Salmon with the Vermont Maple Glaze."

"But I thought you—"

"I was merely helping you learn an important concept. Perhaps someday you will thank me, though I doubt it."

The young man opened his mouth as if to say something,

then seemed to think better of it. He stared toward a black-board on the wall. It said SEATTLE'S GREATEST SELECTION OF CRAFT BEERS in chalk. His expression signaled that he yearned to sample all of them as soon as possible.

Mrs. Rhee ordered the Gluten-Free Pasta with Sun-Dried Marinara Sauce. Stephen picked the salmon. I rejected the specials and went straight for the Artisanal Gourmet Burger with Locally Sourced Onion Rings, the most unhealthy-sounding item on the menu. I wondered what the meddlesome Dr. Garabedian would think of that. I hoped he'd be aghast.

As for "the mother," no one seemed interested in ordering it. Or her. The server left, his eyes more glazed than the salmon could ever be.

I turned toward Mrs. Rhee. "I see on the Internet that you're an artist."

Mrs. Rhee brightened. "A sculptor, yes."

"As in statues? Clay pots? Or . . ."

"Fabric sculpture, mostly."

"Really."

Suddenly Dr. Rhee straightened up. "You may as well know now," he announced to no one in particular. "I don't want to do a book."

My eyes widened. So did Stephen's.

Mrs. Rhee's, on the other hand, retained their usual circumference. Perhaps she was used to this sort of thing.

I cleared my throat. "You mean you don't want to—"

"That *is* why we're here, isn't it?" Rhee asked. "Your publishing company would like to do a book about my so-called whistleblowing."

"That did occur to us," I said.

"I'm sure it did. But I came forward on the subject of Milletinor because it was right, not because I wanted notoriety. Or money."

"Of course not. But this is a great opportunity to get your message out to millions of people."

"I don't *have* a message."

I was confused. "Don't you want the public to know that big companies like UniMerritt are greedy and deceptive and couldn't care less about sick people?"

"No. I want to equip patients to make more informed decisions about their treatment."

I shrugged. "Sounds pretty much the same to me."

"There's a *difference*," he said, settling back in the booth. "Please try to be precise."

I frowned. Mr. Science was starting to get on my nerves.

The glowing green EXIT sign across the room seemed to beckon. *All you have to do is get up and walk out*, it whispered. Stephen looked like he was ready to do that himself.

But I couldn't, of course. This book had to happen. It was inevitable, like the meteor that wiped out the dinosaurs. Or *The New York Review of Books*, or the invention of magnetic eyelashes.

I lowered my gaze to the glass that sat before me. The menu had described it as Sommelier-Curated Tap Water with a Slice of Pesticide-Free Lemon.

Taking a sip, I wished for something stronger.

\* \* \*

The next 11 minutes and 27 seconds were remarkably awkward. It was a period of small talk so tiny the ear could barely pick it up.

When at last we received our food, our server was nowhere to be seen. His replacement was a young woman, one of those bespectacled waifs from *Les Miz*. Apparently the hapless young man with the bun had quit and wandered away in a fog, never to be seen again.

"This looks lovely," Mrs. Rhee said of her dish, the lengthy name of which isn't worth repeating here, especially with all that unnecessary capitalization.

Stephen looked at my platter of artsy hamburger, which reeked of frying and decadence. "So does yours," he said, the aroma of onion rings apparently having overcome his disinterest in the conversation.

Dr. Rhee gingerly lifted his butter knife from the table as if it were a scalpel. After making the first incision in his salmon, he placed the flesh in his mouth and began to chew slowly. If he approved of his meal, he didn't say so.

Turning to Mrs. Rhee, I smiled. "And how is yours?"

She smiled back. "Quite excellent, thank you."

Stephen held up a forkful of salmon. "Great minds think alike," he said with a nod at Dr. Rhee.

"If you say so," Rhee said, shuddering at the comparison.

"You know, Mrs. Rhee," I said, "I'd guess we have a lot in common."

"Please, call me Olivia."

"Okay, you're a livia."

I felt myself blush. It was the kind of awful pun my older brother had tormented me with throughout our childhoods. Somehow it had slipped out.

But Mrs. Rhee giggled, then covered her lips with her hand. She glanced at her husband, who kept chewing.

I put my hand on Mrs. Rhee's arm. "Olivia, even though the subject of this book is very serious, we might have a good time working together. I've never been to Seattle before. I'll bet you could show me some outstanding places."

She tilted her head to one side. "We do have wonderful museums. I think you'd love the Chihuly exhibit."

"And of course we'd have to go out to lunch at every opportunity. Though I'd let you pick the restaurants. I'm sure you'd do a better job than we did with this one."

She chuckled.

Stephen looked a little queasy at all the synonyms for gentle laughter. Dr. Rhee cleared his throat and set down his surgical tools.

He pivoted toward his wife. "You are assuming, of course, that I will say yes to the book."

She lowered her head slightly. "Not assuming. Merely encouraging you to reconsider."

He frowned. "Has something changed in the last ten minutes? Perhaps I missed it."

I put down my fork. "Dr. Rhee, I can see you're a man of principle. I would guess you've found certain causes you support."

He didn't respond, but his wife nodded.

"I'd also guess you've found certain organizations promoting those causes. Maybe in the sciences or the arts. Or politics, or hunger relief. What if you could donate your share of the proceeds from this project to those groups?"

His frown didn't budge. But he did raise an eyebrow.

"Even if you feel the book isn't an absolute necessity, think of all the things you could accomplish with that money," I said.

He watched me with narrowed eyes. "Exactly how much are we talking about?" he asked finally.

"Well, publishing is a speculative enterprise," I said. "It's impossible to know how a particular book will sell."

After taking a pen from my purse, I positioned a napkin printed with the words 100% BIODEGRADABLE on the table in front of me. "You'd get an advance against royalties. And judging from the enthusiasm at Pendleton House for this project, I'd expect it to be substantial." I wrote a number on the napkin. "This is in the ballpark, I think." I reached across the table, rotated it with two fingers, and placed it in front of him.

His eyebrows went up, but he said nothing. Then he slid the napkin over so that his wife could read it.

"Oh, my," she said.

They looked at each other.

"Kelvin, that's a lot of good," she said.

He sat there for a moment. He picked up his water glass and took a sip.

Finally he pulled a pen from his shirt pocket, turned the napkin over, and scribbled what looked like long division. Even the thought of all those numbers gave me math anxiety.

He turned to his wife. "The Foundation, do you think?"

"Oh, yes," she said.

He lowered his head again and scribbled more numbers. "We could double our usual giving," he mumbled without looking up. "And with a matching grant . . ."

He returned the pen to his pocket, then folded his hands on the table again. He looked at me, then at Stephen. "My parents didn't teach me only to be self-disciplined and precise. They also believed in doing what was honorable, even when it meant personal sacrifice. The honorable individual puts the interests of others above his own."

There was a pause.

"Is that . . . a yes?" I asked.

He glanced at his wife. "I suppose it is."

"You won't regret it," I said.

"I already do." He turned the napkin around and slid it toward me.

"We can have a contract ready in a day or so. Our Friends in Legal are waiting to hear from us."

Rhee looked me in the eye. "One other thing, Ms. Neville. I wish to have a diagram of the double helix on the cover," he said.

I blinked. "The what?"

"The winding strands of a DNA molecule. A most beautiful structure, and quite pertinent to the subject at hand."

Stephen gave me a warning glance. "Cover approval? We can't put that in the—"

Rhee's formidable eyebrows lowered.

I leapt to the rescue. "Our marketing department and art director deal with cover design. I'm sure that when the time comes, you'll be able to find an approach everyone will be happy with." I gave Stephen a warning glance of my own.

Rhee nodded somberly, then went back to operating on his salmon. His wife, beaming, patted his arm.

"We're looking forward to working with both of you," I said cheerily.

Stephen grunted.

I grabbed an onion ring and chewed as quickly as I could. The thought of spending the next four months trying to wring an instant, personal book out of this emotionless turnip felt more life-threatening than a whole bucket of saturated fat.

But the greasy, golden ring was little comfort.

I was going to need another order.

# CHAPTER 3

"So, what rights did you get?"

Hunter spun his black leather chair around, no longer gazing through his office window. It was not an interesting view, mostly Manhattan traffic and two tacky souvenir shops that sold postcards and crudely painted pewter models of more famous New York tourist traps. But it was better than the view from my office, which showcased an alley lined with dumpsters and an occasional bicycle courier with a poor sense of direction.

"The contract isn't actually signed yet," I said. "Dr. Rhee wants his lawyer to look at it."

Hunter shook his head. "Bad idea."

"Not if you're the author," I said.

"Which I'm not," he replied. "Let's make sure we get all rights. There could be a movie in this. The board likes to hear it when we get a property like that."

I nodded. It was always good to know how the deities on Mt. Olympus felt about things.

"What's this guy like?" Hunter asked.

Stephen and I looked at each other. "Precise," we said, more or less in unison.

"Exacting," I added. "Grumpy. No social skills. I think he may have Asperger's Syndrome."

"You're not supposed to call it that anymore," Stephen chided. "You can only say he's 'on the spectrum.'"

"Whatever you call it, he seems to resist normal human interaction. He'll refuse to talk about his feelings. I dread the thought of having to drag a book out of him one word at a time."

"You'll find a way," Hunter said. It sounded more like a threat than encouragement.

"The guy is a scientist. Not the kind who explains stuff in laymen's terms. The kind who says things that sound like entries on a Martian tax return."

He shook his head. "Science isn't so hard. Remember the words of Alfred Einstein. The guy with the crazy hair."

"*Albert* Einstein?" I asked.

"I don't think so. He said, 'The definition of doing things the same way over and over is getting different results.' In other words, just keep doing what you've always done, Carolyn, and this book will come together."

I looked away, wondering who had dropped Hunter on his head shortly after birth. It was sad, really.

"And in the meantime," he continued, "I have a little something to thank the two of you for reeling this guy in." Grinning, he backed his chair away from the desk and pulled out the main drawer. After poking around for a few seconds, he took out what looked like a pair of business cards.

He leaned over the desk and handed one to each of us. Under the Pendleton logo, the following message was printed in 12-point Helvetica Condensed:

THIS COUPON ENTITLES THE BEARER TO 15% OFF
ANY LUNCH ENTRÉE AT THE GOLDEN QUILL

The Golden Quill was the Pendleton House cafeteria. It was somewhat renowned, at least in this building, for having real bacon bits on the salad bar.

"I believe in recognizing employee achievement," Hunter said solemnly.

I stared at the card. "I . . . don't know what to say."

Stephen looked like he knew what to say, but wisely kept it to himself.

"One more thing," Hunter said. "Every time I tell people what a touchdown this project is going to be, they want to know if the whistleblower has a fan base. A hashtag. If he tweets. If he's on Facebook. Marketing people especially."

Stephen put the card in his pocket and pulled out his phone. "He doesn't seem like the type to me, but you never know. I'll Google him again."

He poked at the phone. "I have to remember to type in *Kelvin*, not Kevin. What kind of name is Kelvin?"

"It's shorter than Fahrenheit and Centigrade," I said.

He snickered, but Hunter looked puzzled.

"Okay," Stephen said, frowning. "Just found something on CNN.com. Posted fifty-seven minutes ago." He poked again. There was a pause as he read the article.

He gasped. "Oh, God. You won't believe this."

"What?" I asked.

"He's dead."

He looked up from his phone.

"The guy is dead."

"How?"

"Nobody seems to know. But everybody knows who did it."

I had to admit, though not out loud, that my feelings were mixed.

On the one hand, I was sorry his life was over.

On the other, I had the feeling mine was about to get a lot more complicated.

* * *

We took turns looking at each other. No one spoke. Hunter's chair squeaked.

Someone had to say it, so I did. "Are you sure?"

Stephen cleared his throat and started reading the post aloud. And slowly, as if trying to find a loophole in an eviction notice.

*A researcher who recently gained fame as a pharmaceutical whistleblower was found dead this morning, according to Seattle police. Dr. Kelvin Rhee, 51, died of undetermined causes. The body was discovered by his wife, Olivia.*

*A biochemist, Rhee was employed by drugmaker UniMerritt Laboratories. In a March 3 letter to the Food and Drug Administration and The Seattle Times, he alleged that UniMerritt had concealed a series of memos in which he had warned management that its new diabetes drug, Milletinor, might increase the risk of pancreatic cancer. The alleged cover-up drew national attention from the media as well as from public officials who called for legal action and a congressional investigation.*

*One of those officials, Representative Constance Griffith (D-Mass.), issued a statement at 11:15 a.m. EDT. "Our hearts go out to the family and friends of this brave American," she said. "As we've seen so many times before, the siren song of profit must not be allowed to drown out the voice of truth. No corporation is above the law, and this one must be held accountable." It was not clear whether the statement referred to UniMerritt's role in the alleged cover-up or was meant to imply its involvement in Rhee's death.*

Hunter swiveled his chair toward the window. "Oh, crap," he said. "Tell me this isn't happening."

Stephen kept reading.

*A police spokesperson declined to comment further on the case. Police Chief Peter Everly has scheduled a news conference for tomorrow morning. An autopsy is pending.*

We took turns looking at each other again. Hunter's chair squeaked once more.

I thought of Rhee sitting at the restaurant table, frown lines deep, operating on his salmon. I saw his wife patting his arm. For a moment I imagined what he might look like with his eyes closed. And his wife, her hands covering her face.

My throat tightened. I wished I could take back everything I'd said—and thought—about him in the last 24 hours.

Stephen tapped and swiped his phone for another half minute or so, then sighed. "Just to answer your question, I'm not seeing him on Facebook. Or Twitter. No fan club that I can find. Lots of comments on the CNN story, though. Mostly blaming the drug company."

Hunter shook his head. "God. Things change in a second, don't they?" He sounded sincerely dazed. "I mean . . . one minute you're eating dinner with him, and the next thing you know, he's . . ."

"Dead?" Stephen asked.

"Well, yeah." Hunter rubbed the side of his face, as if his

jaw hurt. "We're screwed," he said, almost to himself. "You can't interview a dead man. We've got no book."

I couldn't say I was sad about losing the project. I didn't know what to say.

Hunter rapped his desktop with a single whack. "We can't just let it go. We've gotten people's hopes up. Important people. They're expecting great things."

"We?" I said. "I don't recall telling anybody—"

"The board is excited. It's already penciled in on the schedule."

"How did that happen?"

He tried to look innocent. "You know how Our Friends in Marketing are."

There was another long silence. He seemed to have run out of things to say on the subject. At least I hoped he had.

Unfortunately, he had one more terrible idea left in him.

"That's *it*," he said suddenly, smacking his palm on the desk. He rolled his chair back and stood up. "When life gives you lemons, the tough get going."

"Excuse me?"

"Sure, this is a setback. Our subject may be gone. But he's not forgotten. And the two of you are going to make sure he never is."

I had no inkling what he meant. But his statement made me slightly seasick. Stephen's expression indicated he was feeling a similar sensation.

I looked at Hunter. "You have something in mind," I said, knowing nothing was actually in there.

"If we can't do a book *by* the whistleblower, we do one *about* him," he said. "A true-crime story about the heroic science guy who was murdered by Big Pharma."

"But we don't know who killed him," I protested.

"Sure we do. Just a matter of time before the verdict is in."

"But you wanted an *instant* book," I said.

"Right. Strike while the iron's hot. Get it on the shelves in four months."

Stephen and I looked at each other, then at Hunter.

"No one can do a book like this in a time frame like that," I said. "Especially when the facts aren't in."

He looked puzzled. "Facts?"

"Such as who killed Dr. Rhee."

Hunter spread his arms wide. "Everybody knows the drug company did it. We just don't know *how*. That's where you two come in."

Stephen emitted a whimper. There were no words, but it sounded like *Please don't hurt me*.

I leaned toward Hunter, trying not to sound as if I wanted to crush his head with an anvil. "If we accuse the drug company without facts, that would be libel. Our Friends in Legal would have a collective stroke."

He waved the notion away. "The cops will get evidence. They've probably got it already, and UniMerritt's paying them to keep it a secret. Stuff like that happens all the time. Don't you listen to talk radio?"

"Not since I misplaced my tinfoil hat."

He turned and stepped toward the window, where things still did not look picturesque. "If the police don't get the facts, you can get your own. I bet your old buddy could do it. The black guy, Marvin."

"He's retired. And he doesn't like instant books. He says—"

"I know, quality takes time." He paused. "We don't have any. The window of opportunity won't stay open for long. People forget. Remember Pee Wee Herman?"

"No."

"*I* do," Stephen said.

Hunter frowned. "Well, maybe he's not the best example. My point is that time is short. We can't let this one get away. The world's on a fast track, and you can change or die."

"I'm working on it," I said. "Especially the dying part."

He shook his head. "Carolyn, the days of the Pony Express are over."

"I know," I said with a sigh. "But I'm getting used to Mr. Morse's telegraph."

He cranked up his own brand of Presentation Smile, the one with teeth that somehow looked as though they'd been sharpened with a file. "I know you two won't let me down."

"We have before," I said.

"Not this time. You know what's on the line."

I nodded, not caring to itemize that list.

"Besides," he added, "I can offer another incentive to keep you motivated."

He pulled open his desk drawer again, gathered a handful of Golden Quill discount cards, and held them up.

"There's more where these came from," he said with a wink.

I looked at Stephen. He looked at me.

*Life is that way*, I thought.

There was, unfortunately, always more where it came from.

# CHAPTER 4

SEATTLE WAS STILL THERE.

So was our lack of interest in visiting the Space Needle. This time we had good reason to jump from its pinnacle ourselves, but didn't want to tempt fate.

We may have flown over the place, though, as our Boeing 757 descended like a blind and hissing whale through the dense clouds that imprisoned Sea-Tac. The airport hadn't changed its odd name, nor the city its dismal weather.

It was just as well. At the moment, Haiti would have been a more desirable destination. The closer our Delta flight got to Seattle, the more unlikely it looked that we would ever earn another Golden Quill coupon, much less keep the ability to pay our bills.

That got even clearer when we finally stepped into Terminal 4, Gate 38.

Stephen looked around, then stopped short after spotting the nearest television screen. His wheeled carry-on trundled to a halt. "Wait a minute," he said, frowning. "Didn't that CNN report say the police chief was going to have a press conference this morning?"

I squinted at the screen. It showed a local news broadcast. The crawl at the bottom was yammering about temperatures and chances of rain and creating a safe space for traumatized ducks. Nothing about a press conference.

"Maybe we missed it," I said. "Or it hasn't happened yet."

He took out his phone. "Maybe it already happened, and they've posted some of it online." The TV showed the station's URL, and he started poking his phone. "Here it is," he said after a pause. Leaning my bag against a seat, I sat and waited.

This time the crawl said POLICE CHIEF ADDRESSES DEARTH OF DRUG WHISTLEBLOWER.

"*Dearth?*" I said, shaking my head. "They can spell *whistle-blower*, but not—"

"Shhh."

It was a press conference, already in progress on the front steps of some glassy building that reflected the leaden sky. To the podium was affixed the seal of the City of Seattle, a circled Native American face undergirded by what appeared to be a quartet of fish and pine cones. At the microphone stood a silent man, late forties, in a dark blue uniform with four gold stripes and a small constellation of stars on each sleeve. The outfit seemed too big for him.

"So that's Everly," I said.

He was pale and slender, an aging surfer boy, with thinning blond hair that flipped and feathered in the breeze. Gripping the lectern with both hands, his eyes smoldering beneath lowered brows, he seemed ready to condemn something, somebody, or everybody.

His mouth moved, but the din around us overpowered his voice. Stephen drove the volume as high as it would go.

"At this point we don't know a great deal," Everly said. His words were clipped, reedy, like Bobby Kennedy but without the Boston accent. "We do know Dr. Rhee died during the night at his home. A 911 call requesting assistance was placed by his wife, Olivia, at 6:37 a.m. Officers and paramedics were dispatched. Dr. Rhee was pronounced dead at 7:09 a.m."

I wondered whether I should be writing this down. I always made notes when Marvin Ainsley Pitts reeled off bits of information like this over the phone, but a check of my purse revealed no pen.

Everly squared his narrow shoulders. "Our evidence team, as always, made a thorough examination of the scene. There were no signs of a struggle. When the results of his autopsy are available, we will share them with the public."

He paused, as if observing a moment of silence, then raised his chin slightly. "There has been a great deal of speculation about whether Dr. Rhee was the victim of foul play. I want to assure every person in this community that we are considering all possibilities and will follow wherever the evidence leads. As long as I have the privilege of serving the people of Seattle, that will be the policy of this department."

"He's running for something," I mumbled.

"I'll take just a few questions at this time," he said. The camera bobbled as reporters raised hands and yelped for attention. He pointed to someone toward the back of the crowd. A faint query was voiced, but the microphone didn't pick it up.

Everly nodded impatiently. "In case you didn't hear that, the question was, 'Will you pursue an investigation of UniMerritt Laboratories?'" He gazed skyward as if seeking divine guidance. Apparently he got it. "From the very beginning, when Dr. Rhee first spoke out against the criminal behavior of his employer, many people I deeply respect have asked for investigations by the U.S. Department of Justice and the Food and Drug Administration. Now that Dr. Rhee has died under . . . unclear circumstances, it is my responsibility to do what I can to uncover the truth. I will not rest until the whole story is known."

"He's running for president," I said. "Or at least Congress."

Stephen shushed me again.

The view on the phone swung left. There stood about a dozen protesters, many of whom resembled the servers at GreenGenes. The rest looked old enough to know who Jack Kerouac was. All held up signs saying things like BREAK BIG PHARMA and DR. RHEE WAS TERMINATED and NO MORE MERCHANTS OF DEATH.

"At least *they* can spell death," I said.

They began to chant, sounding as if they'd done this sort of thing before.

*"Pharma, pharma, whaddaya say? How many hearts did you stop today?"*

They got in about half a dozen repetitions. But when the camera panned back to the lectern, they seemed to lose interest. Their voices fell off raggedly.

Everly nodded. "I hear you. We can only hope that Washington, D.C. hears you, too." He surveyed the pool of reporters. "One more question."

There was another faraway inquiry, too far from the microphone. "The question," he said, "is how the public can expect a thorough investigation when UniMerritt is such a powerful force in the city's economy." His frown deepened. He pointed a finger, presumably at the questioner. "You can expect a thorough investigation because the Seattle Police Department is not for sale. Not on my watch."

I rolled my eyes.

"That's all we know at this point," he concluded. "Our thoughts are with the family and friends of Dr. Rhee, and with our city. We'll keep you updated as we have new information."

A microphone bumped; the picture lurched slightly. The video faded to black.

I shook my head. "He doesn't sound like a police chief," I said. "Or look like one, either."

Stephen turned off his phone. "This is Seattle. They do things differently here, remember?"

"Not differently enough. Political weasels can be found everywhere."

"That's a pretty snap judgment, isn't it? We don't really know him at all."

*Maybe not*, I thought. But I had a most unsettled feeling I was going to.

* * *

At the Avis counter we rented a yellow Prius, not wanting to be tarred and feathered by a mob of concerned citizens whose consciousness about fossil fuels had been raised to dangerous levels. For the next 20 minutes we tried to understand the vehicle's START button, which seemed strictly decorative. Every time we pressed it, nothing happened.

We consulted the manual from the glove compartment, then a confusing YouTube video on Stephen's phone, and finally a rather disdainful young bystander with large plugs in his earlobes. The latter revealed that we needed to press the brake pedal before pushing the button.

"At least we'll know what to do next time," Stephen said as I drove over the spiked exit from the lot, which always made me worry that I was making a terrible mistake.

"There won't be a next time."

"You'd never rent a hybrid again?"

"I mean we'll never have another *project* again. This one's going to crash and burn."

He looked out the window. "Consider the bright side. We

get a reasonably nice hotel, not the usual homeless encampment with an ice machine. Hunter's sparing no expense, more or less."

"That's always a bad sign."

"I know he spends the most on the worst ideas, as long as they're his. But look at all the attention this story's getting. We've even got protesters."

I nodded. "All we need is time and answers. Time's a problem. But for answers, we can start with Mrs. Rhee. I just hate to do it so soon. The poor woman just lost her husband."

"There'll never be a good time."

"After we check in." Reaching into my purse, I found a slip of paper with the address. "The hotel should be about two miles from here, on the right. Look for a sign that says Emerald City Extended Stays."

We rode in silence for about a minute. "I wonder how extended our stay will be," Stephen said.

"Until Hunter says, 'Where's that book?' and we say, 'It's not done yet,' and he says, 'You're fired.'"

"There's the sign."

Emerald City Extended Stays, we soon discovered, was indeed more presentable than many lodgings we'd endured. There was a gas fireplace in the lobby, a brass luggage rack on wheels, free coffee next to a basket of individually wrapped chocolate chip cookies, and two desk clerks who didn't look ready to stab us with scissors.

Down the hall we passed a Business Center equipped with laser printer and scanner, FedEx drop box, and three computers so new that their monitors weren't decorated with OUT OF ORDER signs. Further down the hall were a Laundry Center, two Conference Rooms, and a Fitness Center—the latter, of course, being something I wouldn't need. Take that, Dr. Garabedian.

We took our bags upstairs, having the luxury of choosing

between two elevators. Room 428, which was mine, smelled of wood with a hint of Mexican vanilla. The mahogany desk had a built-in USB charging station. On the walls hung black-and-white photos of skyscrapers, not the usual paint-ball approximations of tulip fields and clinically depressed clowns. All the kitchen lacked was a lemon zester and a pair of escargot tongs, both of which I had at home and neither of which had ever produced anything worth eating.

There was a knock at my door. It was Stephen.

He looked around. "Looks just like mine."

I sighed. "Guess one of us needs to call Mrs. Rhee."

He folded his arms. "Hey, don't look at me. You're the one who's formed a bond with her. The one who's promised to go to museums and have lunch with her every day. The one who makes terrible puns she thinks are funny."

"She seems like a very sweet person," I said. "And we need her to sign the contract. We can't write this book without her. Probably not *with* her, either."

"So good luck," he said, and walked out.

The door clicked shut behind him. I sat at the desk and heard the *thunk* of his door down the hall.

I picked up my phone. I wasn't very good at this sort of thing. I could carry on a reasonable conversation, but it was different when the other person was grieving. Maybe it was because of what happened when my grandma died. I was 10, and there was a viewing before the funeral. She looked so cold and waxy, and I didn't know what to say. We all knew she was in heaven, but here it was all so quiet.

I dialed Mrs. Rhee's cell number. Unfortunately, she picked up.

"Olivia," I said, then ran out of script.

"Is this Carolyn?"

"Yes. I'm . . . so sorry to bother you right now. I can't imagine what you're going through."

Her voice was almost too faint to make out. "I'm at the funeral home."

I closed my eyes. "I'll call back."

"No, no, it's all right. We just finished looking at caskets."

I swallowed. "That must have been difficult."

"Kelvin would have wanted something practical, basic. My choice was a little more ornate. I hope he won't mind."

"I'm sure he'd understand."

"It's kind of you to call me all the way from New York."

"Actually, we're here in Seattle."

"Here? Why?"

I bit my lip. "We . . . were hoping to talk with you about the book. Not now. Just when you get a chance."

"Well, I guess there can't be any book now."

"That's what I thought, but our employer had another idea. Are you open to discussing it?"

"I suppose so. How about this afternoon?"

"It's not too much of a burden?"

"No. It helps if I keep busy. Say . . . two-thirty at my house?"

"That would be wonderful."

"See you then."

I collapsed in my chair, then groaned. What horrible timing. At the funeral home, no less. I was so glad she hadn't started crying on the phone. That would have been the worst.

I sat there, wondering whether she was crying now.

* * *

"May I get you something to drink?"

Olivia was standing in the middle of her living room, looking smaller and more ghostly than ever. She still floated wherever she went, but less like a free spirit and more like a wistful one.

"I have apple juice, tea, coffee, water . . ."

Sitting next to Stephen on the ruddy leather sofa, I shook my head. "You don't have to—"

"It helps if I keep moving," she said gently. "Really, it does."

"Of course. I'd love some tea."

"I'm good," Stephen said.

She glided off to the kitchen.

"She seems to be functioning pretty well," I whispered. "Better than I would be."

"Running on adrenaline. Eventually she'll crash."

"I don't want to be there when it happens."

She drifted back, a wan smile on her face. "The tea should be ready soon." She sat on a nearby armchair, also reddish leather.

"Such a beautiful part of the city," I said. "I've never seen so many stairways for getting up and down hills."

She nodded. "I suppose the Queen Anne neighborhood is a bit pretentious sometimes, but it's close to everything. The water. Seattle Center. And so much history."

"And I love what you've done with this room. These must be some of your fabric sculptures."

She nodded. "And a little textile art. A few are from friends. Most are mine."

Directly across from the couch hung a series of something like African drums wrapped in gold and gray nylon stockings. Next to it was a vivid proliferation of silk scarves bursting from a fibrous field of tan.

In the corner sat a pyramid-shaped copper fountain, green and pitted with age. It was burbling.

"Very peaceful," I said.

We all listened to it for a moment.

"Kelvin used to say it restored one's equilibrium," she said.

Suddenly the whistle of a teakettle shrilled from the kitchen. I jumped.

"Excuse me," she said, and floated away.

"You okay?" Stephen whispered.

"Fine," I said, feeling myself blush.

She came back, served the tea, and sat again.

"Olivia," I said, "I'm sorry I intruded when you were at the funeral home."

"Oh, it was no intrusion." She paused. "The people there were very kind."

We listened to the fountain again. If it was restoring my equilibrium, I couldn't feel it.

She squeezed her eyes shut. "So many things to think about," she said, as if straining to think about all of them simultaneously. "Like the memorial service. Kelvin preferred to plan ahead. At least ten years ago he made a list of hymns he wanted sung. 'A Mighty Fortress Is Our God' . . . 'Faith of Our Fathers' . . ."

I raised an eyebrow. "Your husband was . . . a Christian?"

She opened her eyes. "Does that surprise you?"

"I . . . guess I figured he was too scientific to accept the supernatural. As for the Christian part, I thought he'd be something more . . ."

"Korean?"

"No, not that." But of course it was exactly what I'd been thinking. Which was pretty dumb, considering I'd heard so much at church about those giant congregations in places like Seoul.

"It's all right," she said. "As far as science goes, Kelvin liked to say the order of the universe was proof of God's existence. He was always talking about Sir Isaac Newton and Francis

Collins. And very few Korean-Americans are Buddhist. Most are Protestant."

I shifted position on the sofa, wanting to move to a topic on which I was less ignorant. "Speaking of church, would you mind if we attend the memorial service?"

"I'd be honored. My husband may have seemed a bit stern when you met him, but I think he appreciated your honesty. And your love of precision. He'd want both of you to be there."

She sighed. "I'm not sure how he'd feel about the chief of police, though."

I raised both eyebrows. "Chief of police?"

"Mr. Everly's office called yesterday to ask whether he could say a few words at the service. They said he wanted to pay tribute to such a courageous man. I said yes."

I glanced at Stephen, who was already looking at me, then back to Olivia. "I have the impression Mr. Everly believes your husband's employer was behind . . . what happened."

She looked down at her teacup. "So do I."

"Why?"

She shook her head. "I can't prove it. But there were times when Kelvin came home from work and didn't want to talk about what was going on. He said it was better if I didn't know certain things. That was before he sent the letter to the Food and Drug Administration and the newspaper."

Stephen leaned forward. "Did other employees feel that way about the company? Like someone was always looking over their shoulder, maybe?"

She shrugged. "I don't know. Socializing wasn't something Kelvin enjoyed, so I didn't have a lot of contact with the others."

She set down her tea and sank back into the armchair. A tiny groan escaped from somewhere deep inside.

"Are you all right?" I asked.

"Sorry. I'm just so tired."

"We should go," I said.

She turned her head toward us, but the rest of her didn't move. "I want to help. Anything I can do."

I got to my feet. "We'll talk another time, when you're feeling better. Maybe after the service." Stephen stood up, too.

She looked confused for a moment. "Today's Wednesday, isn't it?"

"Yes," I said, glad to redeem myself by getting something right.

"The service is Saturday. Three in the afternoon at our church. Grant Park Presbyterian on McGraw Street."

"We'll find it," I said.

Slowly she stood up. She looked tinier than ever.

"Thanks for the tea," I said. "I hope you can get some rest."

We passed another fabric sculpture on our way to the door. It had stuffed burlap and tendrils of velvet, like a jellyfish suspended in time.

"I wish I knew more about what happened to Kelvin," she said. "I'm not sure how much help I can be. I'm afraid it won't be enough."

The fountain in the corner burbled in the quiet that followed.

I shared her fear, but didn't say so.

* * *

Next morning, I heard a thump in the hall outside my hotel room. Then a series of lesser thumps, receding into the distance. The clock radio next to my bed declared that it was 6:12 a.m.

Opening the door, I found the Thursday edition of *The Seattle Times* on the carpet. It lay upside-down, but the photo just above the fold looked familiar. Bending down and turning it around, I discovered why.

It was Dr. Kelvin Rhee, not smiling.

The headline under the newspaper's American eagle logo wasted no words:

### WHISTLEBLOWER MURDERED, POLICE SAY

I sighed but wasn't surprised.

After bringing the paper inside and tossing it on the bed, I yawned. I had to wake up before I could deal with this.

There was a coffee maker next to the sink. I tore open the packet of Seattle's Best, making sure it was the caffeinated one.

When the brew was finally done, I poured myself a cup and set it on the desk. I watched it steam, then unfolded the newspaper. As ready as I'd ever be, I took a sip and began to read.

*The Seattle Police Department announced late Wednesday that the death of Dr. Kelvin Rhee, who brought to light an alleged cover-up by pharmaceutical giant UniMerritt Laboratories, will be investigated as a homicide. According to department spokesperson Peggy Nygren, a preliminary toxicology report suggests that Rhee died of cyanide poisoning, most likely introduced through a prescription he had been taking.*

*Ironically, the prescription—a recently introduced blood pressure medication called Lexidril—is manufactured by UniMerritt.*

. . .

I shook my head and took another drink. Oh, we were off to the races now.

*The autopsy was conducted by the King County Medical Examiner's Office. Nygren said the final report is expected in two to three weeks.*

*In a separate statement, Police Chief Peter Everly said, "The taking of an innocent individual's life can never be tolerated. Certainly not in a city like ours, which values everyone regardless of race, color, age, gender, sexual orientation, gender identity, national origin, language, immigration status, ethnicity, income, ability, or religion. But when a lone voice in the wilderness is brutally silenced, we must take action. The motto of this department is threefold: Pride, Service, and Integrity. We pledge to expose the person or persons who committed this heinous act, no matter how powerful or privileged they might be."*

I had another sip. "Ick," I said. I was not referring to the coffee.

*UniMerritt officials could not be reached for comment.*

"No kidding," I mumbled.

Just then the room phone rang. It was Stephen.

"Have you seen the paper?"

"Yes."

"Have you seen the reaction?"

"What reaction?"

"On the Internet," he said. "People aren't just saying this

proves UniMerritt did it. Some of them want to close the company down or blow it up."

"Doesn't the Internet say that about everything?"

"Yeah, but—"

"So the story's the center of attention. This is our window, and it's wide open. We've got to jump through it."

He paused. "Are you saying Hunter is *right*?"

"I can't put it that way without throwing up. But that *is* our job."

"So what do we do?"

"Well, we can't wait for the police to make public statements. We need access to what they know but aren't saying."

"Did you have someone in mind?"

"Sort of."

"Who?"

"We know at least one insider who'll be at the memorial service."

Another pause. "Surely you don't mean the chief of police."

"Maybe we could do a little networking."

"At the service?" he cried. "You were worried about bothering the widow at the funeral home, and you want to do this at the actual *service*?"

I took a sip of coffee, which was starting to get cold. "I love Olivia, and I feel terrible for her. But you saw how she was. Even if she weren't in shock, she's out of the loop. Her husband didn't tell her what was going on, and the police probably haven't, either."

"Whatever," he said. "Either way, we know UniMerritt is behind this."

"*I* don't know that."

"Deep down, you do. Everybody does."

"Let's get a little information first. Then make our case. We can leave it to readers to decide who's guilty."

He grunted.

"Just think about it," I said.

"Right." He hung up.

Returning to the coffee maker, I poured what was left into my cup and downed it all at once.

I shook my head.

I'd never liked funerals. But I was going to like this one even less.

# CHAPTER 5

BY SATURDAY AFTERNOON, I WAS MORE CONVINCED THAN EVER that meeting the police chief at the memorial service made sense. Stephen's passion for it remained at room temperature.

He struck back by torturing me with continuous nature-hike commentary as we drove toward the church. "Just look at these trees," he said with needless gusto. "No wonder they call it the Emerald City."

I peered through the windshield. The omnipresence of green foliage was exceeded only by that of the dreary, ash-colored sky.

Every turn our silent Prius took toward Grant Park Pres-byterian brought a new reason for him to check some arbo-real website on his phone. "Norway Maple," he said, pointing at what looked like a giant bush. "They're all over Seattle. So are the European White Elm and Pin Oak, at least in this part of town."

"Enthralling," I said.

"I thought there would be more evergreens. But that's the

Olympic National Forest. Douglas Firs and stuff. Mostly outside the city."

"Thanks for clearing that up."

I reached into the cup holder and pulled out the Google Maps directions I'd printed in the hotel's Business Center. We had just two miles and approximately 50,000 trees to go.

"Uh-oh," he said suddenly.

I stuffed the directions back in the cup holder and looked down the street. There was a blue-and-white police squad car, then another. Then a local TV station's van, topped with a satellite dish. Then a rainbow-hued sign that said GRANT PARK, and the beginnings of a crowd waving placards and posters.

"Is there a way around them?" he asked, sounding worried.

"Not according to the directions."

I slowed to a crawl. There were a lot more trees in the park, but he seemed to have lost interest in identifying them.

I rolled my window down. The closer we got, the louder the chanting grew.

*"Pharma, pharma, whaddaya say? How many hearts did you stop today?"*

In addition to all the old favorite slogans, like DR. RHEE WAS TERMINATED and NO MORE MERCHANTS OF DEATH, there were new ones like WE HAVE THE SMOKING GUN and UNIMERRITT'S BUSINESS PLAN IS MURDER.

"Why are they *doing* this?" he said. "They're supposed to be protesting Rhee's killers, but they're just blocking the road to his funeral."

"Maybe they agree with P.T. Barnum. 'There is no such thing as bad publicity.'"

He turned and looked out the rear window. "Here comes another police car. Traffic's getting backed up."

I checked the rearview mirror. Actually, traffic was completely stopped. A few drivers were getting out of their cars, shading their eyes with their hands and squinting at the crowd.

The police officers, all six of them, lined up on the right side of the road. And stood there.

"Why aren't they doing anything?" he asked.

"Must be the iron fist in the velvet glove. Without the iron fist."

One of the officers, a beefy-looking fellow who looked as if he probably knew better, raised a white bullhorn and addressed the multitude. "You are restricting access to a public throughway," he said. "Clear the street."

I consulted my watch. Unless someone did something, we were going to be late.

I inched the Prius forward. The chanting grew louder. A protester wearing a rubber skull mask and a black sweatsuit emerged from the crowd and stood in the middle of the road, directly in front of us.

I kept going. Slowly, but moving.

Stephen sat up straight. "You're going to hit him."

"Not if he gets out of the way."

"You're playing chicken?"

"I'm committed to promptness," I said.

The symbolic skeleton in front of us seemed determined to become a real one, refusing to back down.

"Let the police handle it," Stephen said.

"They don't seem interested in that possibility."

By now my front bumper had to be touching the protester's shins. He looked down at the yellow hood.

For a second it seemed he'd topple backward and find himself under our tires. But at the last instant he brought his fists down to hammer the hood with a single angry *WHUMP*, dived to the side, and ended up crouched on the pavement.

I passed him, still at a single mile per hour. The crowd parted. The chanting faded, then started again. A check of the mirror showed a few drivers behind me applauding as they climbed back into their cars.

Stephen let out the breath he'd been holding. I moved ahead, feeling like the grand marshal of a parade.

"Oh, great," he mumbled, looking out the back window. "Now you're a hero. This is bound to be on the evening news."

"Someone had to do it," I said modestly.

We spent the remaining mile or so in silence. Stephen didn't regain his interest in identifying the trees.

I still had misgivings about my plans for the service.

But I got us to the church on time.

**\* \* \***

The Grant Park Presbyterian Church parking lot was nearly full. A rare appearance of the sun glinted from the roofs of all sorts of vehicles, from ancient Volkswagen buses to brand new Teslas. I found a place next to a hulking bronze SUV with a bumper sticker that said MY OTHER CAR IS A BICYCLE.

The church itself looked like a castle, with turrets and stained glass and bronze plaques no doubt calling it an historical monument. People in suits and ties and dresses and jeans were all somber as they filed into the building.

It was a little like my church, except mine didn't resemble anything medieval and the jeans people had overrun the snappy dressers a long time ago. Mine wasn't Presbyterian, either, and had managed to avoid being associated with any of the major brands. It was pretty big, kind of artsy, and had sort of saved my life a couple of times.

Stephen was behind me as we ascended the stone stairs

and approached the heavy oaken doors. We were greeted with a nod by a black-suited man who'd perfected a look of sympathy without sorrow, hope without jubilation. The order of service he handed me had a sunrise photograph on the front.

In the foyer was a guest book, watched over by a woman who presumably was in charge of dealing with crises such as pens that suddenly ran out of ink. A short line of signatories had formed.

"Maybe you could write a message for both of us," Stephen whispered.

"Maybe not," I said. "To each his own."

When my turn came, I picked up the pen and added these words:

*Concision in style, precision in thought, decision in life.*

I'd considered using something from Ecclesiastes, my favorite book, but it was too depressing. I'd settled on Victor Hugo. It seemed to describe the deceased, or at least what I knew of him.

The sanctuary, full of flowers, was packed and hushed. Organ music murmured in the background, played by a woman who looked too young to know what an organ was. An enlarged print of Dr. Rhee's photo—still the only one I'd ever seen—sat on an easel in front of the platform.

Sunshine glowed through the stained-glass windows, which depicted an array of biblical scenes. Moses with the tablets, the Annunciation angel, Jesus as Good Shepherd.

Stephen leaned toward me. "That one over the pulpit. Is that Eli Whitney's invention of the cotton gin?"

I sighed. He never tired of needling me about anything remotely spiritual. His commitment to evading commitment seemed absolute. The only time I'd ever seen him in church was three years ago, when one of our associate editors got married and invited him by mistake.

I glanced at the empty front row of pews, which was roped off for family. I wondered when Olivia would enter.

My search for a dark blue uniform with stars and stripes on the sleeves yielded nothing. Perhaps the police chief would enter at the last minute with his entourage, being fanned by palm fronds.

Stephen leaned toward me again. "I wonder how many of these people actually knew him."

"Maybe with all the publicity, they felt they did."

He pointed at the program in my hand. "Does it say whether there'll be time for us to share memories of the deceased?"

I studied the folder. "Doesn't look like it."

"Good. That always takes too long and involves way too many tears and in-jokes."

"You're such a sentimentalist."

"What about Everly? Is he in there?"

"Yeah. Under 'Remarks.'"

"Are you still going to try making friends with him?"

"Uh-huh."

Shrugging, he turned away.

A door at the right side of the sanctuary opened. Olivia, wearing a black dress, was escorted to the middle of the front row by an usher much taller than she. Her head was bowed. This time she didn't float but seemed all too earthbound.

She sat down, alone. Her escort left as he'd come.

"No family?" I whispered.

"Not that I've found on the Internet."

From the side doorway emerged another figure, a strapping, middle-aged man in a brown suit that more or less matched his hair. Bible in hand, he nimbly ascended the steps to the pulpit. The organ ceased.

Adjusting the wireless microphone that looped around his ear, he introduced himself as the senior pastor. His expression kept flickering from joy to melancholy and back, as if he hadn't decided which to favor.

"On behalf of Olivia and our church family, welcome to this celebration of the life of Dr. Kelvin Bartholomew Rhee," he said. After noting that the deceased had chosen the first hymn, he asked us to stand. The lyrics suddenly appeared behind him on two screens the size of Times Square Jumbotrons. I still missed hymnals sometimes.

The organ began to rumble, and the singing began. Stephen abstained. I followed the words carefully, curious to know what Kelvin Rhee had found so appealing about them.

*Faith of our fathers, living still,*
*In spite of dungeon, fire, and sword;*
*Oh, how our hearts beat high with joy*
*Whene'er we hear that glorious Word!*
*Faith of our fathers, holy faith!*
*We will be true to thee till death.*

*Our fathers, chained in prisons dark,*
*Were still in heart and conscience free;*
*How sweet would be their children's fate,*
*If they, like them, could die for thee!*
*Faith of our fathers, holy faith!*
*We will be true to thee till death.*

> *Faith of our fathers, we will love*
> *Both friend and foe in all our strife;*
> *And preach thee, too, as love knows how*
> *By kindly words and virtuous life.*
> *Faith of our fathers, holy faith!*
> *We will be true to thee till death.*

With a lowering of his hand, the pastor gave us clearance to sit down. Plenty about fathers in the song, I thought. And consistency. And death.

Rhee had revered the first. He'd demanded the second. Now he'd experienced the third.

Very precise.

The minister read Psalm 23, then launched into a summary of Rhee's life. It contained little I hadn't read or heard, except that he'd been "a man with a servant's heart." It was hard to imagine the latter, but under the circumstances it seemed only fair to give him the benefit of the doubt. After all, he'd planned to give his royalties away.

My eyes kept straying to the back of Olivia's head. She looked so solitary, forlorn.

The pastor managed to work in two sports analogies, neither of which I grasped, as usual. He also told a tale about an old Vermont farmer that could have come from Hunter's file of anecdotes, but the minister's made more sense.

Finally he reached the last chapter of Rhee's biography, beginning with the whistleblowing, which he described only as "the controversy." He ended with the murder, referring to the latter as "the tragic events of the last week." The story wasn't over, he said. Death would be swallowed up in victory, because Kelvin Rhee had placed his trust in the One who had overcome death.

I glanced at Stephen, wondering what he was thinking. We'd argued about eternal life a few times. He'd always scratch his chin in an agnostic sort of way, not quite convinced and trying to distract me with the question of whether Adam and Eve had bellybuttons.

There followed a flute solo, the words of which I couldn't analyze because there weren't any. Then came another hymn, the Martin Luther classic Rhee had put on his list.

We stood again, and once more I followed the lyrics on the screen.

*A mighty Fortress is our God,*
*A Bulwark never failing;*
*Our Helper He amid the flood*
*Of mortal ills prevailing:*
*For still our ancient foe*
*Doth seek to work us woe;*
*His craft and power are great,*
*And, armed with cruel hate,*
*On earth is not his equal.*


*Did we in our own strength confide,*
*Our striving would be losing;*
*Were not the right Man on our side,*
*The Man of God's own choosing:*
*Dost ask who that may be?*
*Christ Jesus, it is He;*
*Lord Sabaoth His Name,*
*From age to age the same,*

*And He must win the battle.*


*And though this world, with devils filled,*
*Should threaten to undo us,*
*We will not fear, for God hath willed*
*His truth to triumph through us:*
*The Prince of Darkness grim,*
*We tremble not for him;*
*His rage we can endure,*
*For lo! his doom is sure,*
*One little word shall fell him.*


*That word above all earthly powers,*
*No thanks to them, abideth;*
*The Spirit and the gifts are ours*
*Through Him who with us sideth:*
*Let goods and kindred go,*
*This mortal life also;*
*The body they may kill:*
*God's truth abideth still,*
*His Kingdom is forever.*


We sat down. I stared at the last stanza on the screen.


*The body they may kill:*
*God's truth abideth still . . .*

Stephen swiveled toward me, his eyes wide. "It's almost like he knew," he whispered. "That's a little creepy."

Hearing a stirring behind us, I turned around. A thin, determined-looking policeman was striding up the aisle, his jaw set, his blue sleeves gold-striped and starred. He left behind two other officers who stood against the wall in the back.

"Speaking of creepy," Stephen muttered.

Chief of Police Peter Everly made his way to the front, followed by a ripple of murmurs.

"He looks shorter in person," Stephen whispered.

The pastor sat in a chair at the side of the platform, near the organ. Everly stepped to the pulpit and placed a few sheets of paper on it. He gripped it as he had the podium at the news conference and squinted with similar intensity.

"As chief of the Seattle Police Department, it is my honor to pay tribute to Dr. Kelvin Rhee. I want to thank Mrs. Rhee for allowing me to do so." He nodded in her direction.

"I am told that Dr. Rhee was a man of few words. So I will keep mine brief." He looked down at his notes, then up. "Five years ago I was appointed chief of police by Mayor Barbara Carlson," he said. "I recall standing in her office and asking her, 'Barbara, what do you believe the people of Seattle want from their government?'

"She looked at me with that strength and compassion for which she is so rightly known, and said, 'They want justice, and they want transparency.'"

He paused, as if we all needed time to recover from this profundity.

"Justice and transparency," he repeated, waving a hand toward the stained-glass windows. "The Scriptures tell us the same. Psalm 45:4 says, 'In your majesty ride forth victoriously in the cause of truth, humility and justice; let your right hand achieve awesome deeds.'"

I leaned toward Stephen. "That passage is directed at the Almighty Himself. No wonder Everly thinks it was meant for him."

"Whatever."

The chief's chin lifted like the prow of a battleship. "Kelvin Rhee rode forth victoriously in that cause. He spoke the truth in love, though others vowed to muzzle him. He sought justice for those who had died at the hands of the negligent. And he did it all with great humility."

"Humility?" I muttered. "What does he know about that?"

"And finally," Everly declared, "Kelvin Rhee achieved awesome deeds. At great personal cost. From this day forward, let us dedicate ourselves, no matter our faith or creed or lack thereof, to the task of taking up where he left off. He holds out to us the twin batons of justice and transparency.

"As for me, I take them and run. Join me. May future generations say of us, 'They have run the race. They have fought the good fight.'"

He gazed at the stained-glass windows, probably imagining a new one picturing the time he'd calmed the wind and waves on the Sea of Galilee. Speaking of which, I was feeling nauseous.

"Thank you," he said, and paused as if expecting a standing ovation. There was none. Nodding, he picked up his notes and strode back down the aisle.

I turned to watch him walk out with the other two officers. "I hope he's not leaving," I whispered.

"That would be awful," Stephen said.

"Would it be too gauche if we followed him?"

"You mean leave halfway through the service?"

"It sounds terrible when you put it that way."

A woman sitting two rows in front of us turned around and gave us a disapproving look.

"It would mean missing the rest," I said.

"Then let's go," he whispered.

We got to our feet. I stuffed the order of service into my purse.

We stepped over seven or eight pairs of Earth Shoes, Guccis, and faux combat boots on our way out, raising eyebrows and excusing ourselves repeatedly.

It was too bad, missing the rest of the remarks and hymns and prayers. I was pretty sure God would forgive us.

I could only hope we weren't too late to catch His Anointed One.

\* \* \*

I started running when we hit the vestibule, flying past the guestbook, which was now dangerously unmanned, and an open-mouthed woman who carried a clear plastic punch-bowl. Stephen hung back, just ambling.

I scrambled down the flagstone steps. Everly and the other two officers made their way toward a police cruiser in the lot. Its lights were flashing, as if eulogies were emergencies.

"Excuse me!" I called, waving. One of the officers looked over his shoulder, but the chief kept going.

I stepped slowly down the stairs. The officer who'd looked over his shoulder stopped and faced me. "Can I help you, Ma'am?"

"I need to speak with Chief Everly," I said, breathless.

"Well, we're kind of in a hurry. There's some trouble at the park, and—"

"I just have a couple of questions."

"Are you a reporter?"

"No. We're writing a book about Dr. Rhee."

Everly came to a halt and turned around.

"A book, did you say?"

I repositioned the purse on my shoulder. "I'm Carolyn Neville, and this is Stephen Ames. We're from Pendleton House Publishing." I gave him my business card. "We're doing a book about the UniMerritt case and the investigation into Dr. Rhee's murder."

He examined the card. "New York," he said, then looked up. "This is . . . an actual book? Available in bookstores?"

"In four months, yes. We're on a fast track."

His earnest frown melted into an equally earnest smile. It seemed genuine enough, in an untrustworthy sort of way.

Reaching out, he shook my hand, then Stephen's. His grip was surprisingly fierce for one of his apparent sensitivity, perhaps from squeezing all those lecterns.

"Always glad to meet my friends in the fourth estate. As I mentioned in my remarks about Dr. Rhee, transparency is indispensable. You keep the rest of us honest, public servants *and* crooked corporations."

"We'd love to talk with you about that," I said. "About your role in all this. You've clearly given it a lot of thought."

He gazed around nobly at the evergreens, whose towering grandeur naturally paled before his own. "Justice has always been a passion of mine," he said.

He pulled a business card of his own from the breast pocket of his uniform, then gave it to me. "If I can be of assistance, it would be my pleasure to do so. Call my office, would you? My assistant can set up an appointment."

Touching the brim of his cap, he turned and walked to the squad car. The two other officers followed. The roof lights continued to flash as the three of them pulled away, heralding his presence among the hoi polloi.

"You should never wash your right hand again," Stephen said.

I slipped the card into my purse. "Say what you will. But he's the chief of police. If we handle this right, it could open doors to all kinds of stuff. All kinds of people."

He snorted. "The guy's a publicity hound. Did you see how his eyes lit up at the words *book* and *New York*? This is his dream come true. It's not just some article in the Seattle paper. It's his chance to go national."

"So you think he's using us," I said.

"Of course."

"And we're not using him?"

He spread his arms wide. "We're the *good* guys."

"If you say so. All I know is that if we don't get this book written in time, there'll be a big empty space on the shelf at Barnes & Noble. And in your cubicle. And my office."

He looked up at the Celtic stone cross topping the church. "In other words, it'll be *our* funeral."

"Not if I can help it."

I headed toward the Prius, whose bright paint seemed suddenly out of place.

This was a sobering occasion, after all.

And yellow was such an optimistic color.

# CHAPTER 6

THE OFFICE OF POLICE CHIEF PETER EVERLY DISPLAYED NO guns on the wall, no shadow boxes of famous badges or handcuffs. There wasn't even a certificate for years served nor cats rescued from trees. A few framed photos showed him posing with people who looked like they smiled for a living. Politicians, I guessed. Other than that, the light gray walls were blank.

The desk was a different story. In the center sat a neat stack of papers, a copy of *Walden and Civil Disobedience* by Henry David Thoreau, and a half-empty bottle of Snapple Kiwi Strawberry. At one end of the desk was a surprisingly large municipal flag on a stand, a teal and white affair with undulating ocean waves, the same Native American face that graced the city seal, and a motto that said CITY OF GOODWILL. At the other end sat a translucent plastic terrestrial globe the size of a bowling ball, set on a golden axis like a giant pearl.

When I saw the latter, I started it spinning it with my finger. "Sorry," I said. "Couldn't resist." Stephen sat down in the visitor's chair next to mine.

Everly, now jacketless in his own high-backed chair, raised a reassuring hand. "Half the people who come in here do the same thing. I've been known to do it myself. I keep that globe to remind me of the big picture."

I smiled, though not sincerely. "Today Seattle, tomorrow the world, eh?"

He lifted an eyebrow. "Not exactly. I simply wish to remember that our city is but one small part of humanity. It not only takes a village to raise a child; it takes a *planet* to raise a *village*."

"Thank you for raising our global awareness," I said, thinking mine was high enough already.

"Well," Everly said. "As a public servant, I am at your disposal. How can I help with this book of yours?"

I took a small digital recorder from my purse and set it on the edge of the desk. "Mind if I record this?"

"Not at all. Justice and transparency, remember?"

"I was wondering whether you know anything about Dr. Rhee's death that leads you to believe UniMerritt Laboratories is involved."

He leaned back, hands clasped behind his head. "My, you get right to the point, don't you? Wouldn't have it any other way, of course. That's the press's job. Um . . . how many copies do you think you'll sell?"

"I wouldn't be surprised at a first printing of a hundred thousand."

His lips parted slightly. He unclasped his hands and leaned forward, probably to keep from choking on his own drool.

"Not that numbers matter, of course," he said. "As for your question about the possible involvement of a certain large corporation, let me put it this way. I know a little about how things work in this country. I'll bet you do, too."

"For the sake of argument, let's say I don't. Perhaps you could enlighten me."

His eyes narrowed. "Big business, Ms. Neville. Do you know what Woodrow Wilson said? 'Big business is not dangerous because it is big, but because its bigness is an unwholesome inflation created by privileges and exemptions it ought not to enjoy.'"

"Excellent quote," I said. "But what about Ludwig von Mises? He said, 'The people who think that the power of big business is enormous are mistaken also.'"

He smiled condescendingly. "Just what I would expect. Von Mises was an austrofascist and fan of Ayn Rand."

I paused, having reached the end of the Economists shelf in my mental library. Most of my memorized adages were from Oscar Wilde, C. S. Lewis, and Cyndi Lauper.

I pushed my recorder closer to Everly. "Be that as it may, some of us share the view that large corporations don't have the public's best interests in mind. Politicians don't either."

His smile faded. "I am not a politician."

"Certainly not," I replied. "But some would say if it walks and quacks like a duck, you should turn it into *foie gras* as soon as possible."

His smile seemed to have left the building permanently.

I bit my lip. Maybe I'd gone too far. "Um . . . Do you have any theories on how a company like UniMerritt *could* have played a role in the death of a hypothetical whistleblower?"

He looked up at the ceiling. "Did you see *Silkwood*?"

"Yes. Meryl Streep was wonderful."

"True story. Karen Silkwood uncovered unsafe practices at Kerr-McGee's plutonium plant. Testified before the Atomic Energy Commission. Died in a mysterious car accident. No criminal charges, but there was a civil suit. The company settled for more than a million dollars."

Stephen shook his head. "That doesn't prove—"

"How about *Kill the Messenger?*"

I thought for a moment. "Haven't seen that one."

"Another true story. Gary Webb was a reporter, *San Jose Mercury News*. Did a series of articles about how the CIA was protecting the Contra rebels in Nicaragua, who financed their operations by selling crack. Certain people didn't like the stories, and the paper demoted him. He resigned. They found him with two bullets in his head. A suicide, they said. Two bullets! Who shoots himself in the head *twice?*"

"Nobody *I* know."

Everly reached out and spun the globe. "There's no need to come up with a hypothetical. These things have already happened. Anyone who thinks they aren't the tip of the iceberg is part of the problem. That's not politics; it's reality." He frowned at me, his eyes narrow.

I started chewing a nail. "I'm just being . . . skeptical. Journalists have to do that, right?"

He shook his head. "Ms. Neville, given your attitude, I'm afraid I must withdraw my offer to assist with your project. It's clear you consider me some kind of political hack."

"But—"

His eyes smoldered. "I'd recommend you tread carefully while you're in this city. I don't want to hear that your efforts are impeding my department's investigation."

He rose from his chair. "Nothing personal. In fact, I'll give you a bit of advice. If you want to find out what happened to Dr. Rhee, you should talk to Angus Blackwood."

"The CEO of UniMerritt."

"Not that he's going to admit anything. But one thing can lead to another."

He picked up the digital recorder and handed it to me. Sighing, I pushed the STOP button. There was a single beep.

"Have a nice day," he said, and set the globe spinning again.

\* \* \*

Our Prius wasn't the happiest place on Earth.

Stephen saw to that as we pulled out of the SeaPark Garage and onto Sixth Street. The pale gray blocks of Police Headquarters receded in the rearview mirror.

"With all due respect, you're shooting us both in the foot," he said.

"In the *feet*," I corrected.

"It's self-sabotage. You're trying to ingratiate yourself with the police chief, and you're insulting him. You want this book to die, don't you?"

I shook my head, even though he probably was right. "We don't need Everly. We're better off talking to Angus Blackwood."

"He won't say anything. Why should he?"

"To keep us from writing a catastrophic exposé of his company. He's in enough trouble already."

We rode in silence for a few blocks. "Are we going back to the motel?" he muttered. "I'm hungry."

In a gap between buildings I caught a glimpse of the Space Needle, that flying saucer perched on crossed chopsticks. "There's always the revolving restaurant at the top of that thing."

"Not in the mood. Good food would be wasted on me now."

"Then lousy food it is." I drove a few more blocks, then pulled into a place I'll call Franchise X.

The food really was dreadful. The bright spot was that the ketchup packets didn't leak.

Somewhere between fried mozzarella sticks and the pepper bacon slider with cheese sauce I turned to Stephen. "What do you know about Blackwood?"

"Not much. He's from Scotland."

"Aren't you going to take out your phone and start Googling? You always do that."

"Not in the mood."

I fished the phone from my purse. "If you want something done right . . ."

Finding a two-year-old article on the *Wall Street Journal* website, I proceeded to read it aloud. I started with the third paragraph:

*Blackwood's gregarious exterior is said to hide a take-no-prisoners approach to business. He grew up in Glasgow, a lower-class fast-talker who worked his way through university and started a successful medical device company, HeatherTech. Recruited by UniMerritt Laboratories for its top spot, he found that his iron-fisted, velvet-gloved style perfectly fit the American way. Now, at age 63, he is credited with the aggressive takeover of two promising startups and a bottom line his shareholders love.*

I scrutinized the photo accompanying the article. "This has to be the wrong picture."

"Why?"

I turned the phone around and showed him. "A CEO with scraggly gray hair and a beard?"

"He looks like . . . a pirate."

"And apparently acts like one, too."

He scraped the last of his hot fudge sundae from its clear plastic cup, then threw the container in a paper bag. "Even if he talks to us, we can't trust what he says."

I returned the phone to my pocket. "No one can trust anything *anyone* says."

Fortunately, that didn't keep people from buying books.

\* \* \*

I was right, of course. About Angus Blackwood.

Once I managed to reach his executive assistant that afternoon, a harried woman who sounded as if she'd been babysitting a Scottish madman for the worst half of her life, I explained the situation. We were writing a book about Dr. Kelvin Rhee, and this was the opportunity for UniMerritt Laboratories to tell its side of the story. It was the kind of thing writers like to say because it makes them look less self-serving.

"I'll get back to you," she said.

And she did, asserting that Mr. Blackwood would be happy to meet with us. His schedule was jammed, but he would cancel something to fit us in. It was the kind of thing executives like to say because it makes them look more public-spirited.

So now, 26 hours after typing BLACKWOOD into Google, I was easing the Prius off 15th Place South near the airport, past the big sign with the UniMerritt logo, a *U* that looked like a test tube containing a swoopy gold check mark.

The campus was the size of a half-dozen golf courses, dominated by three mammoth, tan concrete bunkers joined in the center. All were fitted with hundreds of deeply tinted windows that made it impossible to tell what was going on inside.

Stephen shook his head. "It's like approaching the Death Star."

"Only if the Death Star had landscaping. Shouldn't you be telling me about every kind of tree they've put in, preferably in alphabetical order?"

"Later. If we get out alive."

The parking lot seemed vast enough to accommodate Six

Flags Over Everything. I steered into a VISITOR spot, wishing for a tram to take us to the entrance.

The lobby was a hushed space, hung with photos of happy people whose joy was probably maintained by round-the-clock doses of the company's products. After being stickered with guest badges, we were escorted past the front desk by a young woman whose energy level could be explained only by her ingestion of too many free samples.

She dropped us off in the waiting area outside Blackwood's office, nodding at his longsuffering assistant. Before we could sit, the CEO himself popped from his doorway like a slice of Oroweat from a toaster.

"Greetings!" he exclaimed, flinging his arms wide. They were the sort of open arms one could tell were only symbolic, not inviting an actual hug.

The photo we'd seen on the Internet had been no mistake. In fact, he looked even less like the head of a multinational corporation in person. The chaotic hair, beard, collarless black shirt, and khakis were not the only signs of a renegade. His eyes were the surest indicators, sparkling with mischief —or whiskey, though the latter seemed unlikely given his reputation as a peerless negotiator.

"Ms. Neville," he said, shaking my hand. "And Mr. Ames." Another handshake. "What a pleasure!" His brogue was thicker than the mealy stuffing in a platter of haggis, a dish so disgusting I promise not to describe it further. "Let's take a little jaunt, shall we?"

He motioned to the hallway behind us, where sat a cream-colored golf cart with the UniMerritt logo on the front. "Perhaps you've heard of Management by Walking Around. I've modified that a wee bit. I commonly do this most mornings when I'm not traipsing somewhere else, so I hope you'll join me. I can show you what our family is all about."

I took my digital recorder from my purse. "I'd like to record this, if you don't mind."

"I'd have it no other way, lass. Come sit in the front with me." Stephen took the back.

No sooner had I slid into the seat than Blackwood stamped on the accelerator. With a click the vehicle jerked forward, I jerked backward, and we shot down the hall.

"Keep your head!" he said. I grabbed the door next to me as employees in suits and badges whizzed by, a few toadies smiling and waving but most ignoring us.

"We have seven hundred and forty-three staff members at last count," he said, raising his voice even though the electric cart was nearly silent. "Three buildings—Administration, Manufacturing, Research. We're in Administration now. Finance, Marketing, Legal, Compliance, Facilities, Security, that sort of rubbish. Not the most interesting place, I'm afraid. Bear with me, and before you know it, you'll see where the true magic happens."

I held the digital recorder midway between us. "Did you know Dr. Kelvin Rhee?" I asked.

Blackwood shook his shaggy head. "Not personally. But I understand the man was brilliant. We were fortunate to have him and feel his loss most acutely."

"Did you go to his memorial service?"

"I was in Switzerland that week, unfortunately. But several of our team were there. Quite moving, I heard."

I looked around, alarmed at our velocity. "I was surprised not to see any protesters at the gates. Given that emotions are running high about your company."

"Perhaps it's their day off," he said, jerking the cart around a lady in a wheelchair. "How does it go? 'Pharma, pharma, whaddaya say? How many hearts did you stop today?'"

Somehow it sounded like actual poetry when he said it, enriched with echoes of Robert Burns.

"Ach, we have our detractors. I don't mind saying it hurts to hear that kind of havering."

I waited for him to explain what *havering* was, but he moved on. "Hold just a tad," he said, dropping his speed. "We're getting to the good part. Manufacturing."

We entered another endless gray hallway, this one teeming with workers who mostly wore white lab coats with clear plastic hairnets. Some had blue rubber gloves, paper masks, and goggles.

We were headed straight for a double door with no handles. "A goods lock," he said. He turned to me. "Be a bonnie lass and push that handle on the wall, will you?"

When I mashed the square of steel with my palm, the doors sprang away from the cart.

"In the Administration Building, we can be filthy as you please," he said, speeding up again. "Here, it's all spotless as a vicar's breeches. Pressurized locks, fans, filters to eliminate cross-contamination. Temperature and humidity under control. Sterile zones. No margin of error with pharmaceuticals. We never forget how we hold people's lives in our hands."

He pulled alongside two men pushing a stainless-steel cart stacked with boxes. We kept moving slowly, and so did they.

"How's it going, lads?" he asked.

"Never better," the taller one said.

"What have you got there?"

"Titanium dioxide, magnesium stearate, cellulose . . ." said the other.

"Binders, diluents, coatings," said the first. "Mostly inactive. Nothing to write home about."

Blackwood arched an eyebrow. "It's *all* important, lads. Got any great ideas for me today?"

The men looked at each other. "Well . . . we did think of

something a couple weeks ago."

"Music to my ears. Don't keep it to yourselves."

"We were talking about how it might be worth trying to tweak the MRP system," the shorter one said. "In the raw materials warehouse, maybe use apps instead of dedicated scanners to read barcodes, track inventory, bin numbers. Phones can display visual information, not just data."

Blackwood stroked his beard with the hand that wasn't steering. "Hmmm," he said, as if pondering the bouquet of a Zinfandel at a wine tasting.

"Pickers could double-check ingredient IDs by sight," the taller one added.

Blackwood hit the brake. The two men stopped pushing their cart.

"Either of you a Scotsman, lads?"

They shook their heads.

"No matter. Neither was DaVinci. This may be pure deed genius. Send it to me in writing, and we'll talk."

"Yes, sir," the shorter one said, and both men grinned.

Blackwood stomped the accelerator, and we lurched forward. "Belter, boys!" he called over his shoulder.

I sighed. Was I the only one who didn't know more than a handful of Scottish phrases and didn't want to learn any more? Or was everyone else faking?

Blackwood turned to me. "See? Management by Riding Around."

We paused at another "goods lock," then proceeded down the hall. Suddenly we stopped outside a door with a keypad. There was a window in the door.

"Afraid I can't let you in here," he said. "But perhaps you'd like to peek at a Blending Room. Fascinating process."

"Okay," I said.

He stayed in the cart. We stepped out and peered through the glass.

There were diamond-shaped signs here and there on the walls. The closest was green and said NON-FLAMMABLE NON-TOXIC GAS 2. Another was blue, with flames, and said DANGEROUS WHEN WET 4. On a far wall was a white one with skull and crossbones that said TOXIC GAS 2.

"They sound like movie sequels," Stephen mumbled.

Except for the signs and a handful of workers who kept checking gauges and pressing buttons, everything in the room was stainless steel. Pipes ran from giant funnels to what looked like oversized pressure cookers. Heaps of white powder, poured from plastic bags, dissolved in rotating vats churned by paddles.

"Fascinating," I said. Straightening up, I aimed my recorder at Blackwood. "What are we looking at?"

"Active ingredients. Bulking agents. Computers telling about four million dollars' worth of machines how to mix the stuff, and a group of just plain folk telling the computers where to get off."

He paused. "Just plain folk," he repeated. "Highly trained but ordinary individuals working their arses off to make other folk well. That's what we do here, Ms. Neville. It's *all* we do. No matter what anyone else might tell you."

We looked at each other for a long moment.

"So UniMerritt Laboratories is a philanthropic organization," I said drily.

He chuckled. "No. We're a business. But neither do we kill people. 'How many hearts did you stop today?' As far as I know, not a one."

"And how do you answer those who say you stopped Dr. Rhee's?"

He shook his head. "I'll admit I've done a few boggin things in my day. But I'd never take a life."

"Not you personally. But you've got seven hundred and forty-three potential accomplices at your disposal."

"Not partners in crime, Ms. Neville. Partners in compassion."

*Ooh*, I thought. Even if he was telling the truth, he needed better writers.

He checked his watch. "Shall we move on, then? I have one more thing to show you."

"Which is?"

"The Research Building, where Dr. Rhee worked."

Suddenly there was a tiny *beep beep beep* sound. I looked down at my recorder. "Crap. Low battery."

"I trust you have a spare. There's someone I'd like you to meet. Perhaps he can help you discover what happened to Dr. Rhee. If you really want to know, that is."

We piled back into the cart. He mashed the accelerator, spun around, and headed back down the corridor, his hair trailing like a tattered flag behind him.

# CHAPTER 7

Hurtling down the hallway as if bent on winning the luge in the Winter Olympics, Blackwood steered with one hand and waved at his just plain folk with the other. I suspended my questioning, not wanting to distract him into hitting one of his worker bees.

Finally we slowed, passing under a large bronze plaque that said RESEARCH.

White lab coats and ID badges were still the uniform here, but the hairnets, gloves, masks, and goggles were gone. Employees' names were stitched on their breast pockets, most of which held an array of pens. Through the occasional doorway we caught sight of smaller stainless-steel machines, glassware, computers, and microscopes as long as telescopes.

From one of the doorways stepped a squat, balding fellow in a white coat. His silver hair had been forced into a rather ineffective comb-over. Frowning at the screen of a tablet in his hand, he seemed unaware that he was directly in our path.

Blackwood stomped the brake, yanking me forward.

"Ah!" he said. "Just the man we want to see. Dr. Lazard, I presume."

The fellow finally looked up, still frowning. "Yes," he said. "Mr. Blackwood, no?" He had an accent, French. But the words were merely seasoned with it, not sodden like the Scotsman's brogue.

Blackwood climbed out of the cart and shook the man's hand. "Dr. René Lazard, I'd like you to meet Ms. Carolyn Neville and Mr. Stephen Ames. They're writing a book about your predecessor."

Lazard nodded, but looked wary. "A book, yes."

Blackwood turned in our direction. "Dr. Lazard very recently joined us as a lab supervisor."

"*Very* recently," the man said.

"From Parker Klaxton Scientific in Boston, I understand," said Blackwood.

"Quite correct."

"Ms. Neville and Mr. Ames want to know what really happened to Dr. Rhee. Can you shed any light on that subject?"

Lazard shook his head, though not hard enough to disturb the precarious arrangement of his hair. "I am afraid not. I had never met him. I was still in Boston when he died."

Blackwood fiddled with his beard. "True. But I wonder if you might help these two by giving them a list of the folk in your lab who *did* know him."

Lazard lifted his chin. "A list?" he asked with a sniff. "Is that . . . wise?"

"We've got nothing to hide. Unless there's something you need to tell me."

"Of course not. I am thinking only of the company."

"That makes two of us," the CEO said. "And when you send this list, please include your people's contact information. So these journalists can talk to them, eh?"

Lazard looked down and scrawled a note on his tablet. "As soon as I am able."

I leaned out of the cart and handed him my business card. "You can e-mail us."

Lazard did not smile. In fact, he looked at us as though we had spat upon the French flag itself.

"Thank you, Doctor," Blackwood said, getting back in.

Hitting the accelerator, he proceeded to make a tight U-turn and headed back down the hall. "A bit crabbit, that man," he confided over his shoulder. "But fair gifted. Or so they tell me."

He checked his watch again, then sped up. "It seems our time has flown. Dr. Lazard will be in touch, I'm sure."

I clicked open my purse, pulled out two batteries, and snapped them into the recorder. "Just a couple more questions."

"Fire away, lass."

I pointed the device at him. "Why should people believe UniMerritt had nothing to do with Dr. Rhee's death?"

He shook his head. "I'm not daft, Ms. Neville. I'm a realist. I know riding about on a little cart is hardly enough to change anyone's mind about us. I can only hope for a fair hearing. Perhaps your book will help."

He paused. "I grew up on the streets of Glasgow. Not in a posh neighborhood, mind you. Most of my mates are dead now. We didn't have all the drugs then, but we had the drink. The place wasn't crawlin' with social workers then, not that they've helped much. You live in a place like that, and you become a scrapper. I suspect I'll always be one."

"You're going to fight, then. Defend yourself."

"No question."

"How far will you go to do that?"

"Not as far as some people think I've already gone."

My spine tingled. What a sound bite. Not enough to fill a book, but it was a start. Only 50,990 words to go.

The cart slowed, then stopped. I looked around. We were back where we'd begun. There was Blackwood's executive assistant, sighing into the phone, looking as if she'd been trying to herd catfish because herding cats was too easy.

Her boss parked the cart, and we climbed out. I turned off the recorder. *Beep.* Blackwood shook my hand, then Stephen's.

"Thanks for the tour," I said.

"I look forward to reading your book. I only hope I'm not behind bars when I do it."

"I have the feeling you won't."

He chuckled. "Good luck, then. To all of us."

Smoothing his wild hair back with his hand, he disappeared into his office.

* * *

Since the bubbly young woman who'd ushered us from the reception desk to Blackwood's office was absent, we escorted ourselves to the lobby. The photos of happily medicated people still hung there, but our tour had put them in an entirely new light. Now they looked like victims whose medications had been mixed in rooms containing TOXIC GAS 2.

"He's a menace, you know," Stephen said, keeping his voice down.

"Oh, I don't think so. Phony as a thirteen-dollar bill, maybe, but not dangerous."

"It's not like you to be so naïve," he said, gazing around as if to trying to spot a hidden camera.

"He's just concerned with his company's image. And his own. He milks that brogue and his Celtic sayings and his mean-streets stories for all they're worth. He's Scottish with a capital *aye*."

"I noticed. I could hardly keep from asking him to beam us up."

"Thank heaven there were no bagpipes available. But he's not sinister."

He clapped a palm to his forehead. "He may seem harmless, but what about the people behind the scenes? The powers that be will go to any lengths to protect themselves. They have people who don't mind breaking the law. Corporate espionage. Security. Who's in charge of security at UniMerritt?"

"I have no idea."

Suddenly looking resolute, he marched over to the front desk. The receptionist, a fiftyish woman pinned with a loop of purple ribbon representing some disease unknown to me, smiled up at her.

"Can you tell me where the Security Department is?"

The smile faded, but only slightly. "Do you have an appointment?"

"Uh . . . no."

"I'm sorry. You would need one."

He squeezed one eye shut. "Who's the head of Security?"

"That would be Mercedes Pierce."

"Mercedes . . . as in . . . a woman?"

The receptionist raised her eyebrows but didn't speak.

"I—I mean, not that it matters," he stammered. "You just don't usually think of . . ." He frowned at me, as if I'd thought the same thing but had cheated by not saying it out loud.

He tapped a finger on the counter. "Can I call for an appointment?"

The receptionist shrugged. "I suppose so." She lifted a white courtesy phone from her desk and consulted a laminated list. "Extension 3240," she said.

Stephen punched buttons and waited.

"Yes," he said after a pause. "This is Stephen Ames. I'd like to make an appointment with Ms. Pierce." Another pause. "What is it regarding? Well, I'm working on a book about Dr. Kelvin Rhee, and I'd like to get her perspective on—"

A third pause. "Why not?"

Fourth pause. "Yes, I know you're sorry. Everybody's sorry." He hung up.

I studied my fingernails, which were getting a little long. "So?"

"She said Ms. Pierce doesn't do interviews. I'd have to talk to the company spokesperson instead."

"Ah."

"See? This proves it. They obviously have something to hide."

"Mr. Ames, some would say you're showing signs of paranoia."

"Some wouldn't."

"In fact, UniMerritt probably has just the thing for it. An anti-anxiety medication, maybe."

His voice dropped. "And wouldn't they just love to slip it into my next cup of coffee."

At first I thought he was joking. But he looked at me with unnerving urgency.

"Let's get out of here," he whispered, and walked as quickly as he could toward the doors, his footsteps clacking like bones on the marble floor.

\* \* \*

In the parking lot Stephen refused to get in the car. He hung back at least 20 feet, shielded by a gray Hyundai SUV.

"Someone could have planted a bomb in it. While we were taking the tour."

"That's ridiculous." I pressed the unlock button on the remote. I could hear the locks clunk, but nothing exploded.

"I'll wait 'til after you start it," he said, taking another step back.

Shaking my head, I climbed into the Prius and pressed the brake. I reached for the START button, but hesitated. It was ridiculous, but I couldn't seem to help it. My finger hung there, suspended, for about five seconds. I knew the longer I waited, the harder it would be to go on with my life. And the easier it would be to join Stephen in flirting with neurosis. If not psychosis.

Finally I stabbed the button. There was no sound, this being a hybrid, but now I welcomed it. I rolled the windows down. "There!" I called. "No bomb, all right?"

He opened the door. "Not this time, anyway," he replied, lowering himself into the passenger seat.

I pulled past the giant *U* logo and into traffic. Rush hour hadn't begun, but we were near the airport, and things could get worse anytime. "If your panic attack is over, you may as well settle in," I said. "This could take a while."

Pouting, he took out his phone and poked at it. "That was no panic attack."

"From now on, do I have to check the car for bombs every time we go somewhere?"

"No. And I don't want to talk about it anymore."

"Fine."

A minute or so later he sat up straight. "Boy, that was fast."

"What?"

"The research guy, Dr. Lazard. He's already sent that e-mail."

"Probably didn't want to lose his job. Blackwood wasn't too happy with him."

"It's pretty short. 'As promised, contact information for

research personnel formerly supervised by Dr. Rhee.' He's got three names here."

"What are they?"

"Douglas Brickman, Wesley Goldblum, and Neera Patel. Along with e-mail addresses and phone numbers."

"Excellent. So who's this Mercedes Pierce, then? Can we find out anything about her?"

"Give me a minute."

Sixty seconds later he said, "Hmm. Give me another minute."

Finally he started to say something, but I beat him to it. "Don't tell me. You're not finding anything. She doesn't exist."

"Well, there's a little official bio on the UniMerritt site. She was in information technology at the Pentagon. Worked for a civilian defense contractor. Doesn't say how old she is, but from the photo I'd say late fifties." He paused. "You know Frances McDormand?"

"The actress?"

"This woman reminds me of her. Sort of . . . plain. But at least Frances McDormand knows how to smile."

"Oh. Is that all the Internet says about her?"

"Yeah. There's a little on where she went to college, but not much else. You can't get more shadowy than that."

I shrugged. "Doesn't mean she's some sort of evil mastermind. We don't all crave notoriety. Dr. Rhee didn't."

Traffic was slowing, so I felt it was best to do the same. Soon we were crawling. I stared in the rearview mirror, watching vehicles inch forward like a ramshackle river of steel and glass.

I swung my gaze back to the front, but something nagged at the edge of my brain. Something about what I'd just seen. One of the cars.

I looked at the mirror again. There it was, just behind us, to the right. A gray Hyundai SUV.

I twisted around to get a better look. Hadn't I just seen one of those in the UniMerritt parking lot? The one Stephen had hidden behind?

I couldn't remember whether it had been occupied in the lot. I couldn't tell who was driving it now, either, with the sun glinting off the windshield.

Were we being followed?

It was irrational, of course. There must have been hundreds of gray Hyundai SUVs on the road in Seattle alone. Even if it was the same one, we probably just happened to be taking the same route. If I wasn't careful, I might get as paranoid as Stephen.

"What are you looking at?" he asked suddenly.

Swallowing, I twisted back toward the front.

No, I couldn't tell him. It would only feed his obsession.

"Nothing. Nothing at all."

For the next few minutes I kept glancing at the mirror, but couldn't glimpse the driver. Finally the car turned right and was gone.

Clearly it was nothing. Nothing at all.

# CHAPTER 8

I PUT THE SUV INCIDENT OUT OF MY MIND. OR TRIED TO.

Instead, I focused on talking to the three researchers on Lazard's list, the ones who'd worked for Rhee.

The first available was Wesley Goldblum, who according to the Internet seemed to have spent the last six of his twenty-four years doing nothing but winning awards and scholarships. There was no shortage of photos showing the baby-faced whiz kid standing next to lab-coated science types, bearded academics, and overweight businessmen, accepting checks and certificates with a slightly goofy grin.

We'd set up an appointment at his apartment for the following evening. Now Stephen and I were ascending the front steps of his building as the porch lights winked on around us like cigarette lighters held aloft at a Green Day concert.

"Never met a prodigy before," Stephen said.

"Neither have I. A few wunderkinds, but that's it."

"He had his master's degree by the time he was twenty-two. When I was that age, I was still trying to decide whether to be an astronaut or an editor."

I raised an eyebrow. "An astronaut? Astronauts have to know math and science."

"That's why I'm an editor."

We found apartment 6D. I was about to ring the doorbell when a muffled male voice came from inside.

"You need to die," it said gruffly.

"Don't count on it," a woman growled.

"I haven't got all day," said the first voice. There was a harsh popping sound, then a rapid series of them.

I looked at Stephen.

"Don't ask *me*," he whispered.

Not knowing what else to do, I rang the doorbell.

A few moments later the door opened. "Oh, hi," said the impossibly young man from the Internet pictures, his caramel-colored hair disheveled and a wireless headset looped around his neck. He smiled that goofy smile.

"You're playing a video game," Stephen said.

Wesley combed his hair quickly with his fingers, looking a little sheepish. "*HellHeart Nine*. You know it?"

"Not really," said Stephen.

He looked at me.

"Somehow I missed that one," I replied.

Wesley nodded. "You must be the guys with the book."

"That's us," I said.

"Come on in."

The apartment was crowded, not with people but things. Practically every wall was bolted with shelves, and nearly every shelf was laden with a video game console or TV screen or a row of Japanese-looking plastic figures with eerily large eyes. Purple controllers and what looked like Skittles were strewn across the floor.

Occasional bursts of dialogue and gunfire continued to drift from another room.

"Portal breached."

"Entering next level."

"Eat this, Parthian scum."

*Blam blam blam blam blam.*

"Wes Goldblum," he said, shaking my hand, then Stephen's. We introduced ourselves.

"So you're doing a book, huh? Cool."

He sat on one end of the couch, which looked like it might be brown under all the papers and game cartridges. We cleared an area at the other end and did the same.

I took my recorder from her purse. "Okay if I take some electronic notes?"

"Actually, no."

"How come?"

"I've got my whole life ahead of me. I won't make it very far if people think I can't keep my mouth shut. It's a *really* competitive industry."

"But Angus Blackwood already knows you're talking with us. He was all for it."

"Yeah, but without a recording nobody can prove who said what, or that you guys didn't just make it up."

The kid really *was* smart. Sighing, I put the device away and pulled out a pad of paper and a pen instead.

"We understand you worked with Dr. Rhee," I said.

He nodded. "Yeah, it's hard to know what to say about that. I mean, it's terrible what happened to him. But I can't say working for him was something I'd like to repeat."

"Was he hard to work for?"

He reached up and massaged his neck, as if to work a crick out of it. "I have to say yes. I mean, the hours were impossible. He was constantly having me redo experiments that were perfectly okay. Just because I didn't indent a line in the log, or I made a funny little comment under 'Output,' or he couldn't figure out an abbreviation on a label I'd put on a flash drive. He was such a perfectionist."

I looked at Stephen. "Hard to imagine," I said.

"Supposedly it was all for my own good," Wesley added.

"That must've made you pretty angry," I said. "From what we've heard, you're not exactly a slacker."

He shrugged. "I mean, I've gotten a little recognition."

"What kind of research were you doing?"

"For the last couple years, mostly diabetes."

"Did you have any idea there was a problem with Milletinor?"

He shook his head. "We weren't involved in the clinical trials."

"What happened when Dr. Rhee blew the whistle?"

"He just got worse. Secretive. I didn't know he was going to do it. I don't think anybody in the lab did."

I leaned forward. "Dr. Rhee was making things difficult for you. Maybe you would have been glad to see something— or someone—remove him from your life."

The young man started to say something, then stopped. "Hey, wait a minute. Are you saying I had something to do with what happened to him? Because it's not like he was just picking on *me*. He treated everybody that way."

"We're not here to accuse you of anything," I said. "We just need to know what happened."

"I don't *know* what happened. Look, UniMerritt can be a lousy place to work, but I'm not going to *kill* anybody to make it a little nicer."

There was a pause. It was long enough that we could hear the sounds of the video game again.

"Locked on target."

"No! Not my son!"

There was a scream.

*Brrraaaaaaaaaaaaap*, went some kind of automatic weapon.

I folded my arms. "You're not the type to kill anybody, then?"

He rolled his eyes. "I know the difference between a first-person shooter and real life. Games don't make you violent. They're a safety valve. You get that stuff out of your system."

"Right," I said.

"Besides, I have . . . what do they call it? An alibi."

I raised an eyebrow. "Which is?"

"Just a minute." He got up and went into another room. Less than a minute later he was back.

"This is Jade," he said, nodding at a young lady whose hand he was holding. She was skinny, her hair dyed an iridescent pink, wearing jeans and a black T-shirt with something in Japanese on it. A headset matching Wesley's circled her throat, and a butterfly tattoo decorated her left bicep.

"Jade is my . . ."

"Girlfriend," she finished.

"Also my alibi. The night Dr. Rhee . . ."

"Died," she said.

"Yeah, died . . . we were in the middle of a totally intense online *HellHeart* tournament."

"We lost, but it was totally fantastic," she added.

"How does that work, exactly?" I asked. "Could the other players vouch for you?"

He shook his head. "Theoretically, somebody else could have been using our account."

"But we know it was us," the young woman said.

*Now there's an ironclad alibi,* I thought.

I looked at my watch. "We won't keep you much longer, Wesley. Can you tell us anything about Mercedes Pierce?"

He frowned. "Who?"

"The head of security at UniMerritt."

"Oh. Guess I've heard her name. Don't know her. Never seen her, as far as I know. Don't know anything about her."

I sighed. "Seems nobody else does, either."

I rose from the couch. When I did, a box that said *Viper*

*Rot III* slid off and fell to the floor. The cover art depicted a decaying rattler with red eyes and fangs the size of shish kabob skewers.

"Very nice," I said. I handed Wesley a business card. "If you think of anything else, let us know."

"Sure. Are you talking to the others from the lab?"

"That's the plan," she said.

"They're both liars." He paused. "Just kidding." But he wasn't smiling.

The porch lights still glowed like Zippos as Stephen and I worked our way down the front steps of the building.

"Interesting young man," I said. "For one so bright, he seems a little . . . dim."

"Maybe being a prodigy deprived him of a normal childhood. Now he's making up for lost time." He paused. "Interesting alibi, too."

I stopped and looked up at the stars. "Alibis from wives, mothers, and significant others aren't reliable. Surely you know that from your extensive media consumption."

"So you don't believe them about the video game marathon?"

"I'm not sure. But I find it even harder to believe something else."

"What?"

"That a geek like Wesley could have a girlfriend."

He snickered. "Are you jealous?"

"Never," I said.

But in a way, I was.

\* \* \*

Neera Patel didn't look happy to see us.

On the other hand, she didn't look unhappy. She didn't seem to have emotions at all.

That was clear when we met at a park near the UniMerritt campus the next morning. Her slender face, its outstanding cheekbones framed by upswept black hair, appeared incapable of expression. The most one could say was that she looked poised.

The three of us sat on a bench, the kind made of recycled plastic, avoiding the evidence that a stray seagull or two had recently visited. I tried not to look up at the trees, fearing it might stimulate whatever portion of Stephen's brain caused him to catalog flora at great length.

"Thanks for seeing us," I said. "I'd be taking my digital recorder out of my purse about now and asking if I could use it, but I'm thinking you'd rather I didn't."

Ms. Patel, hands folded in her lap, blinked her unusually long lashes. "You would be correct."

"That was a timesaver," I said, pulling pad and pen from my purse. "How long did you work with Dr. Rhee?"

"Just the last eighteen months. I'd come from the lab at Texas A&M, where I'd worked for almost nine years."

"Why did you leave your previous job?"

"We lost our funding. The grant dried up."

"How would you describe Dr. Rhee?"

She blinked twice. "A tyrannical purist." Her face remained inert.

I drew back, startled.

"A pedantic, obsessive hairsplitter," she continued, still not gathering steam.

"Your verbal dexterity is impressive," I said. "I take it you weren't satisfied in your new environment."

"I don't think anyone was. Including Dr. Rhee. He was never content with our performance. Especially mine."

"If you were so unhappy, why didn't you go elsewhere?"

"I hadn't been there long enough. It would not have

looked good on my resumé." She paused. "And I suppose I understood Dr. Rhee to some extent."

"How so?"

"As I understand it, his parents in Korea were also scientists, and rather . . . exacting. My parents in India are in the medical profession, and similar in their expectations."

"But there the similarities ended."

"Yes. He failed to take me seriously, perhaps because I'm a woman. Or possibly because I'm Indian-American. He would at least listen to Wesley and Douglas. My opinions and conclusions were often dismissed."

She hesitated. "And there was the glassware incident."

"What was that?"

"About six months ago, we got a major shipment of lab glassware. Beakers, retorts, flasks, test tubes. I spent half the night unpacking it. About 1:30 I was so tired I couldn't see and managed to trip and knock a whole bunch of it off the wall service bench. I didn't have the energy to clean it up, so I left it and figured I'd take care of it in the morning. But Dr. Rhee discovered it before I got there and said I'd done it deliberately."

I put down my pad. "Why would he think that?"

"I'd asked him for a raise the week before, and he'd turned me down. This was my retaliation, he said."

"Did he . . . punish you?"

"He demoted me a pay grade."

I shook my head. "If that had happened to me, I might have gotten a little violent myself."

"You don't think *I* killed him, do you?"

I cleared my throat. "You did have a motive. But we're not jumping to any conclusions."

"Nor should you. I am not given to crimes of passion."

"I can believe that."

"Wesley and Douglas had their reasons, too, but none of us fits the profile I assume you're looking for."

"Maybe not. Do you remember the night Dr. Rhee died?"

"Yes. Well, mostly I remember the next day, when we all found out."

"What were you doing the night before?"

"Sleeping."

"Alone?"

"Very much so." She paused. "Are you asking whether I have an alibi?"

"You could put it that way."

"I don't have one. But for the purposes of the book you're writing, isn't the question whether my employer is capable of murdering its enemies?"

"I guess so."

She looked around the park as if for spies. All I saw was a mother watching her two preschoolers spin on the merry-go-round. There was no gray Hyundai SUV.

She lowered her voice. "Let's just say that people are capable of anything."

"People like . . . Mercedes Pierce?"

"Possibly."

Stephen perked up. "You know her?"

"Not really. I'm not sure anybody does. I sat next to her once at a luncheon for female employees. She spent the whole time doing e-mail on her phone. Kind of rude, I thought."

"Not a crime," I said, "but we're making progress."

She tapped her watch. "I really have to get back to the lab. I'm running a *mycoplasma pneumonia* culture and have to check the colony every two hours."

"I hate it when that happens," I said.

We all stood. I put my pad away and gave Ms. Patel

another business card. At this rate, I was going to have to reorder. "If you think of anything else—"

Suddenly, right behind and overhead, there was a *caw* sound, and a flapping. Jerking up our heads, we saw a marauding seagull, all white-gray feathers and brash persistence.

*A seagull? Here?* We had to be at least 10 miles from—

It dive-bombed the bench, its screech matching Stephen's. We all scattered.

Ms. Patel maintained her composure, her brown eyes staring down the oncoming banshee. The bird banked up and back, then deposited a squib of white on her dark green dress. Finally it fluttered into the trees.

The children on the merry-go-round were shrieking, and their mother herded them toward their car. Stephen sprinted toward our Prius.

There was another screech. The bird was back, headed toward Ms. Patel.

"Excuse me, Ms. Neville," she said calmly. "You might want to stand back."

I retreated further. She doubled the strap on her substantial-looking black purse and drew it back over her shoulder like a baseball bat.

The gull dove. Gripping the strap, she swung with all her might.

The purse met the attacker with a sickening crunch. In a second the bird was on the ground, its wings thumping pathetically against the russet bark dust.

The thumping stopped.

Holding her purse in front of her, she stepped over the carcass and headed for her car.

"Perhaps we'll meet again," she said, and kept going.

Speechless, I stared at what was left of the bird.

It was good to see she had no violent tendencies.

\* \* \*

Douglas Brickman had agreed to meet us for lunch. The place was called Sunrise Eatery, in a strip mall just down the highway from UniMerritt.

Dining was apparently an activity in which he engaged frequently, judging from his appearance. He looked about 35, moon-faced, with an undersized nose fixed to the center like a pushpin. His graying crewcut was as high as his double chin was deep. The collar of his white shirt, probably purchased in the Big department of a Big and Tall Men's Store, was unbuttoned to avoid strangulation.

"I don't recommend the food here," he muttered, wedging his bulk behind the table as he squeezed into the booth. "It's so bad that it's nearly always empty."

I studied the menu, which looked like a compendium of all the least interesting dishes one could make at home in ten minutes or less, using nothing more than white bread, canned food, and a microwave. "Then why did you suggest it?" I asked.

"Like I said, nobody comes here. I'd rather not have this conversation in a crowded room."

Sighing, I reached into my purse. I left the recorder untouched and took out my pad and pen.

He sat there waiting, his expression sour.

"You've been at UniMerritt for how long?" I asked.

"Nine years. Longest in the department."

"Any idea who might have killed Dr. Rhee?"

"Not the foggiest."

"We've heard he had a . . . unique management style."

Brickman snorted. "You might call it that."

"What would you call it?"

He folded his pudgy hands on the table. "My colleagues had more of a problem with his personality than I did.

Maybe because I'm more experienced. My expectations are lower."

"How would you describe your relationship with him?"

He scrunched up his face in a parody of thinking hard. "How shall I put this? In the beginning, not too bad. In the end, not too good." He looked at us as if daring us to guess what he meant.

I put the pad down. "My mind-reading skills don't work on an empty stomach."

He glanced around the room. "When he first came to the department, we talked a lot at first. I told him my theory about the role of mitochondrial activity in gene therapy. He seemed pretty interested."

"Who wouldn't be?" Stephen mumbled.

"In fact, he produced a paper on the subject. Got it published in a peer-reviewed journal, *Biomolecular Research & Therapeutics*. I should have been listed as first writer. All I got was a citation."

"You thought he stole your idea?"

"I'm sure he wouldn't put it that way. He'd say I only had the *germ* of an idea. Or it was necessary to make me humble. Or it got us a grant, which kept us employed."

"How did that make you feel?"

He rolled his eyes. "Oh, peachy."

I looked down at the empty space on the table in front of me, wondering if anyone would ever take our order. "And how did you feel when Dr. Rhee blew the whistle?"

"Peachy again. I love it when a self-righteous plagiarist gets national attention as a hero."

He leaned toward me as far as his abdomen would allow, which wasn't much. "Have you ever noticed how the Asians are taking over the sciences in this country?"

"Well, I—"

"The Chinese, the Koreans, the Indians. The Chinese—all

they really know how to do is steal our inventions. Everything from drug patents to movie copyrights. I realize Rhee was Korean, but the apple doesn't fall far from the tree."

The image of Hunter Thicke came to mind. Perhaps the two gentlemen were distantly related.

"So you had plenty of reason to resent Dr. Rhee," I said.

He leaned back, looking cautious. "We all did."

"Where were you the night he died?"

"As a matter of fact, I was still at the lab."

"Doing what?"

"Euthanizing rats."

"What?" Stephen asked.

"You don't want to know," he said.

Stephen frowned. "Yes, I do."

Brickman leaned a chubby cheek against his hand. "We induce certain conditions—tumors, for instance. Then we remove them for study. The rats are euthanized before the surgery, of course."

"As if that makes it okay."

"Do we have to get into this now?" Brickman asked, almost whining.

"No," I said. I looked at Stephen. "Another time, alright?"

"All right," he muttered.

"Anyway," Brickman said, "Rhee said I had to double-check my results. Said they were suspect. He never stopped riding us."

"Until somebody stopped *him*," I said.

He shrugged. "One way to look at it, I guess."

"Can you prove how late you were there that night?"

He thought for a moment. "No. Does that make me a murderer?"

"Not at all. It just raises questions."

He spread his arms wide in frustration, though they couldn't stretch much wider than his torso. "Don't you get it?

Rhee stole my work. Thanks to him, I've been stuck playing Igor for the last nine years. I'll probably be stuck there the rest of my life, scrubbing test tubes for this new French guy. What is it with all the foreigners? Aren't there any *real* Americans left in this country?"

I stopped taking notes, figuring anything else would be a waste of paper. "One more question. Do you know Mercedes Pierce?"

"Head of security."

"What do you think of her?"

"I don't. Have you seen that face?"

I stuffed the pad and pen into my purse.

Brickman looked at the wall clock, which had apparently stopped working long ago. Then he checked his watch. "Gotta go."

"But we haven't even placed our order," Stephen said.

"Well, the food isn't the only thing wrong with this dump. The service is lousy, too."

He grunted his way out of the booth, then lumbered out the door.

Stephen turned to me. "Aren't you going to give him your business card?"

"Are you kidding? I don't want this guy to call us. Ever."

He raised an eyebrow. "Because he's . . . unusually large?"

"No, because he's a xenophobic, misogynistic animal abuser."

"Oh, that."

We waited another few minutes to see whether anyone would show up to take our order.

Fortunately, no one did.

# CHAPTER 9

HAVING GIVEN UP ON THE SUNRISE EATERY AND HAVING SEEN the walking cautionary tale that was Douglas Brickman, I almost decided to swear off eating altogether. But Stephen insisted we stop somewhere, preferably a place that didn't serve white bread and wasn't being attacked by seagulls.

We were sitting in such a place, eating Mexican food with far too much cilantro, when the sound of the *1812 Overture* burst from my pocket. I'd used that ringtone so long Stephen claimed I'd installed it during the actual War of 1812.

Hunter Thicke's number was on the screen. That alone would have been reason to destroy the phone immediately, but I abandoned that plan when I realized its financial implications.

"Carolyn, this is—"

"I know. How peachy to hear from you."

"Is the book done yet?"

I hesitated. "All except for the research and the writing."

"Great. So who killed the whistleblower?"

"I haven't a clue."

He paused. "Surely you're not serious."

"I'm *always* serious. Uncovering the truth takes time, like peeling the layers of an onion. Sometimes it even makes you cry."

"What are you talking—"

"It reminds me of an anecdote involving President Woodrow Wilson. It seems that a member of his cabinet had been accused of—"

"Hold it," he said. "I'm the one who tells the stories. It's a gift. You're either born with it or you're not. And frankly, you don't seem to have it. No offense."

"None taken." I crossed my fingers under the table.

"We're talking about an instant book here. I can't have you turning it into the kind where you slowly roast the beans, grind them, and brew them into the perfect cup of . . . words."

"You do know how to turn a phrase."

"Exactly what have you accomplished so far?"

"We've interviewed Mrs. Rhee, the chief of police, the CEO of UniMerritt, and all three of the researchers who worked for the deceased. Not to mention a skinny young woman with pink hair and a butterfly tattoo."

"And you still don't know *anything?*"

"Well, I wouldn't say that. We know what happens when you push the START button on a Prius without pressing the brake pedal first."

"What happens?"

"Nothing."

His voice iced over. "I wish we had time for jokes, Carolyn. Here's how this is gonna go. You and Stephen will deliver a finished manuscript in four weeks."

"Four *weeks?* But I thought—"

"We're losing our window. You'll do whatever it takes to get the goods on the drug company. I want a progress report every seven days."

"But—"

"I know you'll come through. You know how I know?"

"How?"

"Because you're not stupid. A pain in the neck, maybe, but not stupid."

"That's the nicest thing anyone's said to me all day. Thank you."

"I'm going to hang up now, Carolyn."

"If you insist."

I pressed the END button.

Stephen finished the last of his chili rellenos. "Hunter," she said.

"How did you know?"

"You don't talk to anybody else like that. I swear you have a death wish."

"So you *do* understand me after all."

"Sounds like he's getting impatient," he said, picking up a churro.

"We have four weeks. And he wants progress reports."

He sighed. "That's what happens when you create the earth in six days. You expect everyone else to work at the same pace."

He smiled a fake smile. I did my best to do the same.

But something unpleasant was starting to happen in my gut, the kind of thing that happens when your enchilada makes you gassy.

Or when you see your doom approaching.

\* \* \*

By the time we reached our car, I'd made a momentous decision.

"I'm calling Marvin," I said.

Stephen shook his head. "Why? That's like asking a guy to

fix your bathroom sink because he knows how to wash his hands."

I got into the driver's seat. "That's one of the worst similes I've ever heard. Marvin writes about real crimes. He knows how killers think. He knows the system."

"He's good at *writing* about crimes, not *solving* them."

"At least he's an actual person. You're always looking to fictional characters for advice."

"They don't torment you like he does."

"He doesn't torment me. He's practically my grandfather."

"He's almost old enough to be. Another reason not to get him involved."

"You just don't like him because he's African-American."

He folded his arms. "I won't go there. Go ahead, call him. See if I care."

I dialed his number in Florida. Someone picked up, but there was no hello. Only background hiss, then a fumbling noise.

Finally Marvin got on the line. "Yeah?"

"Marvin, it's Carolyn Neville."

"Oh. Kind of in the middle of something, Cranberry. With Tracy. We're having a little disagreement."

"Oh."

"About a boat. Sea Hunt BX 24 BR. Yamaha F 300 outboard 4.2-liter V6. Bait tank, captain's chairs. Bimini top. Wouldn't call it a yacht, but it's a wonder to behold."

"And Tracy doesn't feel that way."

He cleared his throat. "I seem to have neglected to consult her before signing the papers. But I offered to name it after her."

A muffled female voice sounded in the background. I couldn't make out the words.

More fumbling noise. "What's the point of retiring in St.

Petersburg if you can't have a boat?" Marvin called, apparently turned away from the phone.

There was a pause, and he was back. "What do you need, honey? You only call when you're in trouble."

"I need advice."

"Well, the Word says in a multitude of counselors there's safety. What is it now?"

"Have you heard about the whistleblower who worked for UniMerritt Laboratories? The one who was murdered? It's been in the news recently."

"Sure. The diabetes drug that caused cancer. I keep up with all that stuff about side effects. My medicine cabinet is the size of a walk-in closet."

"We're doing a book about him. An instant book."

"I hate instant books. Quality—"

"I know, quality takes time. I'm not asking you to write it. I need your advice on figuring out who did it."

"Who do *you* think did it?"

"Everyone involved had a motive."

"Then it's obvious. Didn't you see that movie, *Murder on the Orient Express*?"

There was more talking in the background.

"Whatever you say, Tracy," Marvin called.

He sighed. "Look. Everything I've heard points to the drug company."

"Maybe yes, maybe no. We're running out of time trying to answer that question."

"That's why instant books don't work."

There was more talk from Tracy, closer this time. The last part sounded like, "Husbands, love your wives."

"*Ow*," Marvin said. "That's my bursitis shoulder, baby." He paused. "Sorry, Cranberry. A little business to take care of at this end. May not be able to help you anyway. Later, okay?"

The line went dead.

Stephen looked at me. "Solution?"

"He's busy at the moment."

"Did he have any advice?"

"Not in so many words."

He leaned against the headrest, looking smug. "I see."

"Do you?"

"Time to go back to the hotel. We've got a list to make. Suspects, means, motives, opportunities."

I shook my head. "You always suggest that."

"It's what they do on TV."

"It never works. Not for us, anyway."

He shrugged. "Always a first time."

I started the Prius in the usual strange and irritating way. "Nice to see you being optimistic for a change," I said. "Sure you don't have a fever or something?"

"Not sick," he said as I pulled away from the curb. "Just desperate."

* * *

Inexplicably, the conference room at the hotel contained no erasable white boards. I'd thought they were required by some building code.

"I'm not sure this is going to work," I said, sitting at the table. "You always make your lists on white boards."

Stephen took out his pad and pen. "We'll have to make do. The pioneers didn't have erasable boards." He wrote something on his paper. "Step one: Name our suspects."

"Angus Blackwood. Mercedes Pierce. Anybody associated with UniMerritt Laboratories."

He kept writing. "That would include an awful lot of people."

"To be specific, Wesley Goldblum, Neera Patel, and Douglas Brickman."

A picture of the gray Hyundai came to mind, too, but with a blank spot where the driver's face should have been. I kicked it to the back of my mind. No need to bring that up, unless I wanted to spend the rest of my life checking for bombs that existed only in Stephen's imagination.

"So much for the drug company," he said. "Who else?"

"Hunter Thicke."

He put the pen down. "Huh?"

"Maybe he had the victim killed to increase sales of the book."

He snorted. "Much as I'd like to see the guy in jail, no way."

"All right. How about the chief of police?"

"Why?"

"I don't like him anymore. And he obviously doesn't like me."

"I don't have enough paper to cover that segment of the population."

"Fine. Leave him off."

"Step two," he said. "Answer a couple of questions about each suspect. Who had the most to gain from Rhee's death? And who seems most capable of actually killing somebody?"

I felt the urge to stand up and pace back and forth to stimulate my powers of deduction, but the room was too small.

"Well, Angus Blackwood may be capable of murder, but he would have delegated it to someone else," I said. I took out my recorder and beeped my way to the file of the Blackwood interview. When I fast-forwarded, the CEO's sped-up brogue sounded like a Highlands chipmunk.

At last I found the spot I wanted.

. . .

*. . . Understand the man was brilliant. We were fortunate to have him and feel his loss most acutely.*

*Did you go to his memorial service?*

*I was in Switzerland that week, unfortunately. But several of our team were there. Quite moving, I heard.*

"That gives him an alibi," Stephen said. "Not that he needs one. The trick is proving he ordered a hit."

"Or that Mercedes Pierce did. If Neera Patel hadn't met her personally, I'd doubt she even exists."

I paused, staring at the wall and trying to imagine a white board full of names and theories. "People think UniMerritt is behind the murder. But what's the motive? Rhee had already blown the whistle, so it was too late. Unless . . ."

"Unless what?"

"Unless he had more—and maybe worse—revelations to make."

"Like what?"

"I don't know. But without them, the company has no motive except revenge. What would it gain from that?"

"Money?"

"Hard to see how. They had to know they'd be blamed if something happened to the man who blew the whistle."

"Big business does what it wants. Remember what Neera said? 'People are capable of anything.' I think she was talking about Mercedes Pierce."

"People *are* capable of anything," I said. "But we can't put them all on our list."

"Then let's just talk about the researchers. Like Wesley."

"Not too plausible as a murderer. Unless you consider his taste in video games."

"They don't make you violent. He's right."

"He's also the one with the unreliable alibi," I said. "Were he and Ms. Pink Hair really glued to their Nintendos when Rhee died?"

"I think you mean Xboxes."

"Whatever. As for what Wesley would have gained by killing his boss, the answer's obvious. He would have escaped being driven like a slave. But is that really enough to motivate him to commit homicide?"

He looked away. "*I've* certainly felt that way."

I ignored his limitless wit. "What about Ms. Patel?"

"Same motive, only more of it. Rhee disrespected her. Demoted her."

"For allegedly smashing all that glassware. Not to mention the seagull. The woman swung that purse as if she were possessed."

He shuddered. "Thanks for bringing up that mental image."

"She also has no alibi. In fact, I can't think of anything in her favor."

He folded his arms. "And *I* can't think of anything in favor of Brickman. At best, he's a racist vivisectionist."

"Technically, no. Vivisection is dissecting live animals. The rats were dead."

"Sure, after he killed them."

"What would he have gained by poisoning Rhee? It wouldn't have salvaged his career."

"Crazy people don't think that way."

He ran a finger down the list. "What about Rhee's wife?"

"Olivia? That's a non-starter."

He shrugged. "Maybe she had something to gain."

"But she's heartbroken. Maybe you can't see it, but I can."

"What about her husband's life insurance? Maybe she stood to get a big windfall. Wouldn't be the first spouse to do something like that."

"I can't believe she would."

"Afraid to find out?"

"Of course not. How do you propose we do that?"

"We could ask her."

I shook my head. "You, maybe. Not me. Not after what she's been through."

"Okay."

"You'd better brush up on your bedside manner first."

"I'll find a way."

He looked around the room, as if hoping to find a clue. "Anybody else?" he asked.

"Not that I can think of."

"Then we're done here."

"Really? Who did it?"

He looked down at his notes.

"Everybody."

# CHAPTER 10

WHEN OLIVIA RHEE OPENED THE DOOR THE NEXT DAY, MY resolve wavered. I couldn't let Stephen ask The Question. It was cruel.

She was wearing the same outfit she'd worn last time we were here, a billowy housedress that looked like lavender parachute silk. Her fine black hair, braided as usual, was starting to unravel. When she smiled it was with more effort than before. If she'd been fragile before, she was frail now, hollow as an eggshell.

"Thank you for coming," she said, the volume of her voice barely matching the burbling fountain's.

That made it worse, of course, her thanking us for coming to ask whether she'd murdered her husband for his insurance.

We sat on the red leather couch again. She apologized for not having anything to go with the tea, saying she hadn't been to the store for a while.

"Totally understandable," I said.

There was a long silence. The noise of the fountain filled it.

"The memorial service was beautiful," I said.

"It's kind of you to say so. I saw your names in the guest book."

I relaxed a little, relieved that she hadn't noticed our early exit from the sanctuary. Or at least didn't mention it.

Stephen cleared his throat. "Mrs. Rhee, I've been wondering . . ."

I swallowed.

"I've been wondering whether the police have come up with any more information on what happened."

I exhaled. Maybe he was trying to torture me.

She shook her head. "Not that they've told me. They turned the house upside down in the beginning. I got the impression they didn't find very much. They said there were no fingerprints other than ours."

Stephen nodded. "The killer could have worn rubber gloves. Researchers wear rubber gloves. We saw that on our UniMerritt tour." He paused. "Of course, hair stylists, janitors, dental hygienists, food preparers, and police evidence collectors wear them, too."

I turned toward Olivia. "We have very little information about what the police know. That makes it difficult to write the book. I wonder whether you could do us a favor. Could you show us . . . where it happened?"

"The bedroom? I—I'm afraid it's a bit of a mess. I haven't had the energy to keep up with the housework." She looked at the floor.

"That might be a good thing," I said. "The more closely the room resembles the way it was that night, the better our chances of finding something helpful."

She lifted her head. "All right."

We followed her down the hall, then to the left.

It was a large room, big enough for two double beds, two chests of drawers, and an armoire. One bed was rumpled, untidy. The other was perfectly arranged. A single fabric sculpture, a tranquil blue and gold something, hung on the textured white wall. There was a smell of coconut incense and moisturizer. The atmosphere was intimate, hushed, and a little stale.

"I suppose you can tell which bed is mine," Mrs. Rhee said faintly. "Kelvin made his in a very . . . *precise* way."

"And this is where you found him," I said.

"Yes. He usually got up before I did. This time . . . he didn't. The covers were half on the floor, as if he'd kicked them back. I tried to wake him up. He was gone. I called 911 right away. I was surprised at how quickly they got here, but it was too late."

"You didn't hear anything during the night?"

She shook her head. "I've always been a sound sleeper. And I usually wore earplugs. Kelvin tended to snore."

"Were there any signs someone had broken into the house?"

"The window to the guest room was open. But I'd been airing it out, and I must have left it that way. The glass wasn't broken."

"What do the police say happened?"

She sat on the edge of her bed and picked at the blanket. "Kelvin had high blood pressure for years. Last year he started taking this new medicine, Lexidril. Maybe you've heard his company makes it."

"Yes."

"He always took it at bedtime. It seemed to be working. The capsules were yellow. They were in a bottle by the bed."

She pointed. The nightstand held a pair of reading glasses and a digital alarm. The pill bottle was gone, of course. I wondered how long the glasses and alarm would stay there, gathering dust.

"They told me the intruder must have replaced the

capsules with ones containing the cyanide. Or opened the ones in the bottle and reused them."

I nodded. "Do *you* think that's what happened?"

"I suppose so. I didn't ask a lot of questions. I assume the police know what they're doing. They were mostly very nice in the way they treated me."

I paused. "Does their explanation make sense to you?"

She scratched her head. "So far, yes."

I looked around the room, wishing some overlooked cigarette butt or strand of hair would start flashing like a strobe light. But nothing did.

The theory made sense, all right. But it wasn't very satisfying.

It didn't explain who did it—or why.

* * *

Stephen got down on his hands and knees and peered sideways under Rhee's bed.

"What are you looking for?" I asked.

"I don't know. Anything."

"Let me know if you find it."

After a few more moments he got back up. "Can you show me the window that was open?"

"Of course." She led us further down the hall and to the right.

This room was much smaller, with one double bed and dresser. The window was covered by a pair of burgundy curtains on a brass rod. Mrs. Rhee stepped to the side and pulled them open.

"Not very big," Stephen said. "Guess I could get through it if I hadn't eaten much at lunch."

He looked at me. "Are you thinking what I'm thinking?"

"Probably not."

"Douglas Brickman. There's no way he could've climbed through that window."

I raised an eyebrow. "You're right."

"Who is Douglas Brickman?" Olivia asked.

"One of the researchers who worked for your husband," I said. "Did you ever meet him? A rather . . . large man."

"Oh, yes."

"What was your impression of him?" Stephen asked.

She thought for a moment. "I don't want to assume too much from such a brief encounter. But he didn't seem happy."

"That's putting it mildly," Stephen said.

"He appeared to be . . . agitated."

"Did your husband ever talk about him?"

"Not that I recall."

"Did you meet his other two researchers?"

"Only for a few minutes, probably at a company picnic. And a few times when I brought Kelvin his lunch. He was a bit absent-minded."

"What did you think of Wesley Goldblum?" I asked.

"He was the very young man?"

I nodded.

"Well . . . smart, of course. He said something funny, but I can't recall what it was. Kelvin thought he should get a haircut, but I thought the boy was kind of cute."

"And Neera Patel?"

She gave it some thought. "I believe I only met her once. She reminded me a bit of Kelvin."

"In what way?"

"Not very . . . emotional. That surprised me, given what Kelvin told me. He came home one day and said she'd broken a lot of lab equipment or something. It must have bothered him quite a bit, because he hardly ever talked about work."

"Did you ever meet Dr. Lazard?" I asked.

"I don't know who that is."

"He replaced your husband at the company."

She lowered her gaze.

"Not that anyone could replace him," I said quickly.

She shook her head. "I have no ties there anymore. I guess I'll never have a reason to visit again." She sighed. "Would you mind if we go back to the living room and sit down? I seem to get tired earlier these days."

"I'm sorry," I said. "Of course."

We returned to the front room. The fountain seemed louder than ever, babbling and dripping like a hot tub minus the relaxing effect.

I turned to Stephen. "Do you have the list we made?"

He took the notepad from his pocket and handed it to me. As always, his penmanship was nearly unreadable, thanks to his emphasis on speed over clarity.

I managed to make out the names. "It occurs to me," I said, "that everyone on our list had ties to the drug company, whether or not they worked there. I imagine they'd have easier access to poison and empty capsules than most people would."

Stephen scratched his chin. "But most of them wouldn't have known about Dr. Rhee's prescription." He looked at Olivia, the lone exception.

I rushed to her defense. "Anybody could have found out about it. Don't medical records get hacked all the time?"

He shook his head. "Not prescriptions, I don't think."

"Someone could have stood behind him at the pharmacy and heard his conversation with the pharmacist. Or looked in his garbage can for a prescription receipt, or the label on an empty pill bottle he'd thrown away. Or—"

Stephen coughed quietly into his fist. My evasion wasn't going to work. Or as Hunter Thicke might have put it, the elephant in the room could no longer be swept under the rug.

He was going to ask The Question, and I couldn't stop him.

"Mrs. Rhee, did your husband have a life insurance policy? And were you the beneficiary?"

I groaned. "Please forgive Mr. Ames's directness. He—"

Olivia managed a watered-down smile. "It's not a problem. I'm used to directness." She faced Stephen. "I assume you're asking whether I was in a position to gain financially from Kelvin's death."

"Well, yes."

She shook her head. "He had a modest policy through the company. I believe it was for a hundred and fifty percent of his annual salary."

"Not a huge windfall, then," I said.

"But a fairly substantial amount," Stephen countered.

"Yes," said Olivia. "But I was not the beneficiary."

Stephen raised an eyebrow.

"Kelvin believed in tradition," she said. "He was committed to honoring his parents no matter what. The money will go to his father, who just turned eighty."

"I see."

She looked down at the floor. "He is in a memory care home about ten miles from here. Not Alzheimer's, but dementia. Kelvin's mother passed away three years ago. Nursing homes are expensive. I suppose the insurance will help him."

"I hope so," I said softly.

"I visit Kelvin's dad when I can. But he never knows I'm there or who I am. And when you get right down to it, he isn't *my* father. I know that sounds terrible."

"No, it doesn't," I said.

She didn't reply. She seemed to have run out of steam.

The fountain splashed and trickled for a long time.

"I don't know what I'm going to do," she whispered finally.

I couldn't hear it when she started to cry.

But I could see it all too clearly.

# CHAPTER 11

I LIMPED TOWARD THE CAR, EMOTIONALLY SPEAKING. THE watercolor gray sky made the perfect backdrop.

"I hate to leave her that way," I said.

"She said she'd be okay."

I thumbed the remote at the Prius, almost wishing there *was* a bomb underneath.

"Do you still think she killed her husband?" I asked.

"I never said that. I said it was possible."

"Are you having second thoughts?"

He sighed. "I guess so."

I climbed into the car and checked my phone. Hunter Thicke had called again.

I frowned. Couldn't be. It wasn't time for a progress report. I was supposed to have seven days.

Preparing for the worst, I redialed the number. When he answered, his mood seemed much improved.

"Carolyn, I'm on my way to McSorley's Old Ale House. To celebrate our success. Too bad you're not here."

"What success?"

"I've solved the problem. We can get the book written ASAP so we don't lose that release window."

"How?"

"By getting your friend Marvin to help you."

"But we've already covered that. He'd never do it. Not on this schedule."

"Seems he's changed his mind."

"Impossible. I just talked with him yesterday. He still hates instant books."

"Maybe. But he said yes to this one. Has something to do with a boat."

"Oh."

"He said this was the perfect opportunity to get out of the house."

"Ah." Going to Seattle would be the perfect excuse to travel as far as possible from his lovely bride and remain in the continental United States.

"Besides, I'm paying him a lot of money," Hunter added.

Wonderful. Now there was even more at stake.

"I know you'll make this work, Carolyn. And I'm sure you'll get a kick out of seeing your old buddy again."

I wasn't so sure.

"You can thank me later," he said. I heard a horn honk in the background. "Better go. I'll have an extra pint in your honor."

I put the phone down.

"You look worried," Stephen said.

I told him what Hunter had done. Then he looked worried, too.

"Have you ever actually co-written anything with Marvin?" he asked.

"No, I've just edited his books."

"Was he easy to work with?"

"That depends on your definition of 'difficult.'"

He sank back into the seat. "I have my doubts about this. But I'll withhold judgment. After all, he's . . ."

"Black?"

"No, inevitable."

I pressed the Prius' START button.

No bomb went off.

I sighed. Some days were just that way.

* * *

We weren't idle during the next 48 hours as we awaited Marvin's arrival.

Stephen redeemed the time by transcribing his interview with Angus Blackwood. He started an outline for the book.

I, meanwhile, decoded my notes of the interviews with Wesley, Neera, and Brickman. Not to mention beginning to craft what I felt was a fabulous prologue.

When we finally stood at Carousel 4 in Baggage Claim at Sea-Tac, I knew spotting Marvin would be like trying to find a needle in a mountain of pins. Eleven years had passed since I'd seen him. All I could remember was that he stood about six feet tall, wiry to the point of gauntness, and was . . . well . . . black.

"Is that him?" Stephen asked, pointing into the distance at a skinny, denim-clad African-American male with a black baseball cap and green duffel bag.

"No, that guy is too young."

The man waved in our direction.

"Cranberry!" he yelled over the general roar.

I squinted as he made his way toward us through the crowd. "Although I could be mistaken," I murmured.

"I thought that was you," he said, grinning. "Hard to tell, though, now that you've gotten so old."

He gave me a hug, smelling of airline peanuts. I looked

him over. Wiry, yes, but the paunch was paunchier. And his hair was nearly all white.

He turned to Stephen. "You must be Mr. Ames." They shook hands. His grip must have been more than firm, judging by the way Stephen's eyes bugged out.

"So it's all about the boat, is it?" I asked.

Marvin nodded. "Yeah, my helpmeet and I came to an understanding. That's pretty much why I'm here." He paused. "That and the pleasure of working with a true professional. I'm talking about Mr. Ames, of course."

"Of course." I looked at the carousel, where luggage dropped from a chute and thumped the conveyor belt like a series of body bags. "Do you have a suitcase?"

"Yeah. Should be easy to spot. Big, dark blue, the rolling kind, with a piece of red yarn tied to the handle."

"Good idea. Practically all of them match that description."

We stared at the baggage parade. "Mr. Thicke says the book is done except for the research and the writing," he said. "He thought that was pretty good."

"That's because Mr. Thicke's knowledge of publishing is pretty thin."

"So I suspected. But he knows how to sign a check, right?"

"Right."

The suitcases continued to march past our reviewing stand. "Is that one yours?" I asked, pointing.

"Nope. Mine doesn't have a Tinkerbelle nametag. I bet yours does, though."

"I hope you know what you're getting into with this project," I said. "Even with three of us, I don't see how it's going to come out in time. And if it does, it's going to be the biggest piece of junk ever written. At least since L. Ron Hubbard died."

"I see you've been missing your meetings at Optimist International again."

"Marvin, how can you be let yourself be associated with this book? Stephen and I may be nobodies, but you have a reputation to protect."

He shrugged. "I can always keep my name off the cover."

"So can I. But *somebody's* name has to be there."

"Maybe a pseudonym. I've always been partial to M.T. Page."

I pointed at another suitcase. "Yours?"

He followed it with his eyes. "Uhhhhh. . . yes." He reached out and snagged it, then checked the tag. "False alarm." He dumped it back onto the belt.

"So which part of this book do you want to work on?" I asked.

"All of it."

"What does that mean?"

"I'll be taking the long view. Every team needs a leader, right?"

"You almost make it sound like you intend to take over."

"Didn't Thicke tell you? He wants me to oversee the project."

I chuckled. "Good one."

"I'm not kidding, Cranberry. Surely he said something."

I frowned. For a moment I teetered on the line between *He's pulling my leg* and *The world is coming to an end.*

He pulled his phone from his pocket and started tapping on it. "Here's the e-mail he sent me." He handed me the phone.

It was from Hunter, all right. The subject was "Game Changer." About halfway through I came to a paragraph that stopped my breathing:

. . .

*Our team means well, but they've struck out. I'm still the franchise owner, but they need a new coach. That's you. I want you calling the plays so we can win this thing.*

I swallowed. I wanted to say something, but my mental faculties seemed to have been shut down by one of those civilization-leveling electromagnetic pulses you hear so much about.

"A sports metaphor," I said weakly.

Marvin cleared his throat. "I can see you need some time to . . . what do they call it . . . *process* this."

"Just give me a decade or two."

He lifted the cap from his head. "See the *TB*? Doesn't stand for tuberculosis, honey. It's Tampa Bay Rays. Right there in St. Petersburg."

"Is this going to be another sports metaphor?"

"We're on the same side, Cranberry. I may be team captain, but *somebody* has to be, right?"

"That's debatable."

"You'll get over it. You've been in this business a long time. You take a lickin' and go on tickin.'"

"I hate wristwatch metaphors, too."

"There you go. Making jokes already. That's the girl I remember."

He put the cap back on and rocked back on his heels, looking hopeful.

I stared at the baggage on the belt, looking very much the opposite.

\* \* \*

Marvin finally got his suitcase. Not that I cared.

We checked him into Emerald City Extended Stays, then

went out to dinner. He suggested an oyster bar, but Stephen responded with a grimace that belonged on one of those Pacific Northwest Indian totem poles that sprouted like parking meters here. I abstained from voting due to lack of interest.

They compromised on a seafood restaurant not far from the hotel, a place where the servers made you wear a hat shaped like a fish head if it was your birthday. Fortunately, that didn't apply to us. We were seated in a booth under a decorative lobster trap that threatened to tumble onto our heads at any moment.

"Reminds me of the day we met," Marvin said, turning toward me. "You remember that?"

"Lunch at Keen's Steakhouse."

"Man, I'd never been to such a fancy place." He looked at Stephen. "Must have been my turn on the Schmooze the Bestselling Author list. Mine was *Darkness at Dawn*."

Stephen nodded. "I've read it. Kind of grisly, but it deserved all the attention."

"Thank you. Cranberry took me to this steakhouse in Manhattan. They had oysters, but I ordered the Legendary Mutton Chop. Wasn't even sure what a mutton chop was, but it sounded like the thing to get when you're on top of the world. Figured it might be my last chance."

I looked at my watch, hoping to signal boredom, but no one was watching.

"Carolyn got the prime rib," Marvin continued. "I was all nervous, worried I was going to spill something on myself. But about halfway through, my friend here got up to go to the can and upended her little gravy boat in her lap." He grinned. "She walked funny for the rest of the afternoon."

Stephen snickered.

I turned toward Marvin. "I was merely trying to put you at ease."

The two of them laughed. I sat in silence, consoling myself with Dr. Garabedian's prediction that I might die prematurely.

When the food arrived, all seemed to be in order. Marvin took off his cap and placed it next to him on the seat. "Anybody mind if I ask the blessing?"

I felt a twinge of embarrassment, followed by a gust of guilt. I'd gotten used to praying the Manhattan way, with my eyes open to escape detection. Saying grace came as naturally to Marvin as teasing me.

"Go right ahead," Stephen said. He looked more bemused than offended, making me feel worse.

After the prayer, Marvin didn't put his cap back on. He took a few bites of his Parmesan Broiled Tilapia, then put the fork down.

"Something I need to say. I've already said it to Carolyn. Hunter Thicke has some definite ideas on how we'll be working together. Long story short, he wants me to take the lead."

Stephen looked at me. I remained absolutely impassive, a skill I'd perfected while listening to agents pitch books whose working titles made me want to throw myself under a train.

"Mr. Thicke wants us to get off the dime," Marvin continued. "And it's his dime. So here's what I'd like to do.

"First, daily and weekly word-count deadlines. First draft doesn't have to be perfect. Just has to *be*. I had a journalism prof at Lincoln U who always said that."

I sagged.

"Second, the right tools. Speech-to-text software. Hidden camera, maybe."

"*What?*" I cried. "We're editors, not spies."

He looked down at his plate. "I did an article for the *Tribune* once about a guy who robbed an armored car and shot the driver. Wore a wire when I interviewed his accomplice. Another time I did a piece on a nursing home that was neglecting the folks there. This was before the days of cell phones. Used a little camera under my coat to get some very interesting pictures."

He looked at me. "It's called investigative reporting, ma'am. Happens every day."

Stephen raised a hand. "Carolyn's already got a digital recorder," he said, sounding too excited.

"Great. Number three, go after the drug company. Maybe find a mole. Maybe *be* a mole."

"As in *undercover?*" I asked, incredulous.

"Whatever it takes."

I closed my eyes.

Stephen seemed undisturbed. "So who does what?"

"Divide and conquer. You and I take on background research, interviews, write the manuscript. Maybe take turns on alternate chapters."

"Where does that leave me?" I asked, not wanting to know.

"You do the legwork. I'm gettin' too old for that, but I can give you some ideas."

I shook my head, which only made it hurt more. "I don't know the first thing about industrial espionage. I can't—"

"I'm not talking about a license to kill, girl. Nothing dangerous. Well, not *too* dangerous. Besides, nobody would suspect a fine, upstanding lady like yourself."

He went back to work on his food. "You need to get out more. You don't want life to pass you by."

"Actually, I do. The sooner the better."

"You'll do great. Great enough."

He turned to Stephen. They started talking about who to interview and what the word count of the book should be.

I stopped listening and looked over Marvin's shoulder, focusing on a party halfway across the room.

It was a big group, loud. At one end of the table sat an old man with white hair and an outdated suit he couldn't fill anymore. A young female server, flanked by two others, was handing him the hat that looked like a fish head.

He took it gamely, trying to figure out how to put it on. Finally, the server settled it on his cranium and cinched the strap under his chin. The others clapped and cheered as the trio of waiters broke into song, a tuneless, royalty-free substitute for the genuine "Happy Birthday."

The old man tried to smile.

I shook my head. He was my kinsman.

I, too, was about to strap on the fish head and see how badly things could go.

# CHAPTER 12

NEXT MORNING, AFTER BREAKFAST, MARVIN KNOCKED ON THE door to my room.

"You'll need this," he said, handing me a fist-sized cardboard box as the door closed behind him.

"What is it?"

"You'll see. Ordered it from a website about a month ago. Haven't had time to open it. Thought it might come in handy."

"How?"

He lowered his voice. "To find out more on . . . whoever you have the most questions about. Somebody at the drug company."

"Mercedes Pierce, I guess."

"Who's she?"

"Head of security. If she doesn't have a skeleton in her closet, she knows where the bodies are buried."

"And what are your questions?"

"What does she really do? Who works for her? Is she as lethal as she looks? Did she hire anyone to kill Dr. Rhee?"

"Yeah, those are good. Let me know what you find out."
He turned to go.

"Wait!" I said. "How am I supposed to use this . . . whatever's in the box . . . to answer my questions?"

Raising his palms as if to show he was unarmed, he lowered his voice again. "It's mainly a listening device, okay? If you're within about three hundred feet, you can monitor a conversation. At least that's what it said on the website."

"Is that legal?"

He squeezed one eye shut. "That's kind of a gray area."

"Which means what?"

Sighing, he sat down on the edge of the bed. "I looked all this up. In the state of Washington, it's sort of illegal to intercept any private conversation without the permission of all parties concerned."

I frowned. "*Sort of* illegal?"

"Yeah. There are exceptions. Like conversations with threats of extortion, blackmail, bodily harm, or other unlawful requests or demands. So if this woman at the drug company talks to somebody about breaking the law, you're safe. I think."

Last night's headache was descending on me again. "I could end up in jail."

He waved dismissively. "We'd have you out in a jiffy. Your company would spring for bail. Might even be good publicity for the book."

I looked at the little box. "Marvin, this is insane."

"Knew you'd say that. Or something like it. You've always been kind of a . . ."

"Coward?"

He shook his head.

"Wimp?"

"No. A sweetheart."

I just looked at him, wanting to be mad.

He checked his watch. "Well, gotta go. Stephen's gonna catch me up on what the two of you have done so far."

He touched the brim of his cap, then walked out.

Worse, he was humming.

I stared at the door. *So that's how it's going to be.* He would use his grandfatherly charm to manipulate me into doing something I'd regret for the rest of my life.

Well, I had news for him.

It was probably going to work.

* * *

I looked at the box in my hand.

The return address on the label was for something called SecreTech in Oxnard, California. When I opened it I saw bubble wrap and a folded-up slip of paper. A black plastic thing that looked like a cell phone earpiece nestled in a plastic bag. A little gold oval sticker saying MADE IN CHINA was attached.

I unfolded the instructions, which began as follows:

### COVERT OVERHEARING DEVICE MB7890
### OPERATING DIRECTIONS

*Welcome to your purchase of this quality product. Can be listening from a distance of approximately 300 feet (100 m) depending on weather conditions and free standing objects. For mostly results, DO NOT allow unit to come into contact with overhead power lines, water, loud fabrics, etc.*

. . .

It was clear Marvin was sparing no expense. Two AAA batteries were included in the bag, covered with Chinese characters.

Toward the end of the instructions there was this:

## DISCLAIMER

*Use at your own risk. SecreTech LLC assumes no responsibility for the unlawful use of this device. Consult local laws for guidance regarding the interception or recording of private conversations.*

Funny, I thought. Nothing lost in translation there. Must have been the only part they had an American lawyer write. It made Marvin's assurances about legality feel less convincing than ever.

I picked up Covert Overhearing Device MB7890. After nearly breaking the flimsy battery compartment door, I pressed the AAAs into their berth. I'd have to test it. For purely scientific reasons, I chose to monitor the conversation Marvin was having with Stephen next door.

The earpiece must have been made for very small adults or very large and inquisitive four-year-olds. I could already feel it pinching my skin, rubbing it raw every time I turned my head. There was a pea-sized, foam-covered microphone on the front, which I aimed at the wall between our rooms and listened.

At first, there was nothing. Then a hiss, then a muffled exchange of voices. Too faint to make out a single word. I took the thing off my ear and searched for a volume control. There was none.

*Probably not meant to listen through walls*, I thought. I snapped the tiny power switch to OFF.

The jury was still out on this one. I could test it somewhere else later.

First I had to find Mercedes Pierce.

Sitting back down on the edge of the bed, I shut my eyes and tried to concentrate. This technique had always helped me produce ideas, most of which were unusable.

Finding Ms. Pierce would be no small feat. Options drifted through my mind like old photos in a Ken Burns documentary. The first seemed promising, at least for a moment. I could try to discover when and where Ms. Pierce's next lunch appointment was and follow her there. But who would tell me that? Certainly not her assistant, the one who'd given Stephen the runaround.

Then there was Option Two. I could find out where she lived, then sit outside her house in the Prius until she went somewhere. But she'd probably just go to the bank or to pick up her dry cleaning. And we hadn't been able to find her address, not to mention her unlisted phone number.

Shutting my eyes hadn't helped. I opened them and stared at one of the black-and-white skyscraper photos on the wall.

A third possibility stumbled past. It involved sitting in the car outside the company gates until I saw her leave, then following her to her house. But if she was anything like her reputation, I'd be spotted by some guard or surveillance camera and end up like Jimmy Hoffa, reinforcing the concrete foundation of UniMerritt's next building.

I considered a fourth option. I could call a friend at the Department of Motor Vehicles and get her license number, then follow her car. Except I didn't have any friends at the DMV.

Maybe Mercedes Pierce didn't exist after all. Maybe

Neera Patel had only imagined sitting next to her at that women's luncheon.

*Neera Patel.* That gave me a fifth idea.

She'd been the most cooperative of the three researchers. She'd implied that Pierce might have something to hide. And I'd seen her kill a seagull with her purse.

I found her number and dialed. "Hello," she answered, her voice flat.

"This is Carolyn Neville. Remember me? I saw you kill a seagull with your purse."

There was a pause. "Yes."

"I have a favor to ask. Best not to describe it over the phone. Could you meet me at the park where we met before?"

Another pause. "I'm still running that *mycoplasma pneumonia* experiment. It's a bit difficult to get away."

"I'll take as little of your time as possible."

"Very well."

We set a time, right after she checked her petri dishes at 2 p.m. She hung up on me without saying goodbye, but I didn't take it personally. It was just the way androids were.

* * *

There were no seagulls at the park today. I assumed Ms. Patel had scared them all off. We sat on a bench, this one closer to the playground, which was empty.

I described the problem as quickly as I could. "I need someone to tell me when Ms. Pierce is around. When she's at one of those lunches, maybe. Or when she's about to leave the building."

Her face remained frozen, except for the blinking. "Who else will know about this?"

"Just my two co-writers."

She shook her head. "Two too many, I'm afraid."

"Then I won't tell them. It'll be between you and me."

"Please remind me again why this is in my best interest."

I hesitated. She had me there. "Well . . . the sooner we find out who really did this, the sooner you'll be off the suspect list." I'd worn that one right down to the nub.

She nodded. "I will call you when I find out whether another luncheon is scheduled, or when I am aware that Ms. Pierce is on her way out."

"I appreciate that. And what can I do for you in return?"

She gathered up her purse, which looked as if she had recently wiped it clean of blood and feathers.

"You can find out the truth," she said, and walked away.

## CHAPTER 13

In my room I waited to hear from Ms. Patel, not knowing whether that might take five minutes or five months.

I was looking out the window when the call came.

It was almost lunchtime. I'd been sitting on the edge of the bed, weighing whether to eat the leftover pizza in my little refrigerator, when the *1812 Overture* interrupted from my purse.

"Ms. Neville, this is Neera."

"Oh." I swallowed. It was too soon. I wasn't ready.

"There is no women's luncheon scheduled this month. But I was just in the hallway and saw Ms. Pierce walking toward the exit with her purse and her car keys out."

"Do you know what her car looks like?"

"A late-model Volvo, I believe. Black, or perhaps dark blue. I've seen her getting into it a couple of times. I do not know the license number."

I grabbed the box with the listening device, my hand shaking slightly. There'd been no time to test it. "I'd better get out of here," I said.

"I would recommend waiting just off Fifteenth Place South, where it meets the driveway, near the company sign. Perhaps you can get there before she goes further."

"Thank you."

I snatched a pad and pen from the desk and ran out of the room, down the stairs, all the way to the Prius. My heart was already hammering.

Rush hour hadn't arrived, but the lunch crowd was beginning to live up to its name. I picked a path through traffic, doing my best to remember the route I'd taken last time. Every red light sent my blood pressure higher. I imagined Dr. Garabedian sitting in the passenger seat, shaking his head and yapping about the prescription I'd never picked up at the pharmacy.

I drove faster.

At last I reached 15th Place South, then the turnoff. I pulled as far onto the shoulder as I could, dwarfed by the sign with the U-shaped test tube. Judging from the flow of cars on and off the UniMerritt campus, Ms. Pierce wasn't the only one whose gastronomic needs weren't satisfied by the company lunchroom.

Switching off the motor, I focused on the outgoing vehicles coming toward me, trying to filter out everything but dark, late-model Volvos. It wasn't easy, since I'd paid little attention to automotive design for the last 10 years or so. Maybe the boxy models of yesteryear had been superseded by something sportier.

I looked away from the cars just long enough to check my watch. It was 11:57. I'd give it five minutes. After that, I'd have to assume I was too late.

I counted two likely Volvos in the next three minutes, but they were the older, squarish kind and not dark enough. There was another more rounded and dark that may have come from Stockholm, but could have been a Saab.

Finally, at 12:01, I spotted something dark and vaguely Swedish. Squinting, I strained to make out the figure at the wheel. There was a brief gap in traffic, just long enough to glimpse the profile of a plain and flinty woman, the ghost of Frances McDormand.

I hit the brake and the START button, then tried to position myself to make a U-turn. I was pointed the wrong way but hadn't had much choice.

Suddenly there was a break in the flow of cars. I hit the accelerator and yanked the wheel to the left.

Drivers from both directions leaned on their horns. When the noise stopped, I found myself behind the Volvo with a pickup truck between us. I could feel pins, needles, and perspiration in my armpits.

The Volvo turned right; so did the pickup. I nearly lost them as the traffic light shifted from yellow to red but jerked right and stayed in the running. In a block or so the pickup moved to the left lane, and nothing stood between my quarry and me. I dropped back a little, not wanting to be too obvious. But if Ms. Pierce was glancing in her rearview mirror and memorizing my license number, it was too late.

About half a mile later, she signaled right. I did the same.

We turned into the parking lot of a place called Zeno's Grill. It was red brick, and the lettering on the sign looked Greek. The Volvo parked in front; I kept going around the back and found a spot under a tree, which Stephen wasn't present to identify.

Switching off the Prius, I could hear myself panting. I wanted to sink back against the seat and take a nap, but there was no time.

Stuffing the listening device in my pocket, I headed for the entrance.

The small lobby was half full. Ms. Pierce was nowhere to be seen.

I stepped up to the hostess's podium. The young woman there looked up from her reservation book.

"How long is the wait?" I asked, even though I was stuck with it no matter how long it was.

"About ten minutes. Name?"

I drew a blank. "Taylor," I said finally. I had no idea where I'd gotten it, nor whether it was supposed to be my first or last name.

Retreating from the podium, I stood in a corner next to a rack of free newspapers. I took one that said *Seattle Senior Living*, opened it up, and ducked behind it.

A few moments later I heard a familiar voice, somewhere near the podium. "I have a reservation," it said.

Peeking over the top of the paper, I saw the unruly hair, the beard. Angus Blackwood.

I raised the paper, my heart thudding again. If he recognized me, it was all over.

"I'll find my party," he told the hostess, and disappeared into the restaurant.

She checked her list. "Taylor?"

I slid the paper under my arm and followed her, watching to see where Blackwood went. He ended up in a booth against the farthest wall. Across from Mercedes Pierce.

"Here we go," the hostess told me, putting a menu on a table that was too far from Blackwood's booth. Even a bona fide listening device would be insufficient to monitor conversation at this distance, I guessed. And the MB7890 didn't seem to fit that description.

"I wonder whether I could have that table over there," I said, keeping my voice down and pointing at an empty one about 10 yards away.

"I . . . well, okay." Picking up the menu, she led me there and set it down again. "Your server will be with you soon."

"Thank you."

I put the newspaper on the table and held up the menu with one hand, trying to conceal as much of my face as possible. With the other hand I fished the gadget from my pocket.

There was a tiny click as I turned it on. Hoping the other patrons would mistake it for a mobile phone headset or hearing aid, I was about to poke it into my ear when my server appeared. He was a swarthy young man with thick, black, wavy hair. His name badge said NIKOS.

"How you doing?" he asked, looking distracted.

"Fine." I lowered the menu enough to seem slightly less odd. I tried to read it but couldn't concentrate. "What do you recommend?"

"For appetizer, *saganaki*."

"What's that?"

"Feta cheese fried with just a little brandy. Specialty of the house. You love it."

"Okay." I fidgeted. It didn't matter what I ordered, as long as I could hurry and hide behind the menu again.

"And for entrée, gyros. Lamb, sliced thin, with—"

"Yes, I know what they are. I'll take those, too."

"And to drink?"

"Water."

Finally he left. Raising the menu again with one hand, I prodded the contraption into my ear with the other. I aimed my head at Blackwood and Pierce.

There was a hiss, then random popping and rustling. A faint male voice that didn't sound like Blackwood said something like *Couldn't believe my own sister would do something like that.*

I lowered the menu a little. My aim was off. I rotated my head slightly to the left.

More popping and rustling. Then a deeper voice, the Blackwood brogue, but tinny. It faded in and out. *Proprietary information . . . all that blether . . . totally unfair . . .*

I squeezed my eyes shut, trying to pick out more of the words. I jammed the earpiece further into my ear canal, which was as painful as it sounds.

More hissing, then what must have been the voice of Ms. Pierce. It was husky, brusque. *Nondisclosure agreements . . . a question for Legal . . . keep it encrypted . . .*

I grabbed the pen and pad from my pocket and tried to take notes. I was still holding the menu with one hand, even though I'd already ordered. I dropped it and snatched up the senior newspaper, which seemed appropriate because I'd aged at least 10 years in the last 15 minutes.

I'd just scribbled something about *scunners at the FDA* when my server reappeared. In one hand he carried a small plate with a yellowish chunk swimming in brandy. In the other he held a butane fireplace lighter.

Balancing the plate on his palm, he flicked the lighter and touched it to the sauce. With a *whoop* the plate was engulfed in a fireball. I recoiled, smelling the sharp odor of lemon juice and brandy.

"*Opa!*" he said loudly.

Heads turned in my direction. I dipped lower behind the paper.

The smell made my mouth water. I wasn't here for the food, of course, but told myself I had to eat it to avoid suspicion.

It took half a minute to locate the right angle to overhear Blackwood and Pierce again. When I did find the sweet spot, I heard her say something like *longstanding problem* and *off the record.*

Blackwood replied with *fiscal year* and something about spreadsheets. Or deadbeats.

Putting down my pen, I sighed. So far the only thing I'd learned for certain was that Angus Blackwood and Mercedes Pierce were not having an affair.

"Your gyros," announced the voice of Nikos at my other ear.

Again my mouth watered at the odor of peppers and onions and tzatziki sauce. But I only had two hands, and there was no telling when I might have to leave. "Could you box these up to go?" I whispered.

He muttered something in Greek which, fortunately, I didn't understand, then seized the plate and took it away.

I shifted my head back to the sweet spot.

That was when I heard it.

Ms. Pierce said something about *that other matter* and *our friend Mr. Reardon.*

I blinked. Who was Mr. Reardon?

There was another pop, then nothing.

I tapped the device with my fingernail. Still nothing.

I pulled the thing out and shook it, then held it up to my ear. Dead. I dropped it in my pocket.

Lowering the newspaper slightly, I could see their lips moving. Having never learned to read lips, I didn't find this particularly helpful.

Niko returned with my box of gyros. "Anything else?" he mumbled.

"Just the check." He disappeared again.

Suddenly Ms. Pierce rose and nodded at Blackwood, who waved at another server. I ducked behind the newspaper as she passed my table on the way out.

Niko reappeared at my elbow with the bill. I yanked out my wallet and grabbed a $20 bill. "Keep the change," I said.

He didn't look happy. I grabbed another $5 and handed him that, too. He still didn't look happy, but I had the feeling it wasn't unusual.

Turning so Blackwood couldn't see my face, I picked up the box and paper and followed Pierce at a distance. She went out the front door.

Was she just going back to work?

Was she going to see her friend Mr. Reardon?

There was only one way to be sure.

\* \* \*

The second I climbed into the Prius I tossed the MB7890 onto the passenger seat. *Thanks, Marvin,* I thought.

The black Volvo was waiting at a stop sign, ready to leave the lot. *A Mercedes in a Volvo,* I thought. I'd have to remember that hilarious irony in case I lived through this.

I followed it into traffic, trying to keep at least one car between us. Where were we going? Wherever it was, it wasn't back to the office.

Before long we were on Airport Way South, going north. Every other sign seemed to have the word *Boeing* on it. Boeing Field, Boeing Military Flight Center, Aviation Partners Boeing, Boeing Radiation Effects Lab. Overhead, 757s and 767s rose into the clouds. Something called the Museum of Flight was around here somewhere, according to a billboard, and a couple of helicopters cut across the sky in front of me, their shadows rippling on the highway.

The Volvo signaled right. I matched it. I was directly behind Ms. Pierce now, trying not to look conspicuous. We pulled into the industrial district, passing old brick factories, fenced-in patches of electrical transformers, and small but trendy-looking restaurants.

Suddenly, without signaling, the Volvo veered to the right, into an alley. I continued straight down the street, not wanting to follow. A block later I parked in front of an anonymous storefront with boarded-up windows.

I opened my door, then froze. Across the street, in front of a vacant lot, sat another vehicle I hadn't noticed before. There was no one at the wheel.

It was a gray Hyundai SUV.

I hesitated. Was it *the* gray Hyundai SUV?

If it was, what should I do?

I bit my lip. Whatever I did, I had to do it quickly. Ms. Pierce hadn't turned down an alley to freshen her makeup, though it might have been a good idea. If she was meeting someone, the conversation wouldn't be leisurely. She could be gone by the time I got there.

I stepped out and locked the car, then stayed close to the storefronts as I hurried back toward the alley. The smell of curry hung in the air, probably because I was passing a place with a sign that said TASTE OF DELHI. Then came a cell phone repair shop. A bicyclist wearing magenta Spandex and a helmet pedaled past, going the other way. A normal enough neighborhood, I told myself.

My pace slowed as I reached the alley, then came to a full stop. Cautiously I stole a glance around the corner.

At first all I saw was a blue dumpster. Then I saw the rear of the black Volvo further down the alley, parked in the shadows.

I sidled toward the dumpster, my tweedy brown editor's blazer snagging on the brick wall behind me. Slowly I moved around the edge of the huge metal box, wrinkling my nose at the smell of banana peels and more curry.

Two figures sat in the car, in profile, facing each other. Ms. Pierce was in the driver's seat. On the passenger side was a man I didn't recognize. In the shade his features were indistinct, with no big or small protuberances, no hat or odd hairstyle or unconventional moves.

The two of them seemed to be talking, or at least she did. He looked down and moved his shoulder as if accepting something she was handing him. He nodded.

His head swiveled as he appeared to survey the alley.

Then he looked toward me.

Startled, he hunched lower in the seat and seemed to be talking quickly.

Ms. Pierce turned in my direction. She lowered her head, then lifted a cellphone to her ear. She spoke rapidly as the passenger door flew open and the man sprinted down the alley and out of sight.

I retreated behind the dumpster, trying to decide what to do. I had to catch up with him, at least see what he looked like. Find out whether he got into the gray Hyundai SUV.

Turning around, I retraced my steps past the cell phone repair shop and the Indian restaurant, but faster. I looked down the street. The Hyundai was still there. I turned both ways but saw nobody.

Unlocking the Prius, I proceeded to slide inside. I was panting again, my heart thudding in my chest.

I would wait until the stranger showed up.

If he ever did.

* * *

Five minutes passed. Then seven. Then eleven.

My pulse was halfway to normal. Leaning back against the seat, I took a deep breath and let it out.

If he wasn't here by now, he wasn't coming. Either the Hyundai wasn't his, or he had another escape route. Uber, maybe. Or the monorail.

I pressed the brake, then the START button. My hand was about to touch the gearshift when I heard the sound of an engine. It grew louder.

I frowned. It couldn't be the Prius.

The sound was coming from behind me. I looked in the rearview mirror. Blue and red lights were flashing, getting bigger. There was a blue-and-white squad car. It stopped.

Swallowing, I took my hand from the gearshift and rolled

the window down. I turned the Prius off. I sat there, my heart rate on the rebound.

"License and registration, ma'am." He was young and sunburned. I'd never seen anyone with a sunburn in Seattle. Maybe he'd just returned from California, I thought, then wondered why I'd bothered to think that at a time like this.

He studied my photo and the rental car paperwork, then handed them back. He looked at the passenger seat, where lay the MB7890 and my box of gyros.

"Please step out of the car," he said.

I did so, my legs feeling wobbly. I hoped he wouldn't ask me to walk a straight line.

"Please face your vehicle and put your hands behind your head."

I did that, too. But something was wrong. I'd been stopped for speeding twice in my life, and once for having a taillight out, but this was different.

He patted gingerly under my arms, down my sides. I hoped he wasn't enjoying it. I knew I wasn't.

"Carolyn Neville," he said, "you are under arrest for harassment, stalking, and violating the right of privacy."

A numbness started somewhere in my head, then spread. He was gathering my hands behind me, snapping something hard around my wrists. Telling me how anything I said could be used against me in a court of law.

I tried to look back over my shoulder. "But—"

I paused, finding no words. What could I say? That it was all a mistake? That it was perfectly normal to hide behind newspapers in a restaurant, to listen to other people's conversations with a cheap plastic microphone, to follow them into alleys? To think a mysterious stranger was out to get you?

The officer droned on. He got to the part about a lawyer.

"I think I need one of those," I said, my voice cracking.

"That can be arranged."

The flashing red and blue lights cast shadows on the Prius. "What will happen to my car?" I asked faintly.

"Well, let's see. If it doesn't contain evidence, you have the option of getting a friend or family member to come and claim the vehicle, or we can have it towed. Or you can leave it here and take the risk of it being stolen." He paused. "Frankly, ma'am, in this neighborhood I wouldn't take the chance."

"So . . . does it contain evidence?"

"You tell me. I see you've got a couple things on the passenger seat. Mind if I take a look?"

I sighed. No point in arguing. "Go ahead."

"Let's get you in my car first."

Just then I heard a noise across the street. An engine starting.

I twisted my neck around in time to see the gray Hyundai ease from its parking space. It proceeded to move down the street at a perfectly legal speed, if not less. The officer ignored it.

I knew who was at the wheel. Mr. Reardon, or whoever he was, had been very patient.

I shook my head. I should have known.

And for all my trouble, I'd learned so little about Mercedes Pierce.

But I'd discovered one thing.

She had unusual friends.

Including, apparently, some in high places.

# CHAPTER 14

THEY TOOK AWAY MY GYROS AT THE KING COUNTY JAIL.

Also the MB7890. And my wallet, keys, cellphone, shoes, and tweedy brown editor's blazer. A puffy, middle-aged woman with a bad case of rosacea on her nose stuffed them all in a clear plastic bag along with a checklist I had to sign.

In return for these personal belongings I received a shapeless orange jumpsuit, a pair of plastic sandals, and the chance to be photographed. I couldn't gin up a smile when the mugshot was taken but gave my hair a quick brush to avoid looking like a drunken celebrity.

To my surprise, fingerprinting didn't involve rolling my digits on inkpad and paper. It was an electronic process, putting your palm on a scanner that lit up like a copy machine and made a faint whirring sound. It was nice to keep my fingers clean, but I was in no mood to fully appreciate the innovation.

In fact, I wasn't sure what my mood was. I was in a dreamlike mist, doing the unthinkable. This couldn't be me, under arrest and about to be incarcerated. It had to be someone else, maybe a misunderstood bookkeeper falsely charged with embezzlement.

I was in shock, of course. This frame of mind was useful about 30 minutes later, when I found myself having to shower in a dank and steamy room that reminded me why I'd tried repeatedly to be excused from junior high gym class.

The water was just below the boiling point. The yellow bar of soap smelled like tar and disinfectant, probably formulated to eradicate head lice or fungus or some other curse of the unhygienic class. I lathered and rinsed as quickly as possible in the presence of two female guards who wore dark blue uniforms. They kept looking away as though they, not I, were being punished by my unclothed condition.

My mental fog began to dissipate when I was informed by one of the guards, a woman who looked like a side of beef with hair, that I could make one phone call. I was ushered to a room with four telephones in various stages of disrepair. Two were in use by women for whom English was clearly a second language, one being fluent in Spanish and the other in obscenity.

I dialed Stephen, still not having memorized Marvin's number. To my relief, he picked up.

"I seem to be in jail," I said.

"*What?*"

"I've been arrested."

There was a pause. "Let me put this on speaker. Okay. Now say again."

"I'm in the King County Jail."

"Is this a joke, Cranberry?" Marvin called from somewhere in the background.

"Not from my vantage point."

"Arrested for what?" Stephen asked.

I thought for a moment. "Invasion of privacy, I think. Stalking. Harassment."

"Lady, what did you *do?*" Marvin cried, closer to the phone this time.

"What you *told* me to do."

"I didn't tell you to get arrested." He paused. "Must be a misunderstanding. Bureaucratic nonsense. We'll get you out of there. Bail you out."

"Thank you."

"We'll get you a lawyer."

"Lawyers are expensive. Hunter will be irate enough about paying my bail."

"Maybe we can use one of Pendleton's attorneys," Stephen said. "It'll be cheaper."

"Our Friends in Legal won't fly out here. And they only seem to know about things like intellectual property and libel."

I looked down at the base of the tan plastic phone, which had a knot of chewing gum stuck to the side. "So I'm going to ask for a public defender."

Marvin grunted. "You can't, honey. To get a public defender, the court makes you sign a sworn statement that you can't afford your own attorney. I don't know how much you make, but it's way too much to qualify."

"But—"

"I'll call Mr. Thicke and work it out. Believe me, he's already spending money out the wazoo. He's not gonna stop now."

I heard the guard behind me, clearing her throat.

"I think I'm running out of time. We have to talk about the rental car."

"What about it?"

"I left it where they arrested me. You'll need to go pick it up." I told him where, or at least the names of the nearest cross streets.

"I have a key," Stephen volunteered. "We could take a taxi there and drive it back."

"Don't worry," Marvin said. "We'll figure it out. Then we'll take care of bail."

The guard leaned over my shoulder. "Wrap it up, Princess," she mumbled.

Frowning, I turned to look at her. GREER, said her I.D. badge. I had the urge to put Ms. Greer in her place, at least verbally. But she was just too large.

I turned back and swallowed. I didn't want to say goodbye to Stephen and Marvin. They were in the real world, and my only hope of ever getting back. But I couldn't say that, especially in the time available.

"Keep in touch," I said.

"Keep the faith," Marvin replied, and the line went silent.

The guard pointed at the door through which we'd entered. "Let's go see your new home away from home. You're gonna be spending a lot of time there."

"I don't think so. My friends are going to bail me out."

She chuckled. "Sure they are."

I stood up, which didn't help much in light of her resemblance to an upright freezer. "What could keep them from getting me out?"

She chuckled again. "Things."

She took my arm just above the elbow and guided me toward the door.

I felt myself shiver.

This wasn't happening to somebody else, I suddenly realized.

The shock was wearing off.

I would have paid real money to get it back.

* * *

We took an elevator. Ms. Greer pushed the *11* button. The car smelled like the shower room and moved almost as slowly.

"You're on north wing, upper tier, tank A," she said, sounding less menacing and more mechanical. "That's Eleven NUA. Remember that. Not that you'll have a chance to wander around and get lost."

I stared at the wall. *Eleven NUA. Eleven NUA. . .* By the time the doors creaked open, I'd gone over it at least a dozen times. I wanted to write it on my hand, but they'd confiscated my pen, too.

We stepped into the cellblock. The fluorescent lights were cold. The walls were cinderblock, painted gray. Bare cement covered the floor, reflecting the light as if it were wet. But it was just shiny, coated with some kind of sealant.

The hardness of all the surfaces made every sound bounce off, every noise louder. Curses rang out from somewhere like bird calls, along with the occasional random screech.

We climbed a flight of concrete stairs to the upper tier, then passed a row of cells. To my surprise, there were no bars—only heavy wooden doors with small windows. Instead of *zoo* I thought *classroom*.

"This is your tank," Greer announced, pulling me to a halt. There was an A2 over the door, which she unlocked and opened.

It turned out that classroom was an apt description. The space was about that size. I counted 20 bunk beds. Two blue tables, five seats each. A TV was bolted to the wall. There was a smaller room off the main one, but with no door. A bathroom, I guessed. At least it wasn't a pail in the middle of the cell. Or a hole in the floor.

Two phones hung on the wall, which was concrete. Every sound echoed here, too.

Not that there were a lot of sounds to echo. Nearly 20 women in orange jumpsuits loitered and sat and lay around. Some looked antsy or sick, as if they'd had to skip a heroin injection or two. None of them looked happy. Or friendly.

Most ignored each other. A few glanced my way, but no one ogled me or wolf-whistled or yelled "Fresh meat!" like they did in the movies. I tried not to take it as a personal slight.

There was one empty bed remaining, the upper bunk in the right corner.

"Your new resting place," Ms. Greer said, leading me toward the bed and letting go of my arm. "I'm sure you'll get along fine with your new best friend."

I looked at the figure sitting on the bottom bunk. She was a sort of neon orange clown, her red hair thick and matted, nearly as bright as her jumpsuit. At least one tooth was missing. I guessed her age as somewhere between a prematurely-aged 25 and a well-preserved 70.

She looked sullen and proceeded to prove it. "Think you're so great, don'tcha?" she muttered.

"Shut up, wino," Greer barked.

"I ain't talkin' to you, chief," the inmate said. Her words were slurred.

The guard looked at me and grinned. "You girls play nice. Sorry I can't stick around to see how things turn out."

She turned and shut the door behind her. I didn't bother to check, but assumed it was now locked, this being jail and all.

The Orange Menace glared at me. "You stole it," she growled.

I took a step back. "Stole what?"

"You know what. Don't act like you don't."

I raised my palms innocently. "I just got here. I don't know what you're talking about."

"My radio. When I wasn't looking, you stole my freakin' radio."

I shook my head. "You've got me confused with someone else."

She made a disgusted noise. "What you in for? Stealin'?"

"Invasion of privacy."

"Peekin' in people's windows? Pervert." She squinted, apparently trying to focus.

I gave up and headed for the ladder on the bunk bed. I hadn't tried to climb one of these since age 12. It was at summer church camp, the year I learned how to make a leather wallet and surrender it to a bully named Martha who also demanded $5 to put in it.

Reminding myself that acrophobia was nothing to be ashamed of, I slowly ascended to the upper level and lay down on the thin, coarse blanket.

My stomach growled. They'd taken away my gyros, and I'd only gotten to smell them. I still could.

"Excuse me," I said. "Do you know when dinner is?"

There was a pause, as if the woman below was trying to decide whether she was speaking to me. "Yeah," she finally muttered. "I been here before. I know when everything is. Dinner's at 4:30."

"What's the food like?"

"Crap. Last time I was here, it was beans and rice every other day. Sometimes chicken casserole. At least I think it was chicken. Didn't taste like nothin'. Neither did the beans."

"What about breakfast?"

She snorted. "Alarm wakes you up at 6:00 for head count. Then breakfast. Could be oatmeal or Cheerios, couple slices of bread, coffee, and scooby."

"Scooby?"

"Fake sausage patty. I never been here on a major holiday, but I hear they have Froot Loops then."

I found myself wondering what the next major holiday might be. My stomach growled again.

"Lunch at 10:30 a.m. Usually bologna sandwich on more of that white bread. Once they had spaghetti and salad, but they must have been trying to impress some inspector or something."

I checked my watch, glad I'd chosen a cheap one. Had I owned a Rolex, they probably would have taken it away. Given the absence of wall clocks, it would have been impossible to be punctual.

Just over an hour remained until dinner. I stared at the ceiling, which was made of concrete, too. I started thinking about things to pray for. There seemed to be plenty.

"Hey," said the Orange Menace. "You still there?"

"Yes."

"Just so you know, I'm not forgetting about my radio. You'll be sorry you crossed me."

I sighed. "Okay."

I closed my eyes, then went back to compiling my prayer list. Having nothing to write with, I stopped after the first 25 or so requests. They included things like getting out of here, getting out of here as soon as possible, and getting out of here alive.

After praying my way through the list, I was stuck. Nothing to read. I'd never missed my Kindle so much.

Raising my head, I looked at the TV set on the wall. The sound was at low volume, and only a handful of inmates seemed to be watching. An old black-and-white Western was on. I wondered who'd chosen the channel. Maybe the warden, hoping to keep inmates from returning.

I lay back down and closed my eyes again. My thoughts drifted. The day's events replayed themselves, right up to the point when the man in the gray SUV had driven away, unchallenged. Was it really Mr. Reardon, whoever that might be? If so, I had to tell Stephen and Marvin. The elusive friend of Mercedes Pierce might be the key to everything.

"Are you still down there?" I said.

"No," my bunkmate replied.

"How do we call people on the outside?"

"You don't. Unless you've already put money in your account or call collect. Can't leave messages, either. And they cut you off after fifteen minutes."

"How can people call us?"

"Can't."

Grunting, I sat up. Looking down at the two phones on the wall, I felt a wave of dizziness. Carefully I backed my way to the ladder and climbed down.

My pulse was pounding by the time I picked up one of the phones. I dialed Stephen's number. If he wouldn't accept a collect call, he could kiss his job goodbye.

*You've reached Stephen Ames,* said the voice mail. *Thanks for calling. If you'll leave a message . . .*

I hung up. I'd try again later.

* * *

I picked up the phone again. Stephen and Marvin weren't the only people I knew on the outside.

I looked at my watch. It was late in Connecticut, but wasn't this an emergency? Mikki Flaherty would still be awake. And it was safest to try her at home anyway, since her boss at Icarus Imports broke out in hives whenever she made or took a personal call during work hours.

She picked up. "Who's this?"

"Will you accept a collect call from Carolyn Neville?" the operator asked.

"What? Oh, yeah, of course."

There was a click, and Mikki cleared her throat.

"Carolyn? I didn't know they even *had* collect calls anymore."

"They do here. I'm in jail."

Silence.

"Are you still there?"

"Yeah. Did you say *jail?*"

"The county one." I told her why.

When I was done, there was more silence. "But they're going to bail you out, right?"

"I hope so, but nothing happens fast around here. Nothing you *want* to happen, anyway."

"Are you, like, safe?"

"Can't say I feel that way."

"Okay, I . . . I don't know what to do."

"Tell me it's all going to work out."

"Well, it is." She paused. "Remember the story of Paul and Silas in prison? In the Bible?"

"Yeah. Angel shows up, there's an earthquake, they leave."

"So there you go. Seattle's even on a fault line."

I closed my eyes. "I was thinking of something a little less dramatic. And a lot more likely."

"Oh. Well, how about the time you got locked overnight in the freezer at that butcher shop? Kind of like being in prison."

I opened my eyes. "Close enough."

"And wait 'til you hear the joke my nephew told me on the phone this week. It'll lift your spirits."

I had my doubts.

"I once had a dog named Tax. I opened the door, and in come Tax."

My doubts were confirmed.

"Are you there?"

"Yeah. I'm just doubled over with silent laughter."

"Speaking of bad jokes, did you keep your vow?"

"What vow?"

"To give up doughnuts for a week."

I paused. "Guess I did, come to think of it."

"Are you going to skip them in jail?"

"As far as I know, they don't have any. I could skip scooby instead."

"They let you watch *Scooby-Do* there?"

I explained what I'd heard about this delicacy.

"Giving that up doesn't sound like much of a sacrifice," she said. "But under the circumstances, I'll let it go."

"And I'd better let *you* go. This call is probably costing you a fortune. I'll pay you if I get back."

"*When* you get back."

"Right."

I signed off and hung the receiver back on the wall.

With a sigh I headed toward my bunk, then gingerly ascended. I rolled onto my back, exhausted. The mattress felt thin as a kitchen sponge, but in a few minutes I found myself fading into sleep.

* * *

"Chow time!"

The shout was so close it seemed to come from inside my right ear. It was like shoving the MB7890 Covert Overhearing Device into place.

My eyes snapped open. I turned to see my least favorite guard smiling over the edge of the bunk like a Cheshire cat crossed with a pit bull.

"That you, Neville? If so, answer, 'Here!'"

"Here," I croaked, my ear ringing.

"You'll like our dinner menu. Tastes better than the food."

Dazed, I pushed myself to a sitting position. "Has anyone bailed me out yet?"

She laughed. "Different world here, Princess. Different time zone. If it happens, I'll let you know."

A few minutes later, in a common area dotted with round tables, I sat in front of a tray. Beans and rice, with a cup of applesauce and a half-pint carton of milk, no straw. The only utensil was a dainty-looking plastic spoon with a few fork-like notches.

The Orange Menace was sitting next to me. "Did I call it or what?" she crowed. "Beans and rice."

Now that we were elbow to elbow, I could smell the cheap wine and sweat seeping from her pores. I almost lost my appetite, which was already on life support.

I picked up the spork, or whatever they called it. "How are we supposed to eat with this?"

"You ain't," she said. "But you can't stab anybody with it. That's what they're goin' for."

I sent up a brief and silent prayer of thanks, figuring I couldn't afford to close my eyes here any more than I could at work. I wasn't sure thanks were really in order, but I was about to find out.

Scooping a bit of beans and rice, I tried it. For a moment I thought I'd lost my sense of taste.

My bunkmate grinned, revealing that she was missing two teeth, not one. "Needs salt, right? Or ketchup. Anything." Still, she picked up her own spork and started eating.

I looked around the room. Not all the residents of our tank had joined us for dinner. When I asked my companion if she knew why, she nodded.

"Got the shakes, a lot of 'em. Don't feel like eatin'."

"Shakes? Like withdrawal symptoms?"

"Yeah."

I finished my entree, which was no small feat considering the size of the spork and moved to the applesauce.

"So why are you here?" I asked.

She took a swig of milk from her carton and made a face. "Drunk and disorderly."

"Come here often?"

She frowned. "So what if I do?"

I shrugged. "Just wondered."

She shook her head. "None of your business. Don't start that social worker crap with me."

I put up my hands. "No crap intended."

"You're not such a prize yourself. You're *in* here, aren't you? And you steal radios."

"I didn't—"

"Quit talkin' to me. I got better things to do." She set the applesauce cup on her plate and went to work on it.

I ate the rest without speaking, keeping my head low, listening to the indistinct mumble of conversation from other tables, the tap of plastic utensils, the occasional epithet, the random belch. I wondered what Stephen and Marvin were doing right now. Whatever it was, I was jealous.

After dinner I used the bathroom. The doorless doorway would take some getting used to, but the sink and toilet were serviceable—stainless steel, fused into a single unit. The bowl was low to the floor, the flush startlingly loud. The paper was so thin I could almost see through it.

In minutes we were all back on our bunks. The TV was tuned to one of those shows in which perspiring, crafty people scheme to have each other voted into oblivion. My interest wasn't piqued.

From my perch I could see that roughly half the eyes in the room were directed at the screen, there apparently being nothing else to do. That was when I spotted something in the corner, a bin containing what looked like several magazines. Magazines were no substitute for books, with the possible exception of *Publishers Weekly*, *Booklist*, *Library Journal*, and *The New Yorker*, but this was an emergency. I made my way down the ladder and tried to be invisible as I headed for the bin.

Pickings were slim. There was a tattered issue of *Good Housekeeping*, an untouched copy of *Sunset*, two moderately used issues of *Guideposts*, and a large print edition of *Reader's Digest* in fair condition. All were stamped with the words PROPERTY KING COUNTY DEPARTMENT OF ADULT & JUVENILE DETENTION.

I chose the *Reader's Digest*, not for its large print but its brevity. Returning to my bunk, I sank back on the mattress, such as it was, and proceeded to read every page.

I was about to lower my standards and retrieve the *Sunset*, but the door suddenly opened. It was guard Greer, clipboard in hand. She was accompanied by another officer I hadn't seen before, a flabby gentleman with a crewcut so short it barely qualified as anything other than skin.

"Head count!" the latter snapped. "Everybody in the hall!"

I crawled down the ladder as the room emptied. Several inmates trudged as slowly as they could, muttering imprecations about missing their show. We all lined up, more or less, spreading ourselves down the hallway.

The two guards faced us, frowning. Ms. Greer started barking names. "Bennett!"

"Here."

"Delgado!"

"Here."

"Jackson!"

"Yeah."

"Knauss!"

There was silence.

"Knauss!"

"Oh. Uh, here."

"Neville!"

"Present."

She looked up from her list, then at me. "This your first head count, Ms. Neville?"

"It is."

"I told you to answer 'Here,' didn't I? At dinner time?"

"I . . . don't recall."

"Well, recall it now."

"Okay."

"I mean call it again!" she said. "You retarded?"

"Here," I said.

"Neville, do you know why we do a head count?"

"To . . . make sure we're all present and accounted for."

"You bet. We'd hate to have anyone slip through the cracks. You wouldn't try to do that, would you?"

"Not likely."

"Good." She smiled that wicked smile. "Oh, and Ms. Neville. About your making bail . . ."

She let the words hang.

I waited her out, my pulse quickening.

"Ain't gonna happen."

I swallowed.

She looked back down at the clipboard. "Petrocelli!" she continued.

"Here."

"Salazar!"

"Here."

I stared at the glistening concrete floor as she moved through the list. When she got to Tompkins, I recognized the voice that replied. It was the Orange Menace, standing further down the line.

I'd never asked her name. Good thing to know, now that I was going to be here indefinitely.

\* \* \*

When roll call was over and we'd been herded back to the tank, it was time for lights out.

I clambered up the ladder as quickly as I could, not wanting to get caught halfway up in the dark. But I did anyway, and stopped there until my eyes got accustomed to the lack of light.

With a deep sigh I collapsed on the bed, then rolled onto my back. There was just enough illumination from the window in the door that I could make out the ceiling three feet from my face.

I lay there, listening. No snoring yet. Unidentified footsteps echoing in the hall. A sharp profanity from somewhere.

I'd never been in prison before, not even to visit. Unfortunately, I'd seen an episode of *Orange Is the New Black* on Stephen's recommendation. I wished now that I hadn't.

It was about half an hour until the snoring from other bunks began. But that wasn't the reason I got maybe five minutes of sleep that night.

It was the certainty that, from now on, I couldn't be certain of anything.

# CHAPTER 15

THE ALARM WENT OFF AT 6:00 A.M., AROUND 20 MINUTES after I'd finally sunk into the sleep of the dead. My untimely resurrection was only partial.

I heard a grunt, then a curse, from my bunkmate, who I now vowed to call Tompkins because Orange Menace was such a melodramatic nickname.

At first I was too stupefied to trust myself with climbing down the ladder. When I regained my bearings, I soon found myself staring my first prison breakfast in the face. It was cornflakes, a hard-boiled egg, two slices of bread, and coffee.

"No scooby," I mumbled to Tompkins, who was sitting across the table.

"Shut up," she said, rubbing the heel of her hand against her forehead.

"Hangover?" I asked.

"I said shut up."

I sipped the coffee and closed my eyes, pretending I was at Starbucks. My taste buds weren't fooled. Definitely not Seattle's Best. Still, it was drinkable, though not hot enough that I could hurl it in the face of an obnoxious fellow inmate and inflict third degree burns, not that I had the nerve to do that.

Breakfast was followed by another head count. Apparently Greer had the day off to kick puppies, so the roll call was conducted by Mr. Flabby Crewcut and a female officer who looked tough enough to have stapled her blue cap to her head.

All being present and accounted for, I followed the other inmates who were straggling back into the tank.

"Neville?" the portly guard called behind me.

I turned to see him checking his clipboard. "You have a visitor," he said.

I raised an eyebrow. *Marvin? Stephen?*

"Lawyer," he added.

I raised the other eyebrow.

"I'll take you down there," he said, handing the clipboard to the female guard.

The elevator still smelled like old gym shoes and creaked when it moved. The guard didn't take me by the elbow this time, maybe because I was a woman, or maybe because he had fewer control issues than Greer did.

"Been through this before?" he asked.

"No."

"The conversation with your lawyer won't be recorded," he said. "Not like conversations with any other visitors. Pretty much like you see on TV. No touching. Talk on the phone with the glass between you."

"I understand."

"We got video visitation now, with the little screen. Costs a lot more. Not really worth it unless you're talking to your kids or something, if you ask me. Definitely not if you're just talking to your lawyer."

"I'll stick with talking through the glass."

He nodded. "Yeah, some people don't really want their families to see them. Too embarrassed to be here."

"I'm not embarrassed. I didn't do anything illegal. I think."

He shook his head. "Sounds like your lawyer has her work cut out for her."

"Her?"

"Yeah, it's a woman. Don't know her name."

Ten minutes later I was staring through a window at a long-faced, fiftyish woman I'd never seen before.

She looked seriously jet-lagged. Or as if she'd spent the last week in jail herself. Her hair was gray, straight, and she was dressed in a severe, black suit. With both hands she held a large leather satchel on her lap.

I picked up my phone. She picked up hers.

"Ms. Neville, I'm Gina Casebeer." The sound was slightly tinny. "From the legal department at Pendleton House." She seemed to lack the energy, or the motivation, to smile.

"How can you be here?" I asked. "I mean . . . I was only arrested yesterday."

"I took the redeye out of Newark. Then a cab directly from the Seattle airport. Apparently Mr. Thicke considers this matter a high priority."

"I'm sorry. But I must admit I'm glad you're here."

"Perhaps you shouldn't be. Our department isn't used to cases like this. We mostly handle copyright, trademark, and libel. Permissions. Publishing issues."

"Yes, but—"

"One second," she said. She opened the satchel and pulled out a yellow legal pad. I'd never seen it used in its namesake capacity. It seemed like a special moment.

"Tell me what happened."

I gave her the short version, which still took several minutes. The listening device. The newspaper. The SUV. She took notes, nodding here and there, saying nothing.

When I was done, the only sound I could hear was the guard, standing at a discreet distance, chewing something from the vending machine.

She put the cap back on her pen. "Ms. Neville, you work in Editorial, don't you?"

"Yes. But I can explain why—"

"Is it common for editors to engage in this kind of activity?"

I sighed. "No."

She rubbed her eyelids with her fingers. "I just wondered." She reached into the bag again and retrieved a sheaf of papers. "All right. I did as much research as I could on the plane. It's not nearly enough, but I did discover a few things about the charges against you."

"And?"

"I'm afraid it's not as promising as it might be. Let's begin with harassment. In the state of Washington, it can be a felony or a misdemeanor, depending on whether this is a repeat offense and whether you made a death threat. I assume neither is true of you."

"Of course."

She looked down at the page in front of her. "Well, that's in your favor. Unfortunately, it's still a gross misdemeanor. Punishable by up to 364 days in jail and a five-thousand-dollar fine."

I sank slightly in the chair.

She turned the page. "As for stalking, it's much the same. Felony or gross misdemeanor. In this state it's not necessary for the accuser to warn you that your attentions are unwanted. But it has to have taken place more than once."

"Then I'm in the clear. I'd never even *seen* Mercedes Pierce before yesterday."

"That depends on whether waiting at the drug company gate and the restaurant and the alley are considered separate incidents. If they are, it's another 364 days in jail and another five-thousand-dollar fine."

I put the phone down, partly because my wrist was tired and partly because I wanted to mask the retching noise I felt like making. Finally I pressed the receiver back to my ear. "Is that it?"

"Well, there's still invasion of privacy. Technically, violating right of privacy."

I told her what Marvin had said about that. Gray areas. Things being "sort of illegal," but with exceptions. How he thought I was safe. Probably.

She folded her hands on the sheaf of papers. "Is Mr. Pitts an attorney?"

"Well, no."

"I didn't think so." She paused. "Even if he's correct, violating Washington's wiretapping law would make you vulnerable to a civil suit. Ms. Pierce could claim you damaged her reputation and caused pain and suffering." She picked up a page and consulted it. "Damages could be awarded at the rate of a hundred dollars a day for each day of violation, not to exceed one thousand dollars. Plus attorney's fees and other costs."

I descended further into my chair.

"I wish the news were better," she said, and slid the papers into the satchel. "I'm sure it must be difficult in this environment. That's one reason I stayed away from criminal law."

"Is there anything you can do to get me out of here?"

"Mr. Thicke told me Mr. Pitts and Mr. Ames have been working on your bail. I haven't had a chance to touch base with them yet."

I nodded. "I suppose Hunter must be a little upset about all this."

"I don't know. Is his face usually flushed? Does he talk through his teeth? Does he—"

"Never mind," I said.

She clicked her bag shut. "We'll be in touch," she said, and hung up.

I did the same.

The guard was wiping his fingers with a napkin. "Let's go," he said.

Slowly I got to my feet and started to follow him. Then I realized I had no idea how to contact Ms. Casebeer. I turned around, but she was gone.

"Forget something?" the guard asked.

"Nothing important."

I didn't need to know her number.

But I did know mine was up.

* * *

The door to our tank swung open around 10:30 a.m. It was the gristly female guard.

"Neville?" she called, propping the door open with her foot.

From the top bunk I raised my hand.

"The doc will see you now."

I frowned. "What doc?"

She checked her clipboard. "Haddad. Intake interview. They find out your medical needs, that kind of stuff."

"I had an annual physical about a month ago. I'm fine."

She put her hands on her hips. "I don't care how you are. Get your butt down here. I haven't got all day."

With a grunt I climbed down and followed her down the hall, down the elevator, and to a door labeled INFIRMARY. Inside was another door, then a waiting room. In its center was something like a hospital nurses' station, but with a uniformed guard sitting at the computer.

"Name?"

"Neville. Carolyn."

He jabbed a few keys.

"Intake interview with Dr. Haddad. Nurse will be with you shortly."

Half a dozen inmates sat in the chairs. One chair was left. Unfortunately, it was next to a woman who coughed as if trying to turn her lungs inside out. I chose to stand.

The walls were concrete block, off-white. It looked almost like a conventional clinic, except there were bars on the windows and all the patients were dressed alike. I looked around for something to read. All they had were *Web M.D.* and *Outdoor Life.*

I was halfway through a copy of the former when a nurse in blue scrubs called my name and led me down a hallway. She swiped my forehead with an electronic thermometer and told me to stand on the scale. I took off my plastic sandals before stepping up, as I always did with my shoes at the doctor's office to prevent an unjustifiably high and embarrassing reading. As usual, it didn't help.

She pointed me to an examining room and took my blood pressure, which for some reason had risen since my visit with Dr. Garabedian. She picked up a checklist from the counter, next to the sink.

"On any medications?"

I thought for a moment. Technically, that statin Garabedian prescribed was still sitting unclaimed at a drugstore in Connecticut.

"No," I said.

"Ever been diagnosed with HIV or AIDS?"

"No."

"Any bacterial diseases?"

"No."

"Ever have thoughts of suicide?"

"Always."

She gave me a skeptical look.

"Any special concerns?

"Other than being in jail for crimes I didn't commit?" I asked.

"Uh-huh."

"I'm finding it difficult to sleep."

"I mean *unusual* concerns."

"Oh. No complaints, then."

"Good. Dr. Haddad will be in before you know it." She left and shut the door.

I spent the next 12 minutes staring at a poster about six kinds of what used to be called venereal diseases. I'd pretty well memorized it by the time I heard a rustling of papers in the hallway and a click of the door handle.

"Ms. Neville?"

He stuck out his hand and actually smiled. He looked Middle Eastern, which I'd expected from his surname, and about 10 years younger than I was, which was becoming increasingly common. I shook his hand, wondering where it had been recently.

"How are you?" he asked.

"Ambulatory," I said.

"Excellent. This shouldn't take long. Just need to make sure that while you're in our custody your health doesn't get any worse than it already is."

I frowned, not sure how to take that.

He looked at the nurse's notes, much as Garabedian had done. "Blood pressure's up there. Get much exercise?"

"Not in here." I didn't like where this was going.

"Hop up on the table for me," he said. I complied, though the hopping was more like the ponderous transfer of a flour sack from a loading dock to a flatbed truck. He put his stethoscope to my chest and listened. He pressed the lymph nodes under my jaw. He even took a little rubber mallet out of his pocket and thumped my knee. I felt as if I were in a Norman Rockwell painting on the cover of the *Saturday Evening Post*.

"Well, we're not exactly a fitness club," he said, sitting down and scribbling something at the bottom of a form. "For the short term, I'd suggest you take every opportunity to get outside in the yard. Sometimes it's nothing more than walking around in a circle, but if you keep up the pace, there's some cardiovascular benefit. If you're here long-term, you'll have access to some pretty nice equipment."

I stared at the STD poster, my gaze falling for no particular reason on the syphilis section. "I'm told my stay could be long-term," I said.

"If so, this may be your chance to get in shape. I know that sounds insensitive, but it could lengthen your life."

"Thanks for the warning."

"So could paying attention to what you eat. Even here you can skip the desserts. Not all the snacks in the commissary are loaded with fat and salt."

He kept talking, but I stopped listening. It was bad enough to spend time in jail. It was worse to spend it sitting through another lecture from a celery salesman.

When his mouth stopped moving, I figured he was done. "Words of wisdom," I said.

"I know you weren't listening," he said. "Nobody ever is." He smiled and stuck out his hand, which I shook. "Try to stay out of trouble. Not every person in here is all there, if you know what I mean."

"I've met several already. Thank you."

The guard walked me to the elevator and back to Eleven NUA, which seemed like sufficient exercise to me. When we got to the tank, she checked her list again. "Gottfried!" she called.

A tall woman with a barbed-wire tattoo on her forearm stood up.

"You're next," the guard said, and led her away.

I looked at my bunkbed. Tompkins was gone.

*Wonder where she went*, I thought.

I figured she'd be back. Couldn't have gone far.

About 15 minutes later the other guard, the flabby one, walked in with his clipboard. "Potter!" he yelled. "Your lawyer's here."

"Potter's in the can," another inmate muttered.

"Hurry up!" the guard said.

I turned in his direction. "You know what happened to Tompkins?"

He nodded. "Transferred."

"Why?"

"Don't know."

"Where?"

"Don't know that, either." He paused. "These things happen. It's like being in the army. You want things to make sense? You're in the wrong place."

*You're telling me*, I thought.

It was a place where people could be trapped for a very long time. Or, it seemed, where they might even disappear.

* * *

After lunch, which featured a bologna sandwich to rival those served in the world's finest inner-city rescue missions, I tried calling Stephen's number again using the wall phone. This time it worked.

"Carolyn!" he said, sounding relieved. "We thought maybe you were . . . well, dead."

"Not yet. But I'm working on it."

"Marvin's not back yet. He's interviewing some guy who knew Dr. Rhee in college."

"Great."

"We got the Prius."

"But you didn't get *me*."

He sighed. "We tried. There was a problem with—"

Something thumped in the background. "Oh, wait," he said. "Marvin's here. I'll put us on speaker."

"Marvin, it's Carolyn."

"We got the car, Cranberry," he said.

"I know. Why am I still here?"

"We went to the bail bondsman. Everything was fine, if you consider five hundred bucks a reasonable fee. But when we got to the jail, they said there was a problem with the paperwork."

"What sort of problem?"

"I don't know. Bureaucracy. I can't tell if it's the usual kind of screwup, or . . ."

"Or what?"

He cleared his throat. "It's almost like the cops have orders to slow everything down. Don't know whether they're doing this to everybody, or just you."

"Just me."

"You do something to tick them off?"

"Not that I know of."

"Wait a minute," Stephen said. "Remember when we met with the chief of police?"

"Yes, but—"

"You ticked him off royally. You said he was playing politics. He cut our meeting short. That's why we still don't have an insider at the police department."

"Is that true?" Marvin asked.

"I'm an editor, not a diplomat."

"So you insulted the chief of police. And now he's out to get you."

"I didn't say that. Stephen did."

"Whoever didn't say it, I think it's a crazy idea. Seattle's a big city. The chief of police doesn't have time to play games with the likes of you. Nothing personal."

I paused. "Normally, you'd be right. But this is no ordinary chief of police."

"Carolyn hates him," Stephen said helpfully.

Hate was a strong word, but he was close. But was the feeling mutual? Enough to keep me in jail until Everly thought I'd gotten the message?

"I don't buy that theory, either," Stephen said. "The chief is no friend of big corporations. Why would he do something to help Mercedes Pierce?"

"He's got a point," Marvin said.

"He's a political animal," I said. "He makes alliances that promote his interests. He may knock drug companies in public, but he's not going to alienate one of the city's biggest employers in private. Politics makes strange—"

Suddenly I realized something. I squeezed my eyes shut.

"Carolyn?" Stephen said. "Are you still there?"

"Unfortunately, yes."

"You were saying—"

"I just remembered something one of the guards told me."

"What?"

"Except for conversations with lawyers, everything inmates say on the phone is recorded."

There was a long pause. "And is thereby available to the Seattle Police Department," Marvin said.

"I think I'll be hanging up now," I said.

Shaking my head, I returned the receiver to the wall. If Everly was out to get me, the last two minutes could keep me behind bars for the rest of my unnatural life.

# CHAPTER 16

My new bunkmate had little to say.

From the upper berth I watched as she arrived just before the next head count, delivered by the flabby guard. "This is Ms. Rodriguez," he whispered, as if the latter were a vial of nitroglycerine.

I could see why. The newest denizen of our tank was in her late twenties. Her eyes were snakelike, wary. Tattoos crawled from the collar of her orange jumpsuit, hinting that they were only a preview of the feature presentation underneath. The fact that she was Latino was irrelevant, except to my subconsciously intolerant mind.

"I'm sure you two will get along fine," the guard added, not looking sure at all, then took a few steps backward. "Head count!" he yelled. "Out in the hall."

This time the female guard did the counting.

"Bennett!"

"Here."

"Delgado!"

"Here."

"Jackson!"

"Yeah."

When she got to Rodriguez, my bunkmate responded by spitting on the floor.

The two guards looked at each other. The flabby one shrugged.

"I'll take that as a 'here,'" the female guard muttered.

At dinner, Rodriguez seemed interested in eating as far from my table as possible. She took a seat at the other side of the common area with two other Hispanic inmates whose ethnic heritage I didn't notice and didn't just mention.

As for the meal itself, the pizza was sturdy. One compartment of the tray was devoted to chocolate pudding, a chalky lump I savored despite the best efforts of my physicians.

I missed Tompkins already. She'd at least been willing to share a table, though her most recent conversation had consisted mainly of telling me to shut up.

It was also easier to tell what she was thinking. And in the case of my new bunkmate, I was afraid to guess.

* * *

After dinner, I relaxed on my bed.

If, that is, relaxing can be defined as lying motionless, stiff as the corpse you fear becoming, hyperventilating, staring at the ceiling, and feeling the eyes of an obvious gang member bore into your back like a drill press.

The sound on the TV had been turned up, making it easier for my tankmates to learn important grooming tips from *The Bachelorette*. But when a familiar voice rang from the doorway, I had no trouble hearing it.

"Neville!" called the female guard. "You got visitors."

I sat up. *Visitors? Plural?*

Could it be anyone other than Stephen and Marvin?

Overriding my fear of heights, I wriggled to the ladder and scrambled to the floor. Escaping the seething menace of The Tattooed One was a gift, but to do so by seeing my colleagues was enough to make me pray with my eyes closed for the rest of the day.

This time I was taken to a room with several tables. No phones, no glass. Three of the tables were occupied. Stephen and Marvin sat at one and stood up when they saw me. Their smiles were tinged with guilt or concern or both.

Two guards were posted along the walls, which were plastered with lists of visitation rules. Another guard sat at a desk. Their eyes surveyed the room like motion detectors. There was a vending machine in the corner.

My escort turned to me. "No touching. No profanity. I'll be back."

Stephen looked as if he might want to hug me. Marvin, on the other hand, shook his head as if he couldn't believe I'd managed to get myself into this place. He wasn't wearing his baseball cap. I wondered whether it, too, was against the rules.

"Well, look who the cat dragged in," he said.

Stephen cleared his throat. "You look fine in orange," he lied.

I sat down, and so did they.

"Welcome to my world," I said.

Marvin looked around. "Been in plenty of prisons in my time, usually interviewing. As these things go, this one looks pretty good."

"I'll take your word for it," I said.

"Are they treating you all right?" Stephen asked.

"In the sense that I'm not dead yet."

"How's the food?" Marvin asked.

"Delicious."

"Yeah, I'm sure."

There was an awkward pause.

"I couldn't believe all the rules," Stephen said finally. "We looked them up before we got here. Can't give you a hardcover book. Or food, or cards with glitter on them. They took our cell phones away. No miniskirts. Who wears a miniskirt anymore?" He paused. "They only allow visits a few hours a week. It's according to the floor you're on."

"Sorry it's so inconvenient," I said.

He shook his head. "I didn't mean it that way. It must be miserable for you. We've tried to get you out. Really, we've done everything we could think of."

"It's still that bureaucracy thing," Marvin said, lowering his voice. "Like I said on the phone—"

"Stop," I said. I made a zip-your-lip gesture with my fingers, then looked around to see whether the guards had noticed.

"But they can't hear—"

"Don't count on it. You'd be surprised what you can overhear from a distance. Even without a listening device."

He nodded. "Let's talk about something else."

"How's the book coming?" I asked.

They looked at each other. "If it were on a normal schedule, I'd say it was doing fine," Marvin said. "But it's not a normal book."

Stephen sighed. "It's probably about half done. That's not enough for Hunter."

"Have you heard from him?"

Then looked at each other again. "Only every day or so now," Marvin said. "Phone calls or e-mails."

"Did you tell him I'm in here?" I asked.

"Oh, yeah. He ain't happy. Says he's been patient, but he

can't afford to be anymore. Gonna fire our sorry butts if we miss his deadline."

"He sent a lawyer, you know," I said.

"He's not happy about that, either."

"Have you met her?"

"Not yet."

"She's probably taking a nap. Guess I kept her up all night."

"Maybe she can break this logjam and get you out of here," Marvin said.

Stephen nodded. "We need you. The book is missing something."

"Like what?"

"Your part. A theory about who killed Dr. Rhee, and some evidence to back it up. That's kind of the whole point, right?"

We sat there, staring dolefully at the tabletop. If the guards were watching us, they probably were ready to put us on suicide watch.

"Sorry," Stephen said. "We hoped visiting would encourage you."

"It has," I said. "It encourages me to go back to my cell."

Marvin leaned forward. "Been to the commissary?"

"No."

"We can at least put some cash in your account. They usually have snacks, candy, stuff to write on. Playing cards. Then you got your personal hygiene products."

"Ah. I can hardly wait to get some of those."

He shrugged. "Just trying to make your stay more pleasant."

"I want it to be *shorter*."

"That's up to . . . well, I don't know who it's up to." He zipped his lip.

The door through which I'd entered swung open. It was

the female guard. She leaned against the wall and folded her arms.

"Time to go already?" Marvin called.

She looked at her watch. "Nope. You still got another ten minutes."

We sat in silence.

At length I pushed my red plastic chair back from the table and stood up. "I think we've all had enough for one day. No point in prolonging the agony."

"Call when you can," Marvin said lamely. Stephen looked away.

I turned to the guard. "Past my bedtime," I said. "Can you walk me home?"

"Suit yourself," she said.

I heard the scraping of their chairs as I followed her out.

*Short visit*, I thought. But the elation I'd felt in the beginning seemed to have worn off a long time ago.

* * *

When we got to Eleven NUA, it was in chaos.

I heard yelling while we were still in the hallway. It was in Spanish.

The guard halted, then peeked through the window. Apparently determining there was no danger, she opened the door.

There were two guards inside, the flabby one and another I'd never seen. The latter was a young Latino man, a head taller and 30 pounds heavier than my bunkmate. They were arguing.

Relying on my two semesters of high school Spanish, I tried to determine the nature of the dispute. Something about having to go. Another place. And anglos.

After a minute or so of wrangling, The Tattooed One

made a disgusted noise and went quiet. Somehow she managed not to spit.

She walked out, led by the flabby guard and trailed by the Hispanic one. Passing me, she flashed me a look of warning as if this had all been my fault.

The female guard left, too. My heart was thudding in my ears. The other inmates, most of whom had coagulated in a clot at the other side of the room, returned to their bunks. They went back to their TV show, an educational program about the undead.

I used the bathroom, having barely avoided urinary incontinence when menaced by my former bunkmate's evil eye. No sooner had I started up the ladder when the door clicked open again behind me. It was the female guard, who was apparently very busy this evening.

She was shepherding another prisoner into our fold. She was short, perhaps 40, with shaggy, brown hair and black-pearl eyes that scanned her surroundings in fits and starts. She kept shifting her weight from one foot to the other.

The guard looked at me. "Musical chairs," she said.

"I don't understand."

"This is your new bunkmate."

"What happened to the other one?"

"Wasn't supposed to be here. Somebody screwed up. Belongs in maximum security. Doesn't play well with others."

"What was she in for?"

"Don't ask. You can get acquainted with the new girl in the morning."

She stepped back and lifted her chin. "Lights out!" she shouted.

The lights snapped off. The door shut behind her.

I lay down, waiting for my eyes to adjust to the darkness.

Suddenly there was a rustling from below.

"Hey," Black Eyes whispered.

"What?"

"I'm Kendra."

"Great. See you in the morning."

There was a pause. "What's *your* name?"

I sighed. "Carolyn."

"What you in for?"

"Arson."

"Really? What'd you set fire to?"

"Somebody who kept me awake all night talking."

"Hey, good one. Me, I'm here for defacing public property. But it was legitimate protest. Free speech."

I didn't respond, hoping she'd give up.

"Kind of my specialty," she continued. "They call it vandalism, but it's the only way to wake up the sheep."

"What sheep?"

"The people. They're asleep."

"Wish *I* were."

"The big shots don't like me. They don't want the sheep to know what's going on."

"What *is* going on?"

She paused. Suddenly I felt something poking my mattress from beneath. This went on for about 15 seconds.

"Okay," she whispered. "Just swept for bugs. Can't be too careful. Ever heard of the Bandenberg Group?"

"No."

"Of course not. They control seventy-eight percent of the agribusiness in Canada. Most people don't know it, but they've found a way to weaponize soybeans. Soy protein is used in everything from yogurt to crayons to underwear."

"So?"

"Soy protein increases estrogen levels. Feminizes men, makes them weaker. From politicians to soldiers. The terrorists would just love that, wouldn't they?"

"Maybe, but—"

"That's just one example. I could go on and on."

"Please don't."

"I know what you're thinking. But it's not paranoia if they're really after you. That's why I have to get the truth out."

I grunted. There was no use trying to stop her. Until she got it out of her system, she'd never shut up.

"Maybe you've seen my work," she persisted. "Spray paint on brick or concrete, usually. Signed with two question marks, because I question everything."

"Haven't seen it. I'm not from around here."

"Where you from?"

"New York."

"What do you do?"

"Publishing."

"So why are you in Seattle?"

"Doing a book."

"About what?"

My fists were starting to clench under the blanket. This conversation was like Chinese water torture. "About a drug company whistleblower."

There was a crumpling noise, as if she were sitting up. "You're kidding! The UniMerritt thing?"

"Yes."

"Hey, I'm all over that one. You know Blackwood isn't really Scottish, right?"

"I suspected as much. His accent is excessive."

"Fake birth certificate. The U.K. is in on it. Could be Canadian for all I know. Which might make him a member of the Bandenberg Group. UniMerritt could deliver all kinds of soy protein in its medicine."

"It all fits."

"No, it doesn't. UniMerritt doesn't need weaker men to accomplish its goals. Way too slow. It wants to control the pharmaceutical market by terminating its enemies."

"How do you know?"

"You'll have to ask their head of security. Mercedes something. Mercedes Benz."

"Mercedes Pierce? You know her?"

"Well, no. But that's the whole point. Nobody knows her. What more proof do you need?"

I closed my eyes, which was rather pointless in the dark. It was clear that this woman had inhaled too many fumes from her aerosol cans.

"Besides," she added, "I hear she's cozy with—"

From a nearby bunk someone fired a fusillade of curses. *"Will you morons shut up?"*

"Yeah," another woman groused. "Unless you want to attend an old-fashioned blanket party."

I didn't know what that was. But it sounded like something worth avoiding.

I waited for Black Eyes to keep blabbering, but she didn't. After a couple of minutes I rolled over and tried to go to sleep.

I couldn't, of course. Not right away. I had to keep replaying that last line. About being cozy with somebody.

Was she talking about Mr. Reardon? The police chief? Somebody else?

Or was she just a mental case? At the moment, I was willing to bet on the latter.

I'd have to ask her my questions in the morning. With a grunt I rolled over in the other direction.

I knew I was tired, but I didn't know how much. As it turned out, I even dreamed for a while.

Something about somebody wanting to kill me.

* * *

Next morning my bunkmate was gone.

I discovered it after the alarm sounded and I made it down the ladder. The bottom bunk was empty. Not only that, but the bed was made. The blanket was taut as a trampoline.

It was as if she'd never been there at all.

I just stood there.

First Tompkins. Then Rodriguez. Now Kendra.

Was it me? Bureaucracy? A blanket party?

Or did this nut case actually know something?

The door opened, and in came my least favorite guard. "Head count!" she declared. "Out in the hall!"

The flabby guy awaited us, looking like he'd had a long night. I searched for Kendra, just in case, but didn't see her anywhere.

When we'd formed a ragged line, guard Greer consulted her clipboard.

"Addison!"

"Here."

He made it through the whole list. No Kendra.

The other inmates headed for breakfast. I edged toward Greer.

"Excuse me," I said.

She looked up. "What?"

"What happened to Kendra?"

"Who?"

"Kendra."

"Never heard of her."

"But she was here last night."

Greer stabbed her pen into her shirt pocket. "You got a hearing problem, Princess? Need to see the school nurse?"

"No."

"Then go stuff your face."

Breakfast was oatmeal, two slices of bread. And, for the

first time, scooby. The latter looked like everything Tompkins said it would be—a tepid patty of something sausage-like. Soy protein was my guess. I decided to honor my promise to Mikki and skip it.

I skipped it in honor of Kendra, too.

And wondered who might vanish next.

# CHAPTER 17

GINA CASEBEER LOOKED BETTER RESTED NOW. IN FACT, SHE almost smiled as she looked through the pane of glass that separated us. She picked up the phone.

"Good news," she said, opening the satchel on her knee. "I believe we've resolved your bail situation." Her voice was still tinny, but more hopeful. "We should have you out by the end of the day."

I nearly stood up. "You can't be serious."

She gave me a quizzical look. "Ms. Neville, I'm a lawyer, not a comedian."

I exhaled slowly. "Sorry. I just don't want to fall prey to irrational exuberance."

"Of course. But the police say it was all a misunderstanding, a few numbers transposed on a form that convinced the computer you were pretending to be someone else."

"Who?"

"They didn't say."

I shook my head. "Sounds like Marvin was right. Bureaucratic screwup."

"You could call it that. And there's more. The charges against you are being dropped."

I blinked a few times. "Now I *know* you're making it up."

Chuckling, she took some papers from her bag. "I'm not that creative. The whole thing seems to have been a mistake. Someone overreacted. Misinterpreted the statutes."

"Who?"

"They didn't say that, either."

I frowned. "Who are *they*, exactly?"

"The district attorney's office." She paused. "If I were you, I'd stop searching for the cloud in this silver lining. You do want to be released, don't you?"

"More than I can tell you. It's just that . . ."

She waited.

"I have reason to believe . . ."

I felt the phone against my ear. Conversations with your lawyer weren't recorded, were they? Or was that just what they *wanted* you to believe?

Perhaps Kendra's paranoia was contagious.

I didn't want to find out. I decided to keep quiet.

"I . . . have reason to believe that . . . the situation could change at any time," I said.

"I'm not sure I understand."

"Neither am I. But I appreciate your help."

She shrugged and dropped the papers into her satchel. "Well, it's been an interesting change of pace, I'll say that." She closed the bag. "Good luck, Ms. Neville. Hope to see you back at the office soon."

Returning the phone to its cradle, she nodded once. I did the same, and she was gone.

I sat there, staring at my reflection in the glass. It was faint, streaked with fingerprints.

*You're getting out*, I told myself.

But I could have sworn there was a wet ball of yarn in my stomach. And it wasn't the scooby.

It was knowing that once I got past the walls, the man in the gray Hyundai SUV would still be out there. So would the police chief. Eventually Rodriguez would be there, too, happy to carve some gang symbol on my forehead and spit on the floor.

With a sigh I stood up and looked around the room. I couldn't keep thinking this way.

Gina Casebeer was right. This place was keeping me from seeing it. Not just this room, but the whole building. The locks, the smells, the rules, the sleeplessness. The constant squeeze on my chest and the muscles in my neck. Once I was out, I'd be able to breathe again. Think again.

I just needed time. Then I'd see how lucky I was.

Or maybe they just wanted me to think that.

\* \* \*

At 3:14 p.m., Pacific Standard Time, I was sitting at one of the two blue tables in tank Eleven NUA, trying not to watch an infomercial about a combination frying pan and flashlight that was clearly destined to change the world. The door clicked open.

Greer, who remained my least favorite guard, entered with a clipboard and a sneer. She still resembled a side of beef with hair, though I knew now that she also thought like one. "Neville!" she snapped.

She looked at me, cocking her head to one side. "You're out," she said.

I rose to my feet, lightheaded. "Does 'out' mean—"

"That's right. You're being released. God knows why."

"Thank you," I said.

"Don't thank me. Thank the DA's office. Now get your crap together and let's go."

"I'm crapless." I glanced around the room. Nobody I wanted to say goodbye to, either. The bottom bunk was still empty. I took one last look and followed her out, my plastic sandals flapping against the cement.

She took me downstairs, to the room where I'd checked in three days before. The same puffy, middle-aged woman with the rosacea on her nose sat behind an open window, like a ticket-seller at an old movie theater.

"One to check out," Greer told her, and handed her a form. She looked it over and nodded.

Greer turned to face me, smiling slyly. "You'll be back."

I swallowed.

"Mark my words," she added.

She walked out, keys jangling in her pocket.

The woman in the window handed me a large plastic bag with a label on it. I looked inside. There were my wallet, keys, cellphone. There was the Covert Overhearing Device MB7890. The gyros were gone, apparently eaten by some employee of the criminal justice system.

She also gave me my tweedy brown editor's blazer, my slacks, and my shoes. I couldn't keep the orange jumpsuit or the plastic flip-flops, she said, which didn't bother me in the least. "You can change in there," she added, nodding toward a door on her right.

When I came out, she held up a card. "Bus pass? They're free."

"Please save it for someone more deserving," I said. I was glad to do my part for prison reform.

"Somebody picking you up?"

"I hope so." I turned on my phone. It was still charged.

I called Stephen's number.

"Carolyn! Are you out? Gina Casebeer said they were letting you go."

"Can you come get me?"

"We'll be there in twenty-five minutes, give or take."

"I'll be the one looking like a hardened criminal," I said, and hung up.

The woman at the window pointed me toward the exit. "Good luck," she said.

The sun seemed too bright as I walked out of the building, even though it was only the Seattle sun and the sky was overcast. My legs felt rubbery as I headed for a bench near the sidewalk. I sat down and waited.

Vehicles seemed to whiz past at an alarming rate. Pedestrians appeared to be power-walking, even the preschoolers. I hugged my plastic bag of belongings a little closer, wishing things would slow down. Was I one of those inmates who, rejoining society, would never be able to adapt to it again?

On the other hand, I'd been gone only three days. Perhaps it would all come back to me, like riding a bicycle, except that I'd never quite gotten the hang of that, either.

Pulling my phone from my pocket, I proceeded to check e-mail. It was mostly spam and a note from the pharmacy about picking up a certain prescription.

But there was also a message from Hunter, two days ago. Marvin had forwarded it.

I sagged against the bench. Did I *have* to read it? I already knew Hunter was up in arms. But if I didn't read it, I'd never know exactly what he'd said. And I'd always wonder.

I opened it. It was the one about firing our sorry butts if we failed to meet his deadline. He hadn't used the word *butts*, however, and included this trenchant observation in the final paragraph:

. . .

*I know Carolyn's a personal friend of yours, but this crosses the line. Can't believe she's in jail. She must have [expletive deleted] up royally. Hasn't pulled her own weight in years. Dont [sic] let her drag you down, too.*

I returned to the inbox, then shut the phone down. I watched the cars roar by.

It was so nice to be back in the real world.

**\* \* \***

When the yellow Prius finally eased up to the curb, I stood and tucked the plastic bag under my arm.

Stephen was driving. Marvin tipped his baseball cap to me as I climbed into the back seat.

"Welcome to civilization, such as it is," he said.

"Pardon my musky fragrance. I haven't had a decent shower in three days, though I'm certain I don't have head lice."

"We don't smell anything," Stephen said. "And if we do, we know it's not your fault."

"We want to *celebrate*, Cranberry," Marvin said. "Pick any restaurant you like."

I leaned back against the seat and exhaled for what seemed like a geological period. "Remember that place where they make you wear fish hats?"

"Yeah," he said.

"Let's not go there."

"How about Italian?"

"Anything. As long as they don't have scooby."

"What's that?" Stephen asked.

"I can't talk about it yet," I said, and closed my eyes.

Next thing I knew, we were sitting in the parking lot of a

place called Roma Bella.

"You fell asleep," Stephen said.

"Snored like a tractor," Marvin cackled. "Did you snore like that in jail?"

I grunted. "Don't know."

"You must not have, because they would have killed you."

"Very funny."

He opened his door. "Chow time."

Being early for dinner, we didn't have to wait. Unfortunately, I kept thinking about the last restaurant I'd been to. The Greek place. Or had I just dreamed all that?

"We're glad you're not dead," Stephen said after we placed our orders.

"Not yet," I said.

"What was it like?" he asked.

"Summer camp."

"Well, that doesn't sound so bad," Marvin said. "When we came to visit, you looked like death eatin' a cracker. In a foul mood, too. We thought maybe they were giving you a hard time."

I took a soft breadstick from the basket and dipped it in a saucer of olive oil. "Wasn't like that."

When our food came, I breathed in the scent of marinara sauce, bay leaves, oregano, parmesan. I picked up my genuine fork and started eating without stabbing anyone.

"Let's talk about the book," I said.

"What about it?" Marvin asked.

"I saw Hunter's e-mail."

He shook his head. "Sorry, girl. I didn't want to forward it, but I figured you should know. The man sounds like a real fool."

"Only when you get to know him."

"He's all bark, no bite. When we turn in this manuscript, he'll be so happy he won't even remember what he said."

"*If* we turn it in."

He set his spoon next to his bowl of minestrone. "Well, I've been thinking. Maybe we've been going about this the wrong way. You don't need me to be a sidewalk supervisor. You need me to do what I've done for the last fifty years or so."

"Which is?"

"The writing. All that time at the *Chicago Tribune*. Then the books. I'm an Indian, not a chief."

I nodded slowly, pretending this was a great revelation.

"So who becomes chief?" I asked.

"Nobody. Don't need one."

"Will you be giving up your inflated managerial salary?"

"I'm wise, honey, not crazy. Remember the boat."

"Then what are you proposing, exactly?"

"I'll devote myself completely to the manuscript. You and Stephen find the missing piece—who did it. That job apparently takes two people, judging from what happened to you."

Stephen, who'd been deconstructing a pizza the size of a record album, looked up and shrugged. "Okay," he said.

Marvin smacked his palms together. "That's what I like to hear."

A few nearby heads turned at the sound.

I looked around the room. Suddenly I found myself wondering who could hear us. Someone with a *real* listening device. Someone who didn't wish me well. Or even wish me alive.

"So what do you think, Cranberry?" Marvin was saying. "You think the two of you can figure out who's behind this whole thing?"

"I . . . hope so," I said.

But not just for the book.

*Forget the book,* I thought.

I had my own reasons now.

# CHAPTER 18

"It's a brand new day," Stephen said.

He was standing at the door to my room the next morning, holding up my complimentary copy of *The Seattle Times*. "See? The newspaper says it's a new day. Check the date if you doubt me."

"I'll take your word for it. Are you coming in?"

I was fully dressed, of course, except for my tweedy brown editor's blazer. "I'd offer you coffee, but I drank it all."

"No problem." He tossed the paper on my desk. "When I say it's a brand new day, I mean we have to approach things in a whole new way." He sat in my desk chair, folded his hands in front of him, and tilted his head to one side. "So, what's your plan?"

I looked at him blankly, all that coffee having done nothing for my neurological activity.

"Right," he said. "Well, I thought a lot about it last night. The pizza was keeping me awake anyway. Seems to me everything revolves around Mercedes Pierce."

I remembered Kendra's words in the dark, whispered from the lower bunk. *"I hear she's cozy with . . ."*

I nodded. "But it's been impossible to find out anything about her."

"Yeah. So I see us going inside the company."

"How?"

"You know, like Marvin suggested. Moles."

I rolled my eyes. "That pizza did more than keep you awake. It seems to have influenced your judgment."

"I'm not talking about some big undercover thing. Just for a little while. Say we fill in as low-level employees. Temps, maybe. Research assistants, or whatever they're called."

"To do what?"

"See who comes and goes from her office. Listen to what people say about her. Look for memos or maybe even computer files."

I closed my eyes. "Are you forgetting why I spent the last three days in jail? Amateur surveillance. Playing spy."

"No listening devices, I promise."

"Out of the question. I'm not getting arrested again."

Just then there was a knock at the door. I peered through the peephole. It was Marvin.

"Cranberry, can I borrow your paper? I didn't get one." He stepped inside.

"No," I said. "You're not in charge anymore, remember?"

"And this is the thanks I get."

I turned to Stephen. "Tell Marvin your . . . proposition."

He did.

Marvin started out smiling, but by the time the explanation was done, he looked doubtful. "I have reservations about that one."

"Why?" Stephen asked. "Three days ago you thought toy microphones were a great idea."

"A lot can happen in three days." He jerked a thumb toward me. "Just ask this lady."

I resisted the urge to look emotionally damaged by my imprisonment, having done that so many times already.

"Besides," he continued, "how would you even get access to the building?"

"We know three people who could do that," Stephen said. "Wesley Goldblum, Douglas Brickman, and Neera Patel."

"Wait a minute," I said. "Even if they did get us in, Angus Blackwood knows what we look like."

He waved dismissively. "He's probably not even around most of the time. Travels a lot."

I thought for a moment, then delivered what I hoped would be the crushing blow. "Lazard, the Frenchman. He knows us from the tour. If we were supposed to be research assistants, we'd be around him all day."

He paused, then made an exasperated noise. "You guys are so negative! Let's just *talk* to those three. It can't hurt to talk, can it?"

Marvin shrugged. "I guess not."

I grunted. "Just don't be surprised if they're not excited about wrecking their careers for the sake of some nosy strangers from New York."

*Nobody would do that*, I thought.

At least that's what I was counting on.

* * *

Apartment 6D was quiet this time.

There were no gruff video game exclamations, no *pop pop* of weaponry. When Wesley Goldblum came to the door, there was no wireless headset looped around his neck. His hair was still disheveled, however, and its color was still caramel.

The living room was also in its customary ruin. He cleared a three-foot space for us on the sofa.

The girl with the pink hair, which was now more of a deep purple, and the butterfly tattoo, which was apparently permanent, wandered in and leaned against a door frame. "You remember Jade," Wesley said.

She nodded. Her languid posture seemed made for gum-chewing, but her jaw didn't move. Perhaps it would have been too much effort.

"You two aren't playing a video game," I said. "Taking a break from that sort of thing? Sounds healthy to me."

Ms. Purple Hair shook her head. "Xbox is broken."

"Oh."

Wesley took a bag of Doritos from a chair and sat down. "So, Stephen. You said on the phone you needed a favor."

He nodded. "We have reason to think Mercedes Pierce may have been involved in Dr. Rhee's death."

"Wow," Wesley said. "I mean, that's—kind of shocking, even for UniMerritt."

"But we need help finding out. We want to try spending a few days inside UniMerritt. Without people knowing who we are."

He laughed. "Like going undercover? That is so cool!"

"Yeah, I thought so. But we need somebody with an ID badge to get us in."

Wesley's brow furrowed. He looked down at the carpet, or at least where the carpet wasn't covered by issues of *Wired* and *Mental Floss*. "I mean, I'd love to stick it to the company. But there's no way I can get involved in that."

"Why not?"

"I'd have to do it anonymously. Which I couldn't, because Security could find out whose badge was used." He looked back up. "I mean, I've got my whole career ahead of me. Getting fired would be a major blot on my resumé, you know?"

He turned to Ms. Purple Hair. "What do you think?"

"It *would* be cool. But really stupid."

I shook my head. "Too bad," I said, stifling a sigh of relief.

We sat there, silent.

"Well, I guess that's it," Stephen said.

"Sorry," Wesley said. "If there's anything else I can do, let me know. I mean, anything I can do without screwing up my entire life."

When we got outside, the porch bulbs of the other apartments still glowed like a multitude of butane lighters. "Well, that didn't take long," Stephen said.

"These kids today," I said.

He shrugged. "I can see it from his perspective. Maybe there's something he can do without giving himself away."

"Yes," I said, though I couldn't imagine what it might be.

Nor did I care, of course. The important thing was that he'd sent us packing.

One down, two to go.

\* \* \*

Neera Patel's townhouse wasn't as I'd envisioned it.

There were no statues of Vishnu, no tapestries of elephants, no sitar music, no scents of sandalwood or curry. There wasn't even a wicker chair or brass bell from World Market. I didn't share my expectations with anyone, of course, lest my imperialist stereotypes attract attention.

Her living room, in fact, reminded me of the Rhee household. No fountain burbled in the corner, but the interior design seemed calculated to instill tranquility. Ms. Patel was clearly on a tighter budget than the Rhees, yet the sparse placement of Ansel Adams and Degas prints on the white walls encouraged a sense of calm.

Though not in me, of course. Not when this meeting

could lead to my humiliation, incarceration, termination, or annihilation.

Stephen and I sat on the white couch. Ms. Patel sat in the white chair opposite. She served us cups of chai, even though it was Indian and popular.

"You have a plan," she said.

Stephen nodded. "You've already gone out of your way to help. Thanks to you, we know more about Mercedes Pierce. But not enough."

"Enough to put Ms. Neville in jail, you said on the phone."

"Hardly your fault," I said. "Don't blame yourself."

She raised an eyebrow. "I don't."

"Oh," I said, a bit disappointed.

Stephen explained his proposal. Ms. Patel listened, blinking and sipping chai.

"You wish to infiltrate the campus," she said when he was done.

"Just for a little while."

"Using my badge."

"Yes."

"Which could easily lead to my dismissal."

"Well . . . yes."

I sat up straight. I liked where this was going.

"You want to pose as research assistants," she said. "Temps, perhaps. You won't find many temps in research. But we do get visiting professionals, especially from other countries, who come to observe our work."

There was a long pause. She stared into her tea, as if it might contain leaves for divination.

"I'll do it," she said finally.

I sagged. My cup suddenly felt so heavy I had to set it down on the coffee table.

Ms. Patel did the same. "I'm aware that I will lose my job

if we're found out. But as you probably have sensed, I am no fan of my employer."

"I *have* sensed that," Stephen said, sounding a little too excited.

"In addition, I would like the true killer found in order to remove myself from consideration."

I had only one card left to play. I would have called it a Hail Mary pass, but that phrase was a sports analogy.

"I do have one concern," I said. "Your current supervisor, Dr. Lazard, met us when we toured your facility. He knows what we look like."

She nodded. She picked up her cup and had another sip.

"Can you wait for two days?" she asked.

"If we need to," Stephen said. "Why?"

"Dr. Lazard will be away at an ACRP conference in Toronto for about a week."

"ACRP?"

"Association of Clinical Research Professionals."

I tried not to groan.

Stephen must have heard me, because he smiled at my suffering. "We'll be happy to wait," she said. "Maybe you can use that time to give us a crash course on how to act like researchers."

"We do have lab protocols you'll need to know." She paused. "Have you asked Wesley about this?"

"He said no. Understandable, considering where he is in his career. Haven't talked with Douglas Brickman yet."

"Douglas? I take it you haven't heard."

"Heard what?"

"Dr. Lazard fired him two weeks ago."

"Really?"

"I can't say I was surprised. Douglas was . . . kind of a sloth. He probably deserved it."

Stephen pressed his lips together, no doubt to keep from

smirking. After all, who could deserve it more than a vicious, demented vivisectionist?

"On the other hand," Ms. Patel said, "Dr. Lazard has his own issues. In some ways he is almost as bad as Dr. Rhee. Imperious. Ignores input from others."

Not hard to believe, I thought, given his demeanor when we'd met him. Not to mention his outlandish comb-over.

"Well, I guess we won't need to talk with Mr. Brickman about this," Stephen said. "We can scratch him off our list."

"Yes," I said absently.

I closed my eyes. I was out of arguments.

Maybe sneaking around at UniMerritt wasn't such a bad idea after all.

Perhaps I'd come across some of that cyanide and try a bit of it myself.

# CHAPTER 19

Next day, against my better judgment, we reconvened at Ms. Patel's townhouse.

I felt the way I had in eleventh-grade chemistry class, which I'd somehow passed but never really understood. The only things it left me with were the phrase *covalent bonding* and the stink of sulfur dioxide in my nostrils.

Officially, our mission was to learn how to be mistaken for visiting researchers. Unofficially, mine was to maintain my dignity. I had no illusions that I'd succeed at either.

When we got there, she greeted us with a nod. A stack of books sat on her kitchen table, probably her old college textbooks, bearing witty titles like *Principles and Practice of Clinical Research* and *Laboratory Protocols in Applied Life Sciences*.

"Shall we get started?" she asked.

"My head hurts already," I mumbled.

Her purse, which I still thought of as a deadly weapon, sat on the table next to the books. She started fishing objects from it. I recognized a test tube with a rubber stopper. A few more glass things. A couple of metal objects. Something that looked like an old-fashioned mercury thermometer. A translucent plastic container with a blank label. A tiny spoon.

"I wish I had more examples of the equipment you may be using," she said. "But these were all I could . . . borrow."

Stephen raised an eyebrow. "You swiped office supplies?"

She shrugged. "I am already in trouble. What have I got to lose?"

I picked up the test tube. "I know what this is. It's—"

Suddenly I fumbled, and it fell. Fortunately, it landed on a placemat, bounced once, and came to rest unbroken.

"Slippery," I said.

Ms. Patel shook her head. "Rule One: Don't touch anything."

"Sorry."

"I'm sure you've seen test tubes before." She picked up another piece of glassware. "Do you know what this is?" It looked like a wilting teardrop.

"A beaker," Stephen guessed.

"No, a retort."

"*Ree*-tort," we repeated slowly, like Neanderthals being introduced to fire.

"Retorts are used for distillation."

"Dis-till-*a*-shun," we said.

"No need to do that. We have a lot of ground to cover."

She held up a beaker, then what turned out to be a graduated cylinder, then a pipette, and the classic petri dish. We took notes.

By the time we'd learned about centrifuges, balances, temperatures, milliliters, and some squiggly rubber tube whose purpose I never quite grasped, my eyes were glazing over. But Ms. Patel wouldn't let us take a break.

"This is all very elementary," she said, thumbing through one of her textbooks. "Let's continue."

"We were English majors," I protested.

"Then you know how I felt in English class." She found the page she was looking for and resumed. "Good laboratory practice is all about avoiding cross-contamination, reducing the chance of confusing one reagent with another, cleanliness, environmental control, accurate measurement, and safety. Everything must be correctly labeled, documented, and recorded using standardized terms."

We scribbled as quickly as we could. I hoped I was spelling *reagent* correctly and hid the page with my elbow so Stephen couldn't check it.

"You may be called upon to deal with animal subjects—in our case, mostly mice."

"Uh-oh," Stephen said.

"Are you afraid of them? Allergic?"

He shook his head. "I'm compassionate."

Ms. Patel folded her arms across her chest. "So are we. That's why you may need to feed them or change their bedding or clean up after them. It's not as though you'll be asked to perform a necropsy."

Stephen made a face. "What's that?"

"An autopsy. To find out why the subject died. It involves dissection of—"

I jerked up my hands in a cautionary gesture. "Excuse me. I know from our meeting with Douglas Brinkman that this conversation can't possibly end happily. Or before the sun goes down."

Ms. Patel shrugged. "Very well."

She moved on to labeling specimens and using the electron microscope. But when we got to the metric system and calculating sample sizes, our whining became too much for her to bear.

She closed her textbook. "It's clear that we have reached your limit. You can absorb only so much."

I rubbed my temples with my fingertips. "But we don't really know what we're doing."

"Perhaps not. But being a researcher is not only about what you do. It's about the way you do it. Perhaps the most important thing to learn is attitude." She paused. "A good researcher has consuming curiosity. Hunger for discovery. Dedication to truth. Passion for detail. Loyalty to the scientific method."

"Much like an editor," I said. "Except the scientific part."

"Then perhaps you'll do well." She looked at her watch again. "I should get back to the office. I've already used up half a day of vacation, and I don't have many left. And I have to put these lab supplies back before anyone notices."

"We'll come back tomorrow, then," Stephen said.

She shook her head. "I can't take any more time. I will see you here the next day at 7:45 a.m. Sharp."

"But I'm not ready," I said.

"Frankly," she said, "neither am I."

* * *

Lunch was Kentucky-fried. I considered Extra Crispy, but it sounded too formidable at the moment.

"I can't do this," I said, staring at the little bowl of mashed potatoes and gravy in front of me.

"Can't do what?" Stephen asked.

"Pose as a researcher."

He stuck a straw in his Pepsi. "Of course you can. You're a master of vocabulary, aren't you?"

"Yes, but—"

"Then talk your way through. Throw in a lot of multisyllabic words. Like *multisyllabic*. And don't break anything."

I was about to advance a more eloquent rebuttal when the *1812 Overture* beckoned from my pocket.

It was Hunter.

I couldn't do this, either. But I took the call anyway.

"I called Marvin, Carolyn," he said, his voice eerily quiet. "Couldn't reach him."

"How can I help you?"

"Are you back in jail yet?"

"What?"

"Gina Casebeer in Legal says she got you out. Do you have any idea what that cost me?"

"No. But thank you for doing it."

"Where's my book?"

"In the works."

"I've heard that before. Have you figured out who killed the whistleblower?"

"Almost."

"'Almost' is a weasel word."

"How about 'practically'?"

"The only word I want to hear from you is 'done.'"

"We're . . . close. We have a plan."

"Does it involve bailing you out of jail?"

I hesitated. "Probably not."

"'Probably.' Another weasel word. I don't like working with weasels."

*Of course not*, I thought. He'd always wanted to be the only weasel in the room.

"Have I failed to make it clear what will happen if that deadline isn't met?"

"No," I said, envisioning myself sitting in the Bowery Mission on the Lower East Side, smelling the way I had after three days in jail.

There was a long pause. "I think I'll be going now. Good-bye, Carolyn." His voice was still quiet. I had to admire his self-control, or his Xanax.

I set the phone down next to my mashed potatoes.

"Hunter," I told Stephen.

"What did he want?"

"The book. And to kill me, I think."

"But you told him we have a plan. I heard that part."

"It's a terrible plan. I still can't do it."

But after hearing that unnerving tone in Hunter's voice, I knew one thing.

I'd better try.

# CHAPTER 20

WHEN DAY ONE ARRIVED, I KEPT TELLING MYSELF THERE WAS still time to back out. I almost believed it.

Stephen and I met in the hallway outside our rooms. We headed to the elevator without a word. *Still time to back out.*

I thought the same thing as we parked at the far end of the UniMerritt lot. It wasn't full, since we were so early.

We sat in the car, staring out the windows.

I shook my head. "The place is probably crawling with motion detectors and security cameras. What about people who might see us on camera and recognize us? Blackwood . . . Pierce . . . those two men who were pushing the cart with the boxes on it . . ."

He folded his arms. "None of those people spend time staring at screens to see who's walking down the hall. Other people do it, and *they* won't know who we are."

"You don't know that. Not for sure."

He thought for a moment. "Maybe we could avoid the cameras by hiding our faces with file folders or something when we pass one. I'll bet researchers carry lots of file folders."

"I don't know." We fell silent, then waited until Stephen couldn't stand it any longer. "We'd better go," he said.

*Still time to back out.*

We met Ms. Patel at a small, steel-clad back door of the Research Building. She swiped her badge and slipped us in.

"Follow me," she whispered.

We stepped over the threshold. The door clicked behind us.

No more time to back out.

I glanced at the upper reaches of the hallway on both sides. At least one gray security camera already seemed to have us in its sights.

"File folders," I whispered.

"I don't have any," Stephen replied. "I'm sure they have some where we're going."

"Jail?"

"No."

Ms. Patel swiped her badge again at the door to her lab. I felt a little safer when we were inside, but not much.

"Stay here," she said.

We looked around. "There's a graduated cylinder," Stephen said, obviously proud of himself for remembering.

"There's a file folder." I looked inside. "Something in it. We need empty ones. Extra large."

Ms. Patel returned, her heels clicking on the spotless vinyl floor. In one hand she held a pair of generic clip-on VISITOR badges; in the other were two white lab coats. I traded my tweedy brown blazer for one of the latter. We clipped our badges to our coats.

"I always wanted one of these," Stephen said. "With this on, I could do anything. Brain surgery, maybe."

"Let's start with something simpler, shall we?" Ms. Patel asked. She reached for her own lab coat, which hung from a rack with three others. Hers looked heavier than ours, with N. PATEL stitched in blue over the breast pocket.

She looked at the wall clock. "I have to start working in about ten minutes. Is there anything you need to ask me before then?"

I drew a blank. *Focus*, I thought. I reminded myself how Hunter had sounded on the phone. We had to get some answers.

"Where's Dr. Rhee's office?" I asked.

She pointed at a doorway. "It's Dr. Lazard's now, of course."

"Did Douglas Brickman have an office?"

"No. We have desks." She pointed past me, to my right. "That was his. Everything's gone, as far as I know. When you get a pink slip here, security escorts you off the premises. Too many papers and files a disgruntled employee might erase or stick in a briefcase. And Douglas was definitely unhappy."

"Where's Wesley's desk?"

"Over there, next to mine. If you want to look at his things, you'll have to ask him. He'll be in later."

I expected to see a poster of some hideous video game over his desk, but it all looked very businesslike, if a bit disorganized. The only hint of the Wesley from Apartment 6D—a small plastic effigy of an innocent-looking blue creature with huge eyes and a golden scimitar—sat on the desk.

"You're welcome to go through my workstation if you wish," Ms. Patel said. "But I doubt you'll find anything of interest, and little that you are prepared to interpret."

"Perhaps another time," I said. It was bound to be fruitless. She'd had two days to get rid of anything incriminating.

"Then you are free to go," she said.

"Let's work our way toward Pierce's office," Stephen said.

"It's to the right, then a left, then another two hundred

feet or so," Ms. Patel said. "If you need assistance, come back here. Not that I can be of much help if security gets hold of you."

I swallowed. "Do you have any file folders?"

She blinked. "File folders?"

"Think of them as . . . a security blanket."

"All right." She opened a cabinet, took some out, and handed them to me. "Like these?"

"Do you have any bigger ones?"

"I don't believe they *make* bigger ones."

*Still time to back out,* said a voice in my head.

But there wasn't. Not anymore.

* * *

The door to the hallway clicked behind us. Taking a deep breath, I tried to look scientific and inconspicuous.

I held the manila folders in front of my face.

"That doesn't look natural," Stephen whispered. "Try this." He opened two folders, placed them next to each other, and raised them high enough to examine them as if they were CT scans.

I shook my head. "We're supposed to be researchers, not radiologists. Besides, you can't hold those things up and walk at the same time. You'll run into somebody."

"Okay. Forget the file folders."

"What?"

He shrugged. "I changed my mind."

"Then there's no point in *my* carrying them. Anyone who recognizes you will recognize me."

"Fine. You're the one who was so worried about it in the first place. I never thought they were necessary."

He lowered his folders. I lowered mine.

A couple of white-coated employees passed on the left. "We're holding up traffic," she said.

We headed down the hall at the prevailing rate of speed. I kept my head down, hoping it would be taken as a sign of consuming curiosity, hunger for discovery, and whatever those other two or three qualities were.

About five minutes and two wrong turns later, we found ourselves outside a heavy-looking wooden door with a shoe-box-sized window. Crisscrossed wire was imbedded in the glass. A brown plastic sign that said SECURITY was under the window, and a pushbutton was mounted to the right of the door.

"I think you have to buzz," Stephen whispered.

I pushed the button.

"Yes?" said a muffled male voice.

I froze. I hadn't thought we'd get this far, let alone into Mercedes Pierce's office. What was I supposed to say?

"Hello?" said the voice.

I decided to throw myself off that bridge when I came to it.

"We're . . . here to see Mercedes Pierce," I said.

There was a buzz and a click. I grabbed the door handle and pulled, but I must have been too late.

"Try again," said the voice.

Another buzz and click. I yanked open the door, which barely moved, being about the same weight as a railroad car.

Inside was a desk, manned by an armed guard with military posture and a doubtful expression. To the left sat what looked like an airport X-ray machine. FedEx and UPS cartons were stacked next to it on the floor. It seemed everyone scanned parcels for bombs these days, I thought, even at Pendleton House. You never knew what a crazed zealot, much less a rejected author, might do.

"Is Mercedes Pierce in?" I asked.

The guard pointed at another desk to our right. "There's the lady you want to see." He was pointing at a middle-aged woman whose fingers darted like dragonflies across her computer keyboard. She was probably the assistant Stephen had called for an appointment after our tour, only to be turned down.

The keyboard wizard gave her carpal tunnel a rest. "I'm afraid Ms. Pierce isn't in," she said.

Relieved, I nodded.

"And if she were, you'd need an appointment."

"Of course," I said. "Well, we'll just—"

"Hold on," the guard said, looking at me. "Let me see that name badge."

My breath caught in my throat. With unsteady fingers I unclasped the badge from my lapel and gave it to him.

"Clip's broken. You're about to lose it." He turned around, rummaged in a credenza, and produced a new badge. He tossed the old one in his wastebasket.

I tried to thank him, but my vocal cords seemed to have been disconnected.

"'Bye," Stephen said, waving his file folders. At last they'd come in handy.

Back in the hall I leaned against the wall and started breathing again. A sporadic stream of personnel flowed past, their passion for detail and loyalty to the scientific method causing them to ignore us.

"That was exciting," Stephen said, his face flushed. "Now what?"

"Give me a minute while I have a major cardiac event."

He scratched his chin. "Maybe we should have tried to make an appointment."

"Why? That woman already sent you packing when she found out we were writing a book."

"Yeah, I recognized her voice." He looked around. "So do

we go back to the lab? Maybe this time we can make it without getting—"

"You folks look lost," said someone on my left.

I turned to face a white-coated young woman, apple-cheeked and lemon-haired, a veritable fruit salad grinning at us with a fervor that made me want to call the authorities. Her teeth were almost too bright to behold without protective eyewear.

I looked at the name stitched over her pocket. It said L. VAN METRE.

"I see from your badges that you're visitors," she bubbled. "This place can be pretty confusing."

Stephen and I looked at each other.

"Oh, I'm sorry," the woman said. "Are you part of our international program? Do you speak English?"

*Ah*, I thought. *Pretend you don't and she'll go away.*

"English, no," I said. I didn't attempt an accent, pronunciation never having been my strong suit. Stephen had the good sense to just raise his eyebrows and shake his head.

"Where are you from?" the woman asked.

*Sweden*, I thought. They had drug companies there, didn't they? Or was I thinking of Switzerland? I took a chance on the former, having learned a few terms like *svenska* and *vi ses snart*, the latter simply because it sounded so antisocial.

"*Swe . . . den*," I said slowly, hoping sluggishness would make up for having no accent.

"*Ja*," Stephen added.

"Oh!" cried Ms. Apple Cheeks. "I was a foreign exchange student in Sweden! *Da kan prata svenska med mig.*"

I looked at Stephen. This wasn't going to work.

"So nice to meet you," I said.

"But I thought—"

"You must visit us in our country sometime. At our drug company. It's very . . . large."

We waded into the stream of white coats and tacked left, not looking back.

When we'd turned right at the next corridor, I slackened my pace but kept moving.

"Uh-oh," Stephen said. "When we get to the lab, how do we get in? Neera has her badge."

"I'm . . . not sure."

A minute later we stood in front of the door. Sure enough, we were locked out. No card to swipe. No buttons to push. How else could a person—

I tried knocking. Then again, more loudly. A few white-coated passersby frowned, as if offended by such a primitive form of communication.

At last the door opened. But the face filling the gap wasn't Ms. Patel's. It was Wesley Goldblum's.

"Inside," he whispered.

When the door had clicked behind us, he glanced nervously at it over his shoulder. "If anybody else comes in here, I don't know you. I think I already explained why." He walked over to his desk, opened a big white plastic binder, and started making notes.

Ms. Patel entered from a storage room. "You're back," she said, studying the label on a brown jar in her hand.

We took turns updating her. As always, Stephen was more dramatic but I was more accurate.

She kept nodding and reading the label on the jar. She unscrewed the cap and sniffed its contents. "All very interesting," she said. "But I'm afraid Wesley and I are in the midst of a very complex experiment."

"You can say that again," he said, but kept writing in his binder.

"We're also shorthanded, since Douglas was let go," she added. "Since the two of you have hit a bit of a brick wall, can you help us out? Nothing difficult. Things a fourth-grader could do."

"Thanks for the vote of confidence," I said.

"Stephen, I need you to feed the rats." She pointed toward a door that said ANIMAL FACILITY.

He flinched. "Rats? I thought you had mice."

"Mostly. Is there a problem?"

He tried to smile. "No, of course not."

"You are concerned about the animals' welfare, correct?"

"Always."

Wesley put down his pen, smirking. "They don't bite. Well, hardly ever."

Ms. Patel fished a ring of keys from her pocket and unlocked the door. "Use gloves. There's a first aid kit on the wall. Instructions are on the white Lab Diet bags. The rats in the cages with yellow stickers get Standard Diet; the ones with red stickers get Irradiated Diet."

Stephen squeezed his eyes shut. "White bags . . . yellow stickers . . . red . . ."

Ms. Patel sighed. "Wesley, would you show him?"

"I'm on it," he said, and led Stephen away.

"As for you, Ms. Neville, all you need are steady hands."

"I'm not sure I fit that description right now."

"Your task is to clean part of this bench. The table." She pointed at a nearby piece of furniture, a wooden frame with a dark gray laminate top. Small glass items and tools were scattered on it.

"Just a minute," I said. I pulled my notebook and pen from my pocket. "Go ahead."

"Wear gloves. Take any loose things and put them on that table over there." She pointed across the room. I started jotting.

"Bleach is on that shelf. Mix one part bleach and nine parts water in one of the plastic containers. Dip a paper towel in it and wipe the surface. Ethanol is on this shelf. Mix seven parts ethanol and three parts water. Dip your paper towel in it and wipe the bench with that."

I jotted faster. My ears were starting to ring.

"Let it dry for a couple of minutes. Now take a paper towel, dip it in the bleach solution, and wipe the bottom surfaces of the items you took off the bench. Then replace them as you found them."

"Piece of cake," I said, breathing a little too hard.

She picked up the brown bottle she'd come in with. "I'll be back," she said, and headed for the storeroom.

I stared at my scribbled instructions, then sent up a quick prayer. I was working without a net.

I pulled two white latex gloves from the box. The snap of putting them on sobered me further, as if I were preparing for surgery. The harsh smells of bleach and alcohol cleared what was left of my mind.

After lifting the glassware piece by piece, I relocated it gently to the other table. I tore and dipped and wiped. Determined to go the extra mile, I cleaned the underside and interior of one of the glass dishes on which I'd noticed a streak of mold.

I checked my notes. *Replace them as you found them.* For a moment I regretted not having taken a picture of the original arrangement. I did the best I could to reproduce it from memory.

After washing my hands under the long, curving faucet over the sink, I paused like a child who'd scrubbed his fingernails and now stood ready for inspection.

I waited that way for what seemed like five minutes or so. Finally I plopped into the chair at what had been Douglas Brickman's desk. I closed my eyes.

That was when I heard the scream.

*"Noooooo!"*

It was a kind of yelp, a disbelieving wail. I opened my eyes to see Wesley bent over the table I'd just cleansed so thoroughly.

"What did you *do?*" he cried.

I swallowed. "Are you . . . speaking to me?"

"Where is my *Listeria monocytogenes?*"

"Where did you . . . last see it?"

He pointed at the petri dish I'd cleaned so meticulously. "Right here."

"You mean that little bit of mold?"

"*Mold?* That little bit of mold is one of the keys to bacteria-mediated transgene expression for tumor targeting."

"Oh."

"I can grow more, but this puts us behind at least a week. I can't—"

Ms. Patel was back, this time carrying a green bottle. "What happened?"

"She killed my *Listeria monocytogenes.*"

Ms. Patel gave me a look that made me hope her purse was nowhere in the vicinity.

Just then Stephen returned, looking dazed. I noticed there was a Band-Aid on his finger. "A rat bit me."

Wesley shook his head. "I told you not to—"

"Enough," Ms. Patel declared. "Ms. Neville . . . Stephen . . . It would be best if you take the rest of the day off."

Stephen looked at his finger. "Already?" he asked.

"I will meet you tomorrow at the same time, at the same entrance."

"I thought it was mold," I said.

"We will see you *in the morning.*"

Sadly we took off our lab coats and kept the badges. I put on my blazer.

We didn't spot anyone we knew as we plodded out of the

building and into the parking lot. Whether anyone saw us, I didn't know.

We climbed into the car.

"That went well," I said.

"Did you really think so?"

We drove back to the hotel without speaking, because we both knew the answer.

## CHAPTER 21

THE MOOD WAS SOMBER NEXT MORNING WHEN THE THREE OF us gathered in Marvin's room for breakfast. He was providing coffee and doughnuts, no doubt feeling sorry for us—or perhaps for himself because he had to be associated with us. Either way, it was like a party, except that it was far too early and there was nothing to celebrate.

"What are you doing today?" he asked. "Other than staying away from moldy plates and wild animals, I mean."

"What would *you* do?"

He dunked a doughnut and watched the coffee drip from it. "Seems to me this is your only chance to look for physical evidence in that lab. On the shelves, maybe. In the files. Anything out of the ordinary."

"But we don't even know what would be *in* the ordinary."

He nodded. "Yeah, that's definitely a handicap. Got any better ideas?"

"No."

"Didn't think so."

Which is why, 45 minutes later, we were once again tugging our white lab coats on. Ms. Patel and Wesley watched, as if to make sure we didn't harm ourselves or others.

"Sorry about yesterday," Stephen said, positioning his badge on his pocket.

"How is your finger?" Ms. Patel asked.

"It's fine. I used antibiotic."

Wesley glanced toward the table, probably at the petri dish I'd cleaned too diligently. But he said nothing and went back to his desk to make more notes in his binder.

"We'd like to take a look around," I said.

"At what?" Ms. Patel asked.

"Anything out of the ordinary."

"I'm not sure what that means."

"I think it will become clear after we start looking," I said, not sure what that meant, either.

She shrugged. "Well, we have plenty to keep us busy. If you have a question, let me know." She paused. "Just don't touch anything."

"Or clean anything," Wesley added.

"Where do you keep your supplies?" I asked. "Chemicals, things like that."

"The storeroom," she said, pointing in the direction from which she'd brought her green and brown bottles the day before.

Stephen followed me in. I flipped on the fluorescent lights and shut the door. The HVAC system faintly rumbled. It was cool, almost chilly.

The room was about half the size of a city bus. The walls were lined with stainless steel shelves, nearly all of them full. There was no smell.

"What are we looking for?" he asked.

"Remember how we noticed that most people on our suspect list had a connection to UniMerritt or another drug company?"

"Yeah."

"And how that could give them access to things the killer used? Like the capsules Dr. Rhee's blood pressure medication came in. Mrs. Rhee said they were yellow. And the cyanide."

"Okay."

"Let's start by looking for those."

"I'll take the right side," I said. "You take the left."

The first section on my side was labeled HARDWARE, with boxes of safety glasses and microscope slides and clamps. I skipped them. The next was MEDIA, packed with plastic bottles and jars of Urea Agar and Triple Sugar Iron Agar and half a dozen other agars, along with MIO Medium and LB Broth. Whatever they were.

Then there was Terrific Broth. A one-liter bottle, golden as chicken soup but without the cloudiness.

"Look at this," I said, holding up the container. "Terrific Broth."

He read the label. "What's so terrific about it?"

"I don't know. Maybe we should taste it and find out."

"I'm sure tasting is the last thing you're supposed to do with it."

"Look it up on your smartphone."

"Why?"

"Because it's a fascinating use of language. It can't possibly be any kind of 'terrific' in the conventional sense, yet here it is."

He made an irritated noise, hauled out his phone, and started tapping. "It's for growing stuff in," he said half a minute later. "Like bacteria. In petri dishes."

"Oh," I said solemnly, recalling Wesley's heartrending scream.

He dropped his phone back in his pocket. "Let me know if you find anything else fascinating," he said, and went back to his side of the room.

The next section was labeled REAGENTS. Bottles, jars, canisters. Mostly plastic, a few glass. White, brown, green, blue, amber. They seemed to stretch all the way to the back of the room.

This was going to take a while.

Or was it? All I had to do was find the cyanide. It was alphabetical. If Dr. Rhee hadn't invented that orderly system, I was sure he endorsed it wholeheartedly.

I stepped to the Cs. A lot of Calciums. Some Carbons. Some Chlorines. Chromium something. Quite a few Coppers. Suddenly I hit Cytosine, and realized I'd gone too far. I checked again.

"No cyanide," I said.

Stephen turned toward me. "Maybe the killer took the whole bottle."

I looked around. "Or maybe we're in the wrong part of the alphabet. Can you look up *cyanide* on your phone?"

This time he didn't seem to mind. It took longer to get an answer, though.

"Aha!" he said finally. "What we're actually looking for is *potassium* cyanide."

My pulse quickened. I strode to the Ps.

A great deal of Phosphorous. A bit of Platinum. Plenty of Potassium.

But no potassium cyanide.

I frowned.

"Hold on," Stephen said, putting the phone in his pocket. He looked around the room. "Cyanide isn't just any old chemical, right? It's toxic. Maybe . . ."

He turned to his side of the room, then pointed at a steel mesh cabinet. There was a small, red skull-and-crossbones sticker on the top. He tried the door. It was locked.

I peered inside. It was hard to see amid the shadows, but

there it was. Potassium Cyanide. Small, white plastic bottle. I almost smiled.

"Now let's find the capsules," he said.

We searched for about 15 minutes. Not only were there no yellow ones; there were none at all.

"Looking this up on the Internet isn't going to help," he said. "Also, I'm going stir crazy in here. Let's just ask."

Emerging from the storeroom like Armageddon survivors from an underground bunker, we found Wesley peering at something under a tall, beige microscope.

"Excuse me," I said.

"Yeah," he said, not straightening up.

"We can't find any empty capsules. The kind Dr. Rhee's prescription was in."

"Gelatin capsule shells? We wouldn't have those. We don't compound the drugs."

"Who *would* have them?"

Sighing, he finally stood up. "Manufacturing. They've got all the stuff for making pills and capsules."

"Can you take capsules apart and use them again?"

He shrugged. "Don't know. Never tried."

Just then the hallway door clicked. Ms. Patel stepped in, still holding the ID badge she'd just run through the reader.

"You know much about capsules?" Wesley asked her.

"A little."

"They want to know whether Dr. Rhee's Lexidril came in a capsule you could take apart."

"It depends on whether it was the tapered kind or not."

She went to her desk phone, ran her finger down a list that sat next to it, and punched in four digits. "This is Neera Patel in Research. Can anyone there tell me the capsule type for Lexidril?"

There was a lengthy wait. She looked at her watch.

Finally she lifted her chin, alert. "Can it be opened?" Pause. "Thank you."

She turned to me. "Yes, it can be opened. They don't recommend it, of course, since it's almost impossible to split the dose evenly. But it can be done. Why do you want to know?"

"Just wondering what the killer's options were." I thought for a moment. "Who would have had access to empty capsules?"

"Probably most people in Manufacturing. Or people who knew them. Or supervised them."

"Or people who had prescriptions to Lexidril themselves," Wesley said. "That could be a couple million."

"That certainly narrows it down," Stephen said.

For a second I'd thought we were on to something. Now I couldn't even remember what it was supposed to be.

"Well, at least we found the potassium cyanide," Stephen said.

"So did the police," Ms. Patel said. "They took it with them. The one in there now is a replacement. It should last us a long time, since we almost never use it."

"Who had a key to that cabinet?" I asked.

She turned to Wesley. "We all did, didn't we?"

"Yeah."

There was a moment of silence. They both looked at their watches.

"I need to get back to work," Wesley said.

"As do I," said Ms. Patel.

There seemed to be nothing left to say. She went to her desk and started tapping the keyboard at a highly respectable rate. He switched slides on the microscope and returned to squinting.

Stephen looked at me. "So where does that leave us?" he asked.

"Confused," I said. "Let's have lunch."

* * *

Our brown-bag repast, purchased the night before at a deli near the hotel, was delectable. But then everything tastes better when you're trapped in a research laboratory, fearing for your life.

Ms. Patel and Wesley, having no such limitations, left for lunch. We sat at Douglas Brickman's former desk, which had the best ambience due to his absence. Reaching into the paper bag, I pulled out a plastic-wrapped tuna salad sandwich, BLT, and three bags of chips. Two plastic cups of water from the lab faucet, and we had everything we needed.

Except answers.

I picked up my tuna salad. "Who had access to the cyanide?"

Stephen was already partway into his BLT. "Everyone with a key to the cabinet. Dr. Rhee, Neera, Wesley, Brickman."

"And everyone with access to those who had access. Which I assume included Mrs. Rhee and Wesley's girlfriend." I bit into the tuna salad. The HVAC system was going to have its hands full with the smell.

"But it really doesn't matter who could get hold of empty capsules," he said. "They weren't necessary. Since they could be pulled apart, the killer didn't need new ones. In fact, anybody could have entered the bedroom, opened the capsules, put in a little cyanide, and stuck them back together."

I shook my head. "In the dark? Without making any noise? I don't think so."

He shrugged. "Okay, that cuts it down to a million or so

people. If we start now, maybe we can talk to all of them by sundown."

"Forget the million. They have no motive. It's still the same list of suspects it's always been."

We chewed in silence. We crunched our way through the chips.

"It's time to admit it," he said finally. "This isn't working. Besides the fact that we haven't learned very much, our chances of being found out get worse by the minute. I say we go big and get out."

"Which means what?"

"I was hoping *you'd* know. You're the boss, remember?"

The door clicked. It was Wesley. He was finishing a Snickers bar.

"You guys look like your dog died."

Stephen explained the situation. "Yeah, that's a tough one," Wesley said, and tossed the candy wrapper in the wastebasket under his desk. "Like I said, I wish I could help, but—"

"We know," I said.

The door clicked again. Ms. Patel came in with a handful of mail and set it on her desk. On top was a thick magazine whose cover featured a colorful community of amoebas. Or the results of an experiment involving a small pet and a microwave oven.

"*Microbiology Today* is here," she said.

"Yes!" Wesley cried.

She turned to us. "He and Douglas used to fight over who got to read it first."

"Yeah, I miss that big guy." He snorted. "Not."

"Do you know what he's doing now?" I asked.

He and Ms. Patel looked at each other and shrugged.

He leaned toward me. "Do you think he did it?"

"It's possible. But so are a lot of things."

He bent toward Ms. Patel. "They're stuck," he confided.

This time I explained the situation. Wesley took the opportunity to pick up the magazine and start reading.

When I was done, Ms. Patel looked mystified. "Go big and get out, did you say?"

"That's what Stephen thinks."

Ms. Patel sat down at her desk. "How big do you wish to go?"

He shrugged. "If *big* means *impossible*, the way to answer our questions about Mercedes Pierce is to bypass her assistant. Get into her office and go through the files when no one's around."

"How do you know it's impossible?" Ms. Patel asked.

"Her office is *inside* the security office. Not to mention the cameras."

She rubbed her ID badge with her thumb. "I can make it possible for you to remain in the building after hours. But I can't get you into her office."

Wesley looked up from the magazine. "You'd have to hack the security system," he said. "The doors. The cameras."

"I am a microbiologist, not a computer expert," Ms. Patel said.

Stephen tilted his head to one side. "But . . . *one* of us is," he said slowly.

Wesley sat up straight. "Hey, don't look at me. I already told you I can't stick my neck out on this."

"You're a prodigy," Stephen said.

"Yeah, but I can't—"

"You said you'd help if you could do it anonymously. You wouldn't even have to be in the building. Isn't this something you could do from home?"

He put the magazine down. He seemed to be balancing something carefully in his head. "Maybe."

The room grew quiet. So quiet the HVAC sounded like a freight train.

Wesley looked down at the floor. He ran his hand over his disorderly hair.

"You swear you won't tell anybody else about this?" he asked.

"Absolutely," I said.

"Definitely," Stephen said.

"Never," Ms. Patel added.

He smiled a crooked smile. "Then I'm in. Over my head, maybe, but I'm in."

# CHAPTER 22

IT WAS NOT A DARK AND STORMY NIGHT.

Actually, it *was* rather dark, but no darker than one would expect at 10 p.m. in the Northern Hemisphere on a summer evening. If anything, it would have been nice to have it even darker, so that no one could see what we were about to do.

It had taken Wesley 24 hours to convince himself that he was ready to try the hack. I hadn't the faintest idea what was involved, of course, and even Stephen looked blank when Wesley tried to explain it. Something about firewalls and back doors and encryption. Spoofing. VPN. Eventually he abandoned his efforts to enlighten us.

Ms. Patel, meanwhile, had managed to find out how many security guards would be patrolling the Administration Building and when. After staying late the first night, she said there seemed to be three, one of whom passed the security office every 90 minutes or so.

And now, having gotten ourselves locked in the building after 5:00 p.m., the three of us had been concealed in the laboratory storeroom. There was just enough space for a trio of unpadded steel chairs, none of which had been designed to be sat upon for more than a few minutes at a time. At Ms. Patel's insistence we stood up every half hour to avoid blood clots, though after the first two hours I was hoping for a fatal one.

The fluorescent lights gave us all a greenish tinge, but we seldom looked at each other. Most of the time we stared at our smartphones, except when Ms. Patel had *Microbiology Today* all to herself and read it cover to cover.

Dinner was around 6:00. We broke out the Triscuits, string cheese, beef jerky, and bananas I'd packed after a visit to Safeway. It was action food, Stephen said. The thermos of steaming black coffee Ms. Patel had brought was quickly depleted.

The closer we got to the appointed hour, the less we spoke. I could almost hear the tattoo of snare drums in the background. At one point Stephen searched the shelves for something dark and greasy to smear under his eyes, but found nothing that wasn't likely to cause blindness.

It was 9:49 p.m. when Stephen turned to me. "You know the plan," he said. "First, we—"

"No need to go over it. As you just said, I already know what it is."

"Okay."

Ms. Patel checked her watch. "It seems my work here is done. Wesley will get you the rest of the way, I trust." She stood up and brushed a few crumbs from her skirt. "Please lock this room on your way out. And remember, once you leave the lab, you can't get back in."

At 10:58 my phone began to vibrate in the pocket of my blazer. It was Wesley. He was on speaker, probably with his fingers hovering over the keyboard of his laptop.

"Are you ready?" he asked.

I sighed. "As we'll ever be."

"I'm pretty sure I've knocked out the cameras. I think I

can get you in. But you'll have to hurry. If the system detects a breach, it'll lock us out."

I looked at my watch. "The guard should pass the security office in about five minutes. If we get there right after he leaves, we'll have about ninety minutes to see what we can find in Pierce's office."

"Yeah, but you'll have a lot less than that if we're locked out."

My heart rate, which I'd been studiously ignoring for the last four hours or so, was growing harder to disregard. But I tried anyway.

"I'll call you back when we're at the security door," I said. "But we have to be quiet. I won't say anything until we're inside. You'll do all the talking."

"Sweet!" he said.

"My thoughts exactly," I replied.

It sounded so much better than the truth.

* * *

We crept through the hallway in cheap sneakers with soft soles, wearing latex gloves from the lab.

I looked up at the security cameras. I kept telling myself Wesley was right, that he had poked them in their electronic eyes.

Rounding the last corner, we caught a glimpse of the guard, a broad-shouldered young man testing the door handles, barely pausing as he went, his shadow following him. We hung back until he was gone.

I pulled out my phone and punched in Wesley's number as we neared the door to security.

"I'm here," he said, still on speaker. I turned the volume down. "Hope you're at the door. Try it . . . *now*."

The mechanism clicked. I fumbled the phone, nearly

dropping it, but managed to turn the handle just in time. Stifling a grunt, I pushed the door open.

Inside it was almost dark. I put the phone to my ear, waiting for my eyes to adapt.

"Can't tell whether you're in, but I'll assume you are," Wesley said. "Do the same thing with the door to Pierce's office."

I hustled around the assistant's desk. The door clicked. This time I was too late.

"Try again," I whispered.

He did, and I was in. Stephen was right behind me.

The door clicked shut. There was almost no light at all, save for a few tiny red and green indicators on chargers, surge protectors, and a couple of squarish objects that probably were printers or hard drives. My heart was pounding now.

We fished in our pockets for our flashlights. Nothing special, just aluminum LEDs about the size of champagne flutes. We pressed them to life. Our faint, bluish circles of light converged and parted, then settled on the desk and the wall behind it.

The office was smaller than I'd expected. Maybe I'd assumed it would look like some world headquarters of evil, with maps depicting plans of conquest and at least a few instruments of torture. Instead, there was a painting of a clipper ship and several plaques on the wall over the desk. The opposite wall was a floor-to-ceiling window, with the blinds tightly closed.

Not surprisingly, the desk drawers were locked. So was the credenza.

I put the phone to my ear. "Still there?" I whispered.

"Yeah."

"Have you figured out her password yet?"

"I've got three possibilities."

Stephen sat down in front of the computer. When he touched the mouse, the screen lit up. There was the Windows logo. He held out his hand for my phone.

"Go ahead," he said.

He listened, then carefully typed in eight characters. I looked at the series of dots and waited.

A dialogue box popped up. ERROR: INCORRECT PASS-WORD. PLEASE TRY AGAIN.

"Not it," he whispered into the phone, then listened again.

He put the phone down. His fingers moved slowly, deliberately, over the keyboard. Another string of dots appeared.

ERROR, the box said. INCORRECT PASSWORD. PLEASE TRY AGAIN.

His jaw tightened. "Doesn't like that one, either," he said into the phone.

He listened, then repeated the process. For a few moments nothing happened.

Finally the screen said WELCOME.

He exhaled. "We're in."

Setting the phone down, he stared at the computer. "I'm not sure where to look first," he murmured.

"E-mails, maybe," I said. "Contact lists."

"Okay, yeah."

He launched the e-mail program. As soon as it was up, though, a new box with red letters appeared in the center of the screen: ACCESS RESTRICTED.

"Oh, crap," he said.

Immediately he quit the program. "If that set off an alarm somewhere—"

"Try searching for files that contain 'Reardon,'" I said.

He typed the name into the search box on the taskbar.

ACCESS RESTRICTED, came the reply.

"We're toast," he said.

I took the phone back. "Wesley, all we get is 'Access Restricted.'"

"Uh-oh."

"Can you . . . can you hack your way past that?"

There was silence, then a doubtful sound. "I . . . don't know."

"Can you try?"

"I mean . . . it'll take time. Longer than you can stay there."

I squinted at the hour on the computer screen. "We should have at least forty-five minutes until the guard comes around again. Is that enough to—"

"What's that noise?" Stephen whispered.

I put the phone down, listening.

It was a rattle. From the hall.

Someone was trying the handle on the security office door.

I swallowed. "I thought he wasn't supposed to be back for ninety minutes," I whispered.

"Maybe they changed guards, or schedules, or—"

The rattling stopped. But only because the door was opening.

"Kill the flashlights," I croaked. We did, and the room went black.

There was only one place to hide, at least only one I could remember. Stuffing the phone in my pocket, I dropped to my knees and rolled under the desk.

Unfortunately, Stephen did the same.

"Ow," he whispered.

We were more or less face to face. I smelled carpet dust. I held my breath, partly to avoid making a sound and partly because there'd been no Altoids after that tuna salad.

A light came on in the outer office. Seconds later the handle on Pierce's office door rattled. The beam of a flashlight much brighter than ours flicked over the desk, the walls, the blinds.

My eyes stayed shut. I couldn't bear to open them, even in the flickering half-light. I wondered whether Stephen was doing the same. I wanted to apologize for doing whatever had made him say *Ow*.

The guard's flashlight snapped off. The door closed, then the outer door.

We waited for what seemed like a week before daring to move a muscle. When we finally did, it was like trying to untie the Gordian knot while suffering with rheumatoid arthritis.

"Sorry," I muttered.

He had the good sense to say nothing.

"We've got to get out of here," I whispered.

"Right behind you."

I felt the carpet to make sure we weren't leaving anything behind. All Ms. Pierce needed was a credit card, an earring, a comb. Finding nothing, I turned on my flashlight and we retraced our steps to the hallway.

"I hope the cameras are still shut down."

"This way out," he said. "I think."

My heart continued to work overtime as we half walked, half ran down the corridor. At last we reached the side entrance Ms. Patel had smuggled us through for two days. After looking behind and ahead, we slipped out.

There was no time to sit in the parking lot and watch the stars. The Prius was nearly alone, bright bluish-yellow at the base of a light pole and probably under somebody's watchful eye. We got in and got going.

"Too close," Stephen said, flopping back against the headrest.

"And we don't even know if it was worth it." I got out my

phone and handed it to him. "Hit Redial and see if you can reach Wesley."

There was a pause. "Line's busy," he said.

"Then we'll have to wait to hear from him."

He gave the phone back, then sagged against the door and closed his eyes. Streetlights flashed past over his head.

I kept checking the rearview mirror. So far, nothing.

* * *

Back at the hotel, we were too tired to say goodnight in the hallway. It was all sleeping after that.

Until just past midnight, when my phone suddenly decided to harass me from the nightstand.

"Are you awake?" It was Wesley.

I grunted. "I am now."

"Thought you'd want to know what happened. I think I found something."

I sat up. "What?"

"I did a search for that Reardon guy. Nothing in e-mail, but there was some kind of financial thing. Part of a spreadsheet. Like she was paying a Joseph Reardon to do something. I mean, not just once. A bunch of times."

"Did you save it?"

"I copied it before I had to log off. Lucky to get anything." He paused. "So this is good, right?"

"It could be very good."

"I can e-mail the file as a PDF. But in the morning, okay? I'm used to pulling all-nighters, but this was a little tougher than a *World of Warcraft* tournament."

"Sleep as late as you like," I said. "You did good." It was painful to use an adjective when an adverb was required, but I assumed he preferred it that way. Most people seemed to, except for a few dead poets, English teachers, and myself.

I hung up, returned the phone to the nightstand, and leaned back against the headboard.

I felt myself . . . well, *smile*.

We were finally getting somewhere.

I'd treasure this moment.

I knew it might never happen again.

# CHAPTER 23

WHEN MORNING CAME, I WAS STILL IN TIRED-BUT-HAPPY mode. Like Scrooge buying a giant goose to express his newfound generosity, I found a bakery near the hotel and bought enough scones, brioche, and baklava to feed the Cratchit family.

I brought the bounty to our now-traditional breakfast in Marvin's room, where his pink carton of mere doughnuts paled in comparison. He and Stephen asked whether I was feeling okay.

"Great," I said, pouring myself a cup of coffee. "Wesley has hit pay dirt. Thanks to him, we have proof that Mercedes Pierce has been paying Joseph Reardon for services rendered."

"What services?" Stephen asked.

"Don't know yet. Not a smoking gun, maybe, but I can't wait to see that file."

Marvin raised an eyebrow. "Last time I saw you this excited, you were about to reject your one-thousandth manuscript. Or maybe it was your ten-thousandth."

"Where is this file?" Stephen asked.

"He promised to e-mail it to us."

"See?" Marvin said, choosing a brioche *au chocolate*. "I told you undercover can work. Takes a little nerve, that's all."

I shook my head. "Never again."

Stephen picked a scone. "We went big, all right. Now it's time to get out."

"Let's wait to see what Wesley found," I said. "Then we can decide what to do about Mercedes Pierce."

Marvin sat down on his bed. "I don't want to rain on anybody's parade. But this file Wesley found isn't going to take us where we need to go."

"Well, not all the way," I said, "but—"

"What do we really have? A connection between the drug company and this Reardon guy. But nothing connecting him and the murder. *Any* murder."

"Maybe we will eventually," Stephen said.

He shrugged. "And then what? See, I have a problem with the whole theory that these Brainiacs were dumb enough to kill Dr. Rhee *after* he'd spilled the beans. By then the whole country was watching."

"Yes," I said. "It only makes sense if the company thought he had more shoes to drop. Other incriminating revelations to make."

"So did he?" Marvin asked.

"I don't know."

"Maybe you can find out."

"How?"

He looked up at the ceiling. "Who did Dr. Rhee confide in?"

"Nobody, I would guess," I said.

"Who at least knew him better than anybody else?"

"Probably Mrs. Rhee."

"And of the three of us, who has the greatest rapport with Mrs. Rhee?"

I raised a hand. "I suppose *I* do. But I'm not doing this by myself."

"You could take Stephen with you," he said.

I frowned. "He has a tendency to be . . . undiplomatic."

"Good," Marvin said. "We don't have time to beat around the bush."

I sighed. "All right. On one condition."

"What's that?"

"I get all the baklava."

* * *

Olivia agreed to see Stephen and me at her home two hours later. Marvin had pledged to spend the rest of the day completing a rewrite of chapter four, which he insisted was fraught with emotional minefields only he could navigate and factual hairs that he alone could split.

By the time we reached the Queen Anne neighborhood, the day was clear and balmy. Stephen pointed out two more varieties of trees on the way, one of which was named Pissard Plum. He giggled when he said it. I didn't, having graduated from third grade many years ago.

Olivia looked stronger this time when she came to the door. Her smile was less tentative. She wore a denim jacket and jeans; it was the first time I'd seen her in clothes that didn't trail like seaweed in her wake.

Instead of offering us tea, she said she had Dr. Pepper and vitamin water. We declined, having overindulged in baked goods.

"How is your book?" she asked when we were seated in the living room.

"Not quite done," I said. "That's why we're here."

She leaned forward, expectant. "How can I help?"

"Did your husband keep a journal?" I asked.

She thought for moment. "Not to my knowledge."

"Did he leave any sort of document to be read on the event of his death? In a safety deposit box, maybe?"

"No. At least not according to the will, or that our attorney brought up."

"How about a locked file cabinet or desk drawer, or a computer with a file you couldn't open?"

She shook her head. "I never looked for anything like that. Perhaps I'm less curious than some people. As for computers, I can do e-mail. I finally opened a Facebook account last week. Beyond that, I'm totally lost." She paused. "Why do you ask?"

"We're wondering whether he might have known some things about his employer that he hadn't brought to light yet."

"More . . . secrets," Stephen added.

"If so, he did not share them with me." She looked down at the coffee table. "Now that I think about it . . . I remember the day the newspaper article came out, the one about the diabetes drug. He said now the world knew 'the whole story.'"

"So his whistleblowing days were over?" Stephen asked.

"As far as I know. He really didn't like all the attention, you know. And he didn't like saying negative things about the company. He believed you should respect those in authority." She paused. "Not like that Indian girl, the one who broke all the glassware."

"Neera Patel," Stephen said.

"Yes. She clearly had no qualms about attacking her employer. Kelvin told me she did it all the time. As far as she was concerned, everything the company did was wrong. Or unfair. She was always complaining."

"When did he tell you this?" I asked.

"When he demoted her. She was fortunate he didn't fire

her." She shook her head. "If anyone thought there was more to say about UniMerritt, it was that girl."

I glanced at Stephen. He glanced at me. Maybe there was more to Ms. Patel than we'd thought. Or less.

"I guess that tells us what we need to know," I said, getting to my feet. Stephen did the same.

I paused at the door. "Olivia, I've been wanting to ask how you're doing. Generally speaking, I mean."

Rising from her chair, she sighed. "It gets a little easier each day. There are times when I don't think I can keep going. But it's time to move into the future, isn't it? I can't live in the past, can I?"

"I'm sure your husband wouldn't want you to."

"Please let me know if there's anything else," she said. "I can't help thinking Kelvin wants this book to come out, too."

We walked out the front door, into the sunshine. I squinted.

The door closed behind us. It was then that I realized something about the room we'd just been in. Something had been different, odd.

The fountain, the one that always burbled in the corner. The one Dr. Rhee had said restored one's equilibrium. That brought peace, tranquility.

It hadn't made a sound.

In fact, it hadn't been there at all.

\* \* \*

Ms. Patel was stunned.

At least I thought she was. It was hard to tell when she always looked as if she'd just gotten a Botox injection.

Stephen and I were sitting in the living room of her townhouse, facing the Degas prints on the white walls, having just disturbed her serenity.

"Mrs. Rhee said *what?*" she asked.

"That you were constantly disparaging the company," I said. "Her husband told her."

She shook her head. "That's impossible. He was a wretched man, but he was not a liar. I believed UniMerritt was capable of anything, yes, but I never said that at work. Or anything like it."

"Why would she make it up?" I asked.

"I can't imagine."

"Did you ever talk with her?"

She hesitated. "Not a real conversation. We met at a company picnic or something, just an introduction."

"So anything she knew about you had to come from Dr. Rhee."

She nodded.

"Then it's her word against yours."

"I assume so."

I looked at one of the prints, the one with the ballet dancer frowning at her slippers as if suspecting an ingrown toenail. It provided no insight into our current dilemma.

"Ms. Neville, I have risked everything to be of help to you. I have broken rules, answered questions, stayed up late, spirited you in and out of places you were not supposed to be. What has Mrs. Rhee done?"

"Answered our questions."

"But not truthfully, it seems."

Closing my eyes, I rubbed my temples gingerly. Deciding to do the only logical thing, I changed the subject.

"Do you think Dr. Rhee had any other revelations to make about wrongdoing at UniMerritt?"

"Besides Milletinor?" She shrugged. "If so, he did not confide them to me."

I nodded. "Nor to anyone else, apparently."

I paused, then patted my thighs with my palms. "Thank

you for your cooperation. We'll get back to you." I stood up, trying to look as if I knew what I was doing.

Back in the Prius, I turned to Stephen. "What do you think?"

He shook his head. "I don't know who to believe. Neera's right—she's sacrificed a lot for us. But she's really doing it to get back at her employer. Mrs. Rhee hasn't been much help, but can we really expect her to be? Her husband left her in the dark about his work."

"Exactly," I said. "That's why her story doesn't pass the smell test."

"What do you mean?"

"Remember what she told us after her husband died? She said he didn't like to talk about his work."

"So . . ."

"So why would he have told her so much about Neera? He'd probably mention the glassware incident, but the whole rant about being disrespectful? Does that sound like the guy we met at dinner?"

"I don't know. He *was* into chains of command. And he wasn't into the social graces."

"But he controlled himself. He said no more than he had to."

He threw up his hands. "Like I said, I don't know who to believe."

I pressed the brake, then the START button. "Well, I think *I* do."

"Where we going?" he asked.

"Back to Olivia's. It's time to do what needs to be done."

He groaned. "Can you just drop me off somewhere? I'm starting to get motion sickness."

"Sorry. This is an express bus. No stops along the way."

He hunched down in his seat. "Wake me when it's over," he said, and braced for impact.

# CHAPTER 24

OLIVIA LOOKED SURPRISED TO SEE US. "DID YOU THINK OF something else?"

"Yes," I said, trying not to look too menacing, at least not yet. "May we come in?"

"Of course."

We all sat in the same spots we'd sat in 40 minutes ago.

"Olivia, we have a problem. Or, more specifically, you do."

"What kind of problem?"

"Credibility."

She looked at Stephen, maybe hoping for a second opinion. Stephen looked at the floor.

"We know you've had a terrible loss," I continued. "But we —I—have a hard time believing you've told us everything you know about your husband's death."

She looked confused. "What more could I tell you?"

"You could begin with where you were the night he died."

"Right here. But in the bedroom, of course."

"Doing what?"

"Sleeping."

"And you heard no one come into the room."

"No. As I said before, I was wearing earplugs."

"Yes. But your husband wasn't."

"Well . . . no. But—"

"It seems far more likely that someone tampered with his medication well before bedtime. Someone who had unlimited access to it, and the dexterity to open those capsules and seal them up again."

She shook her head slowly. "You can't be suggesting that I . . . you couldn't possibly . . ."

"I notice the fountain is gone," I said.

She paused. "It stopped working about a week ago. I don't know how to fix it. It's in the garage for now."

"Or maybe you removed it because it reminded you of him. And not all the memories are good ones."

"Neither of us was perfect," she said quietly. "But we loved each other in our own way."

"But he couldn't have been easy to live with."

"That's what love is for. It forgives. It 'keeps no record of wrongs.' That's in First Corinthians 13."

I nodded. "I may not be a Presbyterian, but I know the 'love chapter.'"

My words hung in the silence.

"You think I killed my husband?" she said. "I thought you were my friends. Or at least that *you* were, Carolyn."

"I'd *like* to be. But when you won't—"

Steadying herself with both hands on the arms of her chair, she rose from her chair. "I . . . think I'm going to be sick. Excuse me." She stumbled out of the room.

I covered my eyes. What if she was telling the truth? If so, I had no business saying any of this. She'd suffered enough.

The toilet flushed. A door opened and closed.

Then another.

"Maybe she needs help," I said, getting up. "I'll go—"

A muffled rumble came from somewhere on the other side of the house.

A garage door opener.

Stephen got off the couch, headed for the front window, and looked at the driveway.

"Oh, crap," he said. "She's taking off."

I got to my feet, then jerked the front door open. The garage door was descending with a clacking hum.

I was just in time to watch her silvery Lexus drive away.

\* \* \*

I ran to the Prius. "Where does she think she's *going?*" Latching my seat belt, I waited for Stephen to do the same, then backed into the street as quickly as I could.

"*Why* is she going?" he asked. "What good will it do her to run? Is she planning to fly to some foreign country and retire on all that money she doesn't have? Turn herself in? Go to a—"

"Look," I said. The Lexus had turned right a block or so away. I caught a glimpse of its tail end and pressed the accelerator.

"Okay, you were probably right," Stephen said. "But don't get us killed in some stupid car chase."

I guessed at the speed limit, seeing no signs. We hadn't gone this way before. Trees of various unnamed varieties flashed past. I could see the blue water of Puget Sound beyond their tops.

Stephen was already on his phone, tapping madly. "What are you doing?" I asked.

"Tracking our course. Looking for traffic jams. Seeing which way to go."

"There's only *one* way. After that car."

"Did you know there's an Upper Queen Anne and Lower Queen Anne?"

"Great," I mumbled. Sure enough, we were going down a hill. So was Olivia, only faster. A horn honked as she barely missed a white sedan that had dared to emerge from a side street.

"Hurrying is pointless," he said. "We're about to hit downtown traffic. If we're going to have a car chase, it'll be in slow motion."

I pumped the brake, and suddenly the trees were behind us. A logjam of concrete pylons and overpasses spread before us like an ugly postcard.

The Lexus slowed to a crawl. We were two cars behind it, passing condos and apartments and artsy businesses that sold things like hemp and dulcimers. And then, in the distance, the Space Needle.

I shook my head. "What is she *doing?* She doesn't seem to be thinking about anything. She's boxed in by traffic. If she has a plan, I can't imagine what it is, other than getting as far away from us as possible."

"Maybe that's enough."

We continued our snail's pace for another mile or so. I could see Olivia in profile, her head swiveling one way and then another, apparently searching for a break that was never going to come.

Suddenly, at a prolonged red light, her door swung open. She jumped out, clutching her purse, and began to run. When the light went green, a symphony of horns commenced and built to a crescendo.

"Come on," I told Stephen, switching off the Prius and clambering onto the street.

"You can't just leave the car here!"

"Don't worry, I'll lock it."

He got out. "This is nuts."

We began to run, threading our way around the other vehicles, following Olivia's 20-yard lead. The other motorists addressed us with a cavalcade of clever nicknames I can't repeat.

"Hey!" yelled one of the kinder ones. "Get your butt back in your car and quit blocking traffic!"

Waving politely, I jogged on. Compared to what they'd be yelling if I pulled this in midtown Manhattan, that comment was practically a valentine.

Soon, though, the chase began to take its toll. My breath came in gasps. There was a squeezing in the center of my chest. Not as if an elephant were sitting there; more as if he were thinking seriously about doing it and had sent me a letter of intent.

I could hear Dr. Garabedian's warning. The one he'd delivered with the prescription that was supposed to keep me from having a heart attack. Something like, *Even if you'd rather not take it, maybe your survival instinct will convince you before it's too late.*

Maybe it already was.

\* \* \*

I could smell Puget Sound. Part rotting shellfish, with bold hints of sewage and sulfur. Seagulls wheeled over our heads like buzzards. I tried not to think of Neera Patel, but the association seemed permanent.

We were getting closer. Huffing and wheezing beneath an overpass, I spied a ferryboat, at least as long as a football field, gleaming white with green trim. Packed with cars, it floated with stately bearing toward the docks, which I couldn't see yet.

I trailed Stephen, who panted but didn't seem in danger

of collapse. "Looks like she's . . . headed for . . . the water-front," he managed. "God knows why."

The crush of vehicles was solid now. The white-on-green signs that sprouted like toadstools around us explained why. This was the heart of Seattle, at least for tourists. The ferries, the Space Needle, the Pacific Science Center, and the nearby monorail had attracted every selfie-snapping visitor in the western United States who wasn't at Disneyland. Most were turning right, toward the tree-lined street next to the water.

"Maybe she's trying . . . to lose herself in the crowd," Stephen continued.

I grunted in response, starting to slow down. Soon I was walking, my brown flats providing no more padding than a pair of Dutch clogs.

Olivia turned right, skirting traffic, her petite frame making it hard to keep track of her. If only she'd been wearing one of her wafting, rippling sculptor outfits.

But even she was human, and no athlete as far as I knew, and had been running for at least a mile. She geared down to walking, still clenching her purse as if it contained her life savings. Maybe it did.

"Finally," Stephen said, breaking off his jog and slowing to a wobbly amble. "I thought she'd . . . never stop."

And she hadn't, not completely. She was still weaving through the throng, past one pier after another, past some-thing called Ye Olde Curiosity Shop, then Ivar's Fish Bar. We were beginning to catch up to her.

Then came the ferry dock. The *Kitsap* was coming in, its passengers lined up on the prow, the cars in tidy rows behind them.

The crowds were nearly gridlocked now, but Olivia pushed on. Suddenly she disappeared behind a knot of gangly teenagers with matching baseball caps. We stopped, waiting for her to reappear.

She didn't.

Stephen swore. "We've lost her."

I took a deep breath. "No. Over there."

There was the denim jacket, the purse, the desperate, birdlike movements. She seemed headed toward the incoming ferry. But there sat another boat, the *Chimacum*, already docked. She ducked inside the terminal.

We elbowed our way through the crowd. "So that's where she was going," Stephen said. "Maybe we can get tickets."

The terminal was vast, echoing, a bazaar of people and cafeteria-style restaurants and digital reader boards with arrivals and departures. Passing the ticket kiosks, we hurried directly to the window.

"Two adults for the *Chimicum*," I said, not even knowing where it was going.

The agent shook his head. "Too late," he said.

"Did a woman buy a ticket on that ferry just now? Small, wearing denim clothes, with dark hair?"

"Nope. It's been too late for almost ten minutes now."

Turning around, I surveyed the crowd. "Lost her again."

Stephen pointed toward an exit on the other side of the terminal. "Is that her?"

I squinted. Small, denim clothes, dark hair. "Can't tell."

"He who hesitates is lost," he said, and started running.

I did my best to follow, wondering what my blood pressure was doing. Keeping my eyes on the back of Stephen's head, I watched him dodge and sprint his way across the room.

Moments later we were outside again, the smells of deep-fried and decaying sea life hitting our nostrils. The *Chimicum* was pulling away from the dock.

It was definitely Olivia. She was past the tourists now, apparently headed for the next pier. It was an older, darker conglomeration of roped-together pilings with no attractions and no signs of life.

A deserted gray shack sat on the end of the dock. Rusting gears and pulleys were bolted next to it. Maybe fishing boats had used this landing once upon a time, but no more.

Olivia looked over her shoulder, then vanished in the shadows.

We stood there, my breathing still ragged, the squeezing in my chest more insistent.

There was no place else to go, not that I could see.

For her, and for us, it was the end of the line.

# CHAPTER 25

"Can you see her?" Stephen whispered.

"No."

We looked down at the water far below. It was so dark it could have been crude oil, but with a greenish touch that resembled antifreeze. Lapping gently at the pilings, it stank of dead fish.

Suddenly a hand appeared, curling around from the far side of the shanty. Then a denim-covered knee.

"Don't . . . come any closer," Olivia said, panting.

We were standing where the land met the dock. She was about 30 feet away.

"Olivia," I called. "There's no place for you to go."

"I know." She sounded lost, confused.

"You're not thinking of jumping, are you?"

There was a pause. "I don't know."

I looked around for help. There was no one except Stephen. I wasn't sure he counted.

"Tell me what happened," I said finally.

A long silence followed. Far under our feet, the water sloshed.

Finally she spoke. "Things went wrong," she said faintly.

"How do you mean?"

"It wasn't bad at first. We were opposites. But I thought it would work out."

More silence, more sloshing.

"Kelvin was the first boy I ever went out with. I was young. Maybe he reminded me of my father. Very . . . traditional."

"Did he hit you?"

"No, no. He would never do that. But I couldn't meet his standards. He had to be in control."

"I understand," I said softly.

"He always let me spend time on my sculpture. It was the only way I could be myself. But lately he'd even criticized that. Said he didn't want me to spend time on showings when I could be at home, where I belonged."

"So you *killed* him?" Stephen asked.

I gave him a warning look.

"You have no idea what it was like," she said. "I was . . . suffocating."

"Why didn't you divorce him?" Stephen said.

"I couldn't just go. He didn't believe in divorce and would have fought it every step of the way. Even if I'd managed to leave him, I'd have nothing to live on. Not even his life insurance, since that would all go to his father."

She paused. "It was my last chance. I knew what would happen if he . . . were gone. People would blame the drug company."

"But why did you run?" I asked. "And why *here*?"

"I had to get away. I thought I could take one of the ferries somewhere. But I timed it wrong."

"Well, you don't have to jump," I said. "Life is still worth living." I turned to Stephen. "Tell her. Tell her why life is worth living."

He scratched his chin. "I'm sure it'll come to me at any moment."

"You're *hopeless*," I hissed.

"Exactly."

I turned back toward the end of the pier. "Olivia, your husband was a Christian, right?"

"Yes."

"What about you?"

She hesitated. "I'm not sure anymore. My view changed over the years. Kelvin wasn't much of an advertisement for believing."

"But you know others who are different."

She nodded. "Even so, everything's changed now. After what I did . . ."

"Doesn't God give people second chances? That whole repentance and forgiveness thing?"

She shrugged.

"Olivia, I can't pretend you won't go to prison for what you did. But it's got to be better than ending your life."

She didn't reply.

"At least give yourself time to think it over. Come away from the end of the dock and stand back here with us."

More silence, more sloshing.

"We'll just talk," I said. "That's all."

There was a creaking sound from somewhere near the shanty. "I . . . okay. Just for a minute." Slowly she stepped into view.

There was another sound. A soft splitting, then a crack.

Suddenly the railing at her elbow gave way.

She screamed. Denim and hair flailed. Two seconds later a splash echoed from somewhere below.

Stephen swore.

We ran, then picked our way the closer we got to the

edge. Stepping carefully to where the rail had been, I squinted into the depths.

"Can you see her?" Stephen asked.

I shook my head.

He took out his phone and set it on the weathered wood of the dock. "I'm going in. Call 911."

I stepped back. "Are you—"

Just then my right shoe managed to find a patch of something slimy.

My leg shot out from under me. I toppled sideways over the edge.

Gasping, I did the only thing I could.

Which was to plummet like a rock.

\* \* \*

I'd never been much of a swimmer. Back in Idaho at age 12 I'd taken a six-week Red Cross course but barely made it out of the pool at the final test. I hated the smell of chlorine and couldn't remember the last time I'd gone near a body of water bigger than a bathtub.

And now I smacked it, hard.

I did it so suddenly there was no time to suck in a lungful of air. The sea shut over my head with shocking finality.

There'd been no time to remove my heavy blazer, either. I thrashed and flailed and tried to pray.

There was no sound. I was afraid to open my eyes, having already seen and smelled the primordial soup. Eventually I let the lids part slightly, hoping to avoid the sharp poles and jagged harbor trash I imagined surrounded me.

I held my breath, wondering how long I could keep it up. How long anyone could.

My jaw had already clamped shut. One spasm after

another wracked my chest, which burned as if filled with acid.

I flapped my arms in slow motion, the kind of motion scuba divers made in movies and places like Sea World to propel themselves upward. But I got nowhere. I kicked off my shoes, but it didn't help.

Suddenly something brushed my shoulder. My head jerked to the left. In the murk I could make out a figure— small, female, clothed in denim that now looked blacker than blue. Her hair floated upward, tangled.

I reached out, as if I could save her when I couldn't save myself. She pushed my hand away. Apparently she'd made her choice about whether life was worth living. Drifting backward, she faded into the darkness.

The pain in my lungs was a scalpel. I considered going limp, letting the inevitable happen, hoping to pass out before my mouth sprang open and the water rushed in. But I wasn't ready. I was 99 percent sure where I'd go, but there was too much left to do here.

Thoughts, really just pictures, flashed and stumbled through my head.

The faces of my parents.

A parakeet we'd had when I was seven.

A diagrammed sentence on a chalkboard.

The best doughnut I'd ever tasted, something called an Evil Elvis at a place in Dallas, Texas.

And Stephen.

In my imagination he stood on the dock overhead, searching the water. Or he'd jumped in and couldn't find me.

I tried to swallow, but my throat was too constricted. I gagged.

It was my time after all.

All at once there was light everywhere. So bright it seemed to boil away the ocean itself.

Not a white light, exactly, but with a tincture of purple.
The taste of salt water was in my mouth.
And then there was nothing.

# CHAPTER 26

THE FIRST THING I SAW IN HEAVEN WAS A SAND FLEA.

It turned out not to be heaven, but the flea was real. It was about three inches from my right cheekbone, which was resting on the splintery plank of the pier. The tiny crustacean hopped away just as all the muscles in my torso convulsed, and I began to cough up enough seawater to start my own fjord.

When I'd finished, I leaned my head back on the pier and breathed with a wheeze. The sun was low in the sky. Red and blue lights pulsed at the edges of my vision. Ambulance. Police. My throat was sore, and my chest still burned.

"You still with us?" said a male voice. I turned to see a young man in a dark blue uniform. He was taking my vital signs. There was a plastic clip on my finger. "Blood pressure's up," he said. "Oxygen level's down."

I wanted to tell him how astonishing that was, but when I tried to talk there was only a weak rasping sound. He took out a stethoscope and checked my heart but said nothing.

Then I saw Stephen's face. His hair hung in a wet tangle, his clothes smelling of decaying clams.

"You're back," he said, looking tired but relieved. "How do you feel?"

I pointed at my neck.

"Your throat hurts? You can't talk?"

I nodded.

He looked pained. A woman in a reflective yellow vest walked up and handed him a white towel, which he used to rub at his hair.

"That *smell*," he continued. "Just so you know, I dove in to get you." He looked around. "A policeman—I don't see him now—got Mrs. Rhee. Both of you needed CPR and artificial respiration."

I coughed. Mouth-to-mouth resuscitation? From Stephen or the policeman? I decided not to ask.

With a grunt I pushed myself up on one elbow and surveyed the dock. Two police cars, a fire truck, two ambulances. At least three officers, two paramedics, and the woman in the neon yellow vest.

I glanced back over my shoulder. Behind me sat Olivia, her head in her hands. One of the officers was asking questions, but she wasn't responding.

"Yeah, she made it," Stephen said, draping the towel over his shoulder. "It took longer to bring her back. She was in the water probably four minutes. She's pretty lucky."

I wondered whether Olivia would concur. She didn't look too thankful for her second chance at life.

\* \* \*

The officer who'd been interviewing Olivia was obviously not the one who'd rescued her. First, he was a grizzled old-timer. Second, he didn't even look damp.

He put away his pad and pen, then let the paramedics take over. They helped Olivia onto a gurney and wheeled her into the nearest ambulance, which proceeded to drive away. The siren stayed off.

The officer trudged across the dock in our direction. "Excuse me," he said, peering at me. "You know Mrs. Rhee?"

I nodded.

"How?"

I cleared my throat, then tried again to talk. This time I managed three or four words but sounded like an antique pump organ with a leaky bellows.

"We both know her," Stephen said. He started explaining, and out came the policeman's pad and pen. The officer kept nodding and saying, "Uh-huh." Four or five minutes later, Stephen paused to take a breath.

"Interesting," the policeman said. "She wouldn't tell me zilch. But you say she confessed to killing her husband?"

"Yep."

"I'll need you to make a formal statement at some point."

Stephen looked down at his soggy clothes and made a face. "Now?"

"Nah. I imagine you've got some . . . recovering to do."

"When they take my friend here to the hospital, can I ride with her?"

"Are you family?"

"No, but—"

He shook his head. "Against policy."

Stephen rummaged through his pockets and found a ring with two keys. "Can you at least take me back to our rental car? We left it in the middle of the street."

The officer raised an eyebrow. "If it hasn't been towed away. We generally frown on parking violations."

Standing up, Stephen gave me the thumbs-up sign. "See you at the hospital," he said, and followed the officer.

My ride in the ambulance was uneventful, which seemed like a good thing under the circumstances. I stared at the white plastic ceiling, trying not to think about how I must have smelled. The young paramedic kept puffing up my blood pressure cuff and letting it deflate, his efforts at conversation thwarted by my inability to speak above a whisper.

By the time Stephen arrived a couple of hours later, both of us were more fit to be sniffed. I'd been allowed, even strongly encouraged, by the nurse to take a lengthy and thorough shower. A flimsy but clean hospital gown had replaced my blazer, which had no doubt been consigned to the incinerator with the other biohazards. I could even speak, albeit hoarsely. So far I'd found little to say.

Stephen, meanwhile, looked almost normal. It was as if he'd never dipped his toe in the water, let alone been immersed in it. He must have used the hotel blow dryer for at least half an hour.

He sat in the chair next to the bed. "So they're keeping you for observation."

"To make sure I don't get pneumonia," I rasped. "There's a little water in my lungs. Ironically, they're giving me fluids. Like I don't have enough already."

He shifted in the chair. "I got the car. It hadn't been towed yet. The cop said we deserved a ticket for parking in a loading zone, but he didn't have the heart to give me one. I think it was because I looked and smelled like a wet dog."

He glanced around. "Do they let you use your cell phone here?"

"Not if it's lying at the bottom of Puget Sound, which mine apparently is."

He shook his head. "How's the food?"

"Like prison, but with larger utensils."

We both fell silent.

"I have to ask," he said finally. "What was it like?'

"What?"

"To almost drown."

I sighed. I didn't want to think about it, much less relive it. But he was the one who'd saved my life. I hadn't thought of it quite that way until that moment.

I did the best I could to describe it. When I came to the part about seeing pictures of my life at the end, I told her about the parakeet and the doughnut. He laughed.

Finally I came to the grand finale about the light. The white light with the purple tint.

He shook his head. "Are you serious?"

I nodded.

He rolled his eyes. "A near-death experience, huh? Was there a feeling of peace and love?"

"No, it was mostly choking and gagging."

"Did you see any family members who'd gone on before? Did they welcome you? Was it like . . . paradise? Or oxygen deprivation, which is a heck of a lot more likely?"

I fiddled with the plastic band on my wrist. "No matter what it was, I was ready to move on to the next life."

Suddenly the monitor on my IV pole started beeping. I wasn't sure why. Maybe it was my heart, but I didn't feel anything.

Stephen's eyes widened. I fumbled in the blanket for the call button and pressed it.

Almost a minute later the nurse, a sturdy woman with squeaking sneakers, strode in and bent over the source of the noise. She pushed a button twice, then flicked it with her fingernail. The beeping stopped.

"Sometimes these things are persnickety," she said, and marched out.

I turned to Stephen. "As I was saying, whether or not it was a near-death—"

He held up his hand. "No need to defend the faith. It was what it was." He paused. "How do you feel now?"

"Mostly tired. And sore."

"Sorry. They say you might make it after all, though."

I nodded. "You saved my life. But I forgive you."

* * *

The night passed quickly, in the sense that it was an endless nightmare.

Despite my exhaustion, I didn't sleep more than two or three hours, and only in increments of what seemed like 30 seconds. The automatic blood pressure cuff growled and swelled every 45 minutes or so. The defective monitor kept beeping at odd intervals, followed by the squeaky entrance of the nurse, who was replaced halfway through the night by a woman who apparently was a fan of tap shoes.

I knew it was morning when the nurse tugged the curtains apart, revealing a portion of the Seattle skyline that didn't include the Space Needle, Puget Sound, or anything else I recognized. For a second I wondered whether I'd been abducted and transported to an undisclosed location, but that was probably the saline solution talking.

The nurse handed me a clear plastic pitcher—a graduated cylinder, I knew now—with a tube and mouthpiece attached. "Time to measure your lung power," she said. "Blow into this as hard as you can."

I did my best. She seemed satisfied with the result, which gave me a pathetic feeling of accomplishment.

Around 9:00 a.m. a doctor stepped in and stood about 10 feet away. "How are you feeling?" he asked, not looking up from his iPad.

"Feeble and susceptible to infection."

"Great. Time for you to go home. Stay away from the water for a while, okay?"

He mumbled something about discharge papers, then slipped out.

Stephen showed up an hour later, wheeling my suitcase behind him. "They tell me you're getting out. First jail, now this."

"I haven't seen any papers yet."

He sat in the chair. "Since the clothes you were wearing when you came in probably reek, I brought your stuff from the hotel."

"Thanks."

He took out his phone and started tapping. "Hey," he said. "Wesley Goldblum sent you an e-mail. He copied me."

I sat up. "What does it say?"

"No subject line or message. Just an attachment." He tapped again. "Must be that file he saw on . . . you-know-who's computer." He handed me the phone and went to shut the door.

There was a screen shot, a little hard to read, of a spread-sheet in Excel. There was no heading, just a page of columns:

J. REARDON 1/30 SERVICES RENDERED $1,200
    1/31 640
    2/02 90
    2/17 800
    3/27 490
    4/02 185
    4/15 2,000
    4/31 550
    5/11 775
    7/28 1,600
    7/30 490
    8/02 185
    8/15 2,310

. . .

I frowned. "Not enough to convict anybody. Especially Mercedes Pierce."

"But we don't *have* to convict anybody. Mrs. Rhee confessed to us, remember? That's what I told the police this morning. In my formal statement."

I put the phone down. "If Olivia killed her husband, why was Mr. Reardon following us around?"

There was a pause. "I don't know."

"Don't you want to?"

He shrugged. "I guess I can live with not knowing."

"Well, *I* can't. I hate loose ends."

"Life's not like fiction. Everything doesn't get neatly tied up in the last chapter."

I stared out the window.

*We'll see about that,* I thought.

# CHAPTER 27

TWO HOURS LATER THE HOSPITAL SET US FREE.

My discharge papers were the usual boilerplate about watching for fever and not suing anyone. My diagnosis was listed as NONFATAL SUBMERSION, FIRST ENCOUNTER. It was unsettling to think there could be a second.

Next morning Stephen and Marvin and I gathered one more time. We were back to regular doughnuts.

Marvin waved the newspaper as he sat down. "It's all over the front page of *The Seattle Times*. 'Wife Confesses in Rhee Killing.'"

I took a raspberry doughnut from the box. "Ironic. The same paper that printed the whistleblowing letter. I'm sure they profited mightily from bashing the drug company. Now they'll claim they knew all along who really did it."

Marvin shook his head. "The news business isn't what it used to be. When I was at the *Tribune*, we—"

"Yes, we know," I said.

Frowning, he spread the paper in front of him. "Cranberry, for a gal who came so close to buying space in Davy Jones's Locker, you're pretty sure of yourself."

Stephen looked over his shoulder at the article. "Does it mention me? It was my statement, after all."

Marvin ran his finger down the columns as he read, then turned to the jump inside. "Not that I can see. But it says the chief of police has scheduled a news conference for this morning." He looked at his watch. "Where's your remote?"

I groaned. "Do we have to see it?"

"'Course we do. We'll need it for the epilogue."

By the time he found the right channel, the proceedings were nearly over. Peter Everly stood once again at the podium on the steps of City Hall. His uniform still looked too big. This time he wore his cap, the one with the ornate gold badge and piping on the brim, perhaps hoping it would shield him from awkward questions.

He was leaning forward, frowning, listening to a reporter.

"Chief," the woman called, "you've implied all along that UniMerritt Laboratories was somehow involved in Dr. Rhee's death. Now that—"

He bent toward his microphone. "No, no. I never speculated on who was responsible."

"But you said—"

"Let's be clear. The first priority of every public servant is objectivity. Every citizen . . . and non-citizen . . . is entitled to equal protection under the law. That includes those in the business community as well as those in less advantaged portions of our great city."

I set my doughnut down, feeling queasy. Everly always seemed to have that effect on me.

"I have always maintained my commitment to following every investigation wherever it might lead. That is my pledge to you, the people of Seattle."

Another reporter toward the front waved a notepad in the air. "Chief, how do you answer those who ask why—"

"No more questions," he said, and walked away.

The camera pulled back on the crowd, which was significantly smaller than the previous one.

Marvin shook his head. "Man, he didn't look happy."

"Where were all the protesters?" I asked.

Stephen looked at me, not amused. "Just because Big Pharma didn't kill Dr. Rhee, that doesn't mean it's innocent. There are skeletons in its closet. Not to mention torturing animals."

Marvin turned off the TV. "You know," he said, "I just realized what this means."

"What?" Stephen asked.

"We have everything we need for this book. Including the murderer."

I checked my watch, having forgotten the date. "I can't believe it. We may actually be able to meet Hunter's deadline."

Stephen took out his phone. "Let's call him. He's going to be ecstatic."

I didn't like the sound of that.

If it made Hunter happy, there had to be something wrong with it.

* * *

Hunter was in his office. Stephen put the phone on speaker and cued me with a nod.

"Have you heard the news?" I asked.

"What news?"

"We know who killed the whistleblower."

"You do? Who?"

"His wife. Not the drug company. His wife."

There was a long pause.

"You're kidding," he said.

"No."

Another pause.

He swore, and not under his breath.

"How am I supposed to sell a book like *that?* I told you to bring me a thriller about a corporate conspiracy!"

"No conspiracy. Just old-fashioned—"

"People won't buy a book about a wife killing her husband. They can watch that crap for free on *Dateline* and *20/20* and *48 Hours.*"

He made a disgusted noise. "Is Marvin there?"

Marvin stepped forward. "Hunter, my man. How are—"

"I put you in charge. What are you *doing?*"

"Trying to meet your deadline."

Another robust profanity rang out. "Do you have any idea what the expectations are here for this book? What the marketing budget is? I'm not going to look like a fool when it comes out and flops. There isn't going to *be* a book. I'm canceling. It's done."

Marvin cleared his throat. "Now, Hunter, we have a contract, and—"

"You'll get your money. But the project is dead." He paused. "I should have known better than to hire . . . someone like you."

Marvin raised an eyebrow. "Black, you mean?"

"Not that."

"Old?"

"No. Someone who's a friend of Carolyn."

"Oh. I guess you're right."

There was silence on the line. I tried to imagine exactly what shade of red Hunter's face had turned.

"And Carolyn?" he said.

"Yes."

"If the board wants to know what happened, I'll remind them the book was all your idea in the first place."

"True, but—"

He hung up.

The three of us looked at each other.

"Maybe *ecstatic* wasn't the right word," Stephen said.

Marvin shrugged. "*C'est la vie.*"

"How can you be so laid-back about it?" I asked.

He took another doughnut. "That book saved my life, girl. Got me out of the house. At a time of domestic crisis, as it were."

"Not to mention that you get to keep the money," I said.

He nodded. "But I'll spend it on a peace offering for my lovely bride. Plus a couple options for the boat. I'll need a bait tank leaning post with flip-up bolsters. And a T-top. Safety issues, you understand."

He walked slowly toward the door, then turned. "Sorry. It could have been a mighty good book."

"Yes," I said with a sigh. "I know."

* * *

Two days later the three of us stood at the turnaround in front of Emerald City Extended Stays. Marvin was leaving as he'd arrived, wearing jeans and his black baseball cap. His palm rested on the handle of his dark blue rolling suitcase with the red yarn, and his green duffel bag lay on the sidewalk like a moldy bratwurst.

He was waiting for a taxi. We were waiting for him to go.

He turned to me. "Wish I could say it was a pleasure working with you, Cranberry. But it never is, you know."

"The feeling is mutual," I said, shaking his outstretched hand. He gave me a wink.

"You, too, Mr. Ames," he said, shaking Stephen's hand. "Sorry you can't escape this woman as easily as I can."

He shrugged. "God knows I've tried."

The Yellow Cab pulled up. With a final tip of his cap, Marvin climbed in and was gone.

"Guess he kind of grows on you," Stephen said.

"Like psoriasis," I said.

We went back inside, checked out, and got our bags. Our own flight to LaGuardia would leave in just over three hours. After loading the Prius, I pressed the brake and then the START button.

Nothing happened.

I tried again, with the same result.

Stephen whipped out his phone and called the rental agency. Yes, they said, they could pick up the car. But we'd have to take a taxi to the airport or miss our flight.

Stephen was about to call a cab when one pulled into the turnaround. It was orange.

"How convenient," I said. I went to the cab, opened the rear door, and stuck my head in. "Going to the airport?"

The driver was looking down, writing something on a clipboard. "Sure am."

Stephen and I climbed in the back. The driver loaded the bags, and we were off.

Nothing was said for the first half mile or so. Finally he spoke.

"What airline, Ms. Neville?"

"United."

The word hung in the air for a few seconds before I realized what he'd said. I gulped.

"How do you know my name?"

He didn't answer right away. I used the time to belatedly pay attention to what he looked like. Medium build, dark green hoodie. All I could see of his face was his eyes in the rearview mirror. They were pale blue. I checked his windshield visor for a license and photo, but there was nothing clipped to it.

"Actually, we've met before," he said. "In a way."

I waited for more, but it was a long time coming. "I usually drive a different vehicle," he said finally. "Gray SUV. Hyundai Santa Fe."

I froze. "It's you. Joseph Reardon."

"I can neither confirm nor deny that," he replied. His voice was calm, with no accent I could detect.

I looked down at my door handle, wondering whether I could open it and hit the pavement running.

As if in answer, he pressed a button. All the locks went *thunk*.

*We almost made it*, I thought.

But not quite.

# CHAPTER 28

I SANK BACK INTO THE SEAT. "WHERE ARE WE GOING?"

"To the airport," he said matter-of-factly. "That's what you wanted, isn't it?"

"Then why did you lock the doors?"

"For your own safety. Just wanted us to have a chat."

I looked at Stephen but kept talking to the presumed Mr. Reardon. "We have a lot of questions."

"I'm sure you do."

"Do you work for UniMerritt?"

"What gave you that idea?"

"We found some financial records."

"Oh. Well, in a manner of speaking. I try to help wherever I can."

"You've been following us," Stephen said. "Ever since that day in the parking lot, after we took the tour."

"Possibly."

He turned to me. "See? Who's paranoid now?"

I looked out my window, hoping to see a police car I could wave to and somehow convince to pull us over. All I saw was a woman driving a van full of children, many of whom were picking their noses.

"Why were you following us?" I asked.

He tilted his head to one side, apparently considering how to phrase his reply. "Let's say my employer was very interested in knowing whether Dr. Rhee had come across any further information he planned to share with the rest of the world."

"We wondered the same thing."

"So I have just one question for you." He paused. "Did he?"

"Not that we were able to find."

He nodded. "I'm sure that will be a weight off my employer's mind."

The Sea-Tac exit was coming up on the right. He clicked the turn signal.

I checked my watch. The airport was coming up. This was my last chance to tie up the loose ends, the ones I knew would bother me for the rest of my life if I didn't speak now.

"You may have run out of questions," I said, "but I haven't."

"Go ahead. I'm an open book, unless circumstances force me to be otherwise."

"You know I went to jail."

"Yes. Very unfortunate."

"Two women I met there. They disappeared."

"Really."

"The first was named Tompkins. An alcoholic, red hair. Probably homeless."

"Don't know her."

"The other's name was Kendra. Said she was a graffiti artist. Had some very strong opinions about your employer."

He shook his head. "Doesn't ring a bell."

"One more. There's a young woman at UniMerritt—last name Van Metre, first initial L."

"Never heard of her."

I looked out the window again. *Well, that was pointless.* I couldn't believe anything he said anyway, could I? I'd just have to be bothered for the rest of my life. As if I wouldn't be anyway.

The United departures zone was ahead on the right. We slowed.

"*I* have a question," Stephen said.

"Go ahead," said Reardon.

"How did you just *happen* to show up in a taxi at the hotel when our car broke down? You couldn't possibly have known it wasn't going to start."

Reardon tapped the steering wheel. "Not unless I'd known that a certain wire in the relay assembly might get disconnected during the night. Electric cars are so dependent on all those little parts."

"And how did you get this cab?"

"Perhaps I gave the previous driver a large tip."

He steered to the right, stopped, and let the car idle. "Your destination," he said. Reaching down, he popped the trunk. "If you don't mind, I'll let you get your own bags. I try to avoid airport surveillance cameras."

A few moments later we were standing on the curb next to our luggage. We watched him drive off, his vehicle soon dissolving into the stream of traffic.

Stephen shuddered. "For a while I thought he was going to . . . you know."

I shook my head. "Not today, anyway."

Rolling my suitcase toward the terminal, I smiled.

*And not next time, either, I hope.*

ACKNOWLEDGMENTS

Thanks to my son the doctor, Christopher, for his insights on research and medicine. And for actually reading the book —or pretending to.

And thanks to my brother Paul, who helped me understand Seattle, if that's possible.

## A LOOK AT: MURDER MOST MADDENING (A CAROLYN NEVILLE MYSTERY BOOK 3)

Carolyn Neville decides that her old friend Marvin should update his true-crime bestseller *Darkness at Dawn* for its 50th anniversary. Her skeptical boss agrees—on the condition that she'll quit if it doesn't sell.

Marvin goes to the mountain town of Motherlode, Colorado to gather new information about the unsolved murder of a beloved schoolteacher. When an attack by an unknown assailant puts Marvin in a coma, Carolyn and her sidekick Stephen Ames take up where he left off.

Carolyn makes friends with the murder victim's sister, but tangles with a hostile local historian, a creepy motel manager and a lecherous mine owner. The investigation takes them to the bottom of a mine shaft and strands them in a blizzard as a killer with a gas can tries to send them out in a blaze of glory.

All Carolyn wants is to see her friend honored, his life celebrated, her boss humbled and a killer found.

*For fans of Horace Rumpole, Monk and Stephanie Plum, the Carolyn Neville Mysteries are full of laugh-out-loud suspense.*

*Purchase now!*

## ABOUT THE AUTHOR

**John Duckworth** is a novelist, editor, playwright, scriptwriter, cartoonist, and father of twins. After earning his bachelor's degree at Linfield College, he spent 35 years in the publishing industry as a curmudgeonly editor, product developer, and author, working with people like Ken Blanchard, Dr. Kevin Leman, Richard Foster, and Calvin Miller, producers like VeggieTales, organizations like Focus on the Family and companies like Random House, Thomas Nelson, NavPress, Group Publishing, Zondervan and Rainfall Toys.

After producing nearly 250 issues of weekly publications *Power for Living* and *FreeWay*, he created seven multi-volume series of youth ministry resources. He's edited or rewritten hundreds of books, articles, and lesson plans.